Mythologia IV

THE RELUCTANT HERO

The Story of Bellerophon and the Chimera

Sign-up for the Eagles and Dragons Publishing Newsletter and get a FREE BOOK today.

Subscribers get first access to new releases, special offers, and much more.

Visit:

www.eaglesanddragonspublishing.com

Men come and go as leaves year by year upon the trees. Those of autumn the wind sheds upon the ground, but when the season of spring returns the forest buds forth with fresh vines.

Even so is it with the generations of humankind, the new spring up as the old are passing away. If, then, you would learn my descent, it is one that is well known to many. There is a city in the heart of Argos, pasture land of horses, called Ephyra [Corinthos], where Sisyphus lived, who was the craftiest of all humankind. He was the son of Aeolus, and had a son named Glaukos, who was father to Bellerophon, whom heaven endowed with the most surpassing comeliness and beauty.

— HOMER, *THE ILIAD*

THE RELUCTANT HERO

The Story of Bellerophon and the Chimera

ADAM ALEXANDER HAVIARAS

HYMN I

THE DARKNESS INSIDE

CHAPTER 1

THE SEER

It had been a long, hot summer's day on the island. The inhabitants of that green jewel set in Aegeus' sea waited out the daylight until evening rescued them. It was quiet as the fishermen slept indoors, and the goatherds rested in the shade of mountain pines whilst their flocks cropped at dried grass around them. The mountain pathways that led like arteries from their green and rocky heights to the brilliant sea below were quiet but for the constant whirr of cicadas.

Suddenly, a cacophony broke the silence. From up one of the mountain paths, a troupe of sweating, victorious youths of the village marched in procession toward the gathering place by the seaside. Men and boys, women and girls, emerged from their dwellings to see what the racket was about.

The boys marched past in triumph, each of them carrying a portion of a beast they had slain upon the mountain.

"We've killed it!" one of the boys announced to the villagers as he marched in the lead, carrying a great serpent's head on the tip of a spear. "Our flocks will be safe now!"

Behind him, his fellows lugged the body of the beast as if

carrying a newly-hacked cedar tree. They all grunted and sweat, smiled as they strained to carry the body of the titanic serpent over their shoulders, all except one last youth beyond the tail. He walked slowly, and last, tears in his eyes which he would not have shown the world as he carried the others' spears.

"Well done, boys!" some of the men called out to them, though the local priests wondered if the Gods might take offence at the slaying of so ancient a creature.

But the boys did not care. When they arrived at the teaching stone, beside the white-pebbled beach, they cheered as they dropped their grisly trophy and ran into the sea where the turquoise water turned crimson about them. They splashed, and cheered, and washed. They already retold and embellished the story of their hunt for the serpent, certain they would go down as heroes in the annals of the island.

The last youth arrived while the others bathed, and stood alone before the enormous, crooked piece of death upon the sun-baked rocks. The beast's head, which swayed slightly upon the tall spear that had been plunged between the rocks, stood oddly apart from its blood-caked body. The black eyes stared accusingly at him, a thing to haunt his dreams for years to come.

He had not intended to be a part of the hunting party, for he had never had trouble with the serpent. His father was a fisher-man, not a goatherd. While it was true that the beast had terror-ized the village for a long while, eaten countless goats, and even a few wandering children, it had been a creature of the Gods' design, with a purpose, a part to play in the drama of their island home.

No one else saw it that way, however, except perhaps the

priests, and the old man who usually sat in that place and occasionally told them a story.

"Don't worry, Daxeos!" the oldest of their group yelled at him from the water. "It won't hurt you anymore! Go on! Dig your spear into its side, just once! It's safe now!"

The other boys all laughed and splashed, and began to cook fish they had just caught over a fire on the beach.

The boy did not join them. Though it horrified him to look at the slain beast, he found that he could not leave its side. Its glistening scales of shifting brown, black and green still mesmerized him. He wanted to look upon it while he could, for soon the colours would fade as much as the descending sun in the distance.

Eventually the boys returned to review their work with some of the village men in tow, praising each other's feats of strength and skill, bragging and patting their fellows on the back.

And all through it, Daxeos stood back, not hungry, not thirsty, not interested in the tall tales that already circulated.

The cicada song slowed eventually as the day neared its end, and a fire was built up around the teaching stone. The attendant villagers faded back into their homes, and the boys were alone again, unwilling to let the day of their victory end.

It was then that Daxeos heard the familiar trundle of the old man coming up the path to the stone. He stood and rushed to meet him where the path opened up onto the sprawling rock surrounded by seaside pines.

"Good evening, Daskale!" Daxeos said as he met him upon the path.

"Good evening, Daxeos," the old man answered, stopping in the path. His old, heavily creased face smiled, and his sightless eyes searched for the location of the young voice that had come to greet him. He adjusted the skull cap that protected his bald pate from he sun, and his hands opened and closed upon the staff he carried with him always, tapping slightly on the rocky ground at his feet. "The news in the village is that you have slain a great beast."

The boys about he fire grew silent, the eldest standing up. "We did! The great serpent is finally slain, Daskale! Are you not proud of us?" he puffed out his chest, and nodded to his friends.

"Daxeos," the blind man said. "Give me your arm, please."

"Of course," the boy answered, and the old man laced his arm through Daxeos' who led him across the ground to the rocky seat that jutted up amongst the boys. "Here you are."

"Thank you," the old man said, leaning upon his staff. "Where is the beast?"

"The body is near your feet," one of the boys answered.

The old man was silent as he bent over, leaning upon his staff, to lay his searching hand upon the slain serpent's thick body. "He is dead then."

"Truly," said the eldest youth. "And we shall be remembered for this great deed!"

"Is that what you believe?" the old man said, his voice suddenly curt.

The boys grew silent, and looked from one to another.

"You may have saved a few goats and sheep, even the lives of a few children."

"But that is a good thing!" one of the youths protested. "My father lost many goats to this beast!"

"And mine lost six lambs last month alone!" said another.

"I understand that," the old man said. "I also understand that now that he is slain, there will be countless rats and mice in the village. What then will happen to our grain supplies that he will no longer be there to roam the pathways of our villages at night to devour rodents?"

The boys were quiet, some angry.

"Daskale?" said the eldest. "Do you deny that this beast terrorized our village? Are you telling us that it was not bravely done?" His voice was challenging, tainted with aggression.

"I do not," the old man replied calmly, rallying his patience for the youths about him where he sat upon the rock. "The serpent did both protect and terrorize our village. It was here for a reason, and so you must make offerings for the life you have taken."

"We will all make belts from its skin," said one of the younger boys. "And we will be known as the brave monster-hunters of Chios!"

The boys cheered at that idea.

"Well, all of us except Daxeos," the eldest added, his eyes turning on the boy at the old man's side. "He was afraid to even come with us, let alone throw a spear."

"And were *you* afraid?" the old man asked the eldest.

"No. I was not," the older boy said proudly.

"Were the rest of you?" he asked the others.

"No."

"Was that because you were in a group? Did you feel stronger together?"

They did not answer.

"What is fear?" the old man asked, and in that moment, the cicadas slowed completely in their song and the sea's breeze whistled through the pines about them.

"Fear is weakness," the eldest finally said.

"Is it?" The old man straightened as he leaned on his staff.

"I rather think that fear is the Gods' way of warning us of a great trial to come…or an impending sacrilege."

This last silenced them, but he smiled kindly, though he could not see them.

"You say that Daxeos here," he placed his hand upon the boy's shoulder, "was afraid to come. But he did, despite his fear. One might say that he was the most brave *because* he felt fear. Because he went with you nevertheless."

"Pssht!" the eldest scoffed.

"I knew a man once who felt great fear. Would you like to hear a story about fear, portents, and courage?"

"Yes, Daskale!" they all replied, for they never missed an opportunity for one of the old man's tales when he offered.

"Very well then," he said as they gathered around him in the fading sunlight as the sea lapped at the shore of the beach nearby. He closed his eyes as he searched his mind for the memories, felt the wind upon his face, gently rustling the boughs of pine about them.

"Let me tell you of one hero who lived with fear, but who found the courage to overcome it…"

CHAPTER 2

SHADOW OF THE PAST

There was blood everywhere, as though one stood in the middle of a great battle. Except, there were no armies to speak of. A man stood alone, turning in the dark as he screamed, surrounded by blood-soaked stallions and their gnashing jaws. All was chaos in that moment, and fear filled the man's veins from head to foot as the stallions closed in, kicking with iron hooves, biting with bared teeth that tore into his flesh and cracked his bones as he wailed.

But that was not all. For in the midst of such violence, another beast reared its head. Its roar tore through the air, and a great hissing froze what blood was left in his limbs. And then, all-consuming fire burst forth to close in on the man's terror-stricken eyes before death claimed him…

"FATHER!"

The room was quiet. Bellerophon was struck dumb for a few moments by the dream he had just endured, the dream the Gods had sent him again. Breathless and sweaty, he swung his legs over the edge of his bed to look out of the palace window at the sun. The great chariot was only just cresting the rocky edges of the Acrocorinthos, the high citadel overlooking the city of Corinthos and the surrounding plains.

Breathe...just breathe... he told himself, wiping the sweat from his brow and burying his face in his hands. He hated that dream, hated how weak it made him feel.

A cock crowed somewhere outside, followed by the braying of a donkey. For once, he was happy for their morning racket to invade and break up his thoughts as the remnants of his dream leached away.

Bellerophon, son of Glaucus, grandson of Sisyphus, stood and looked at the plain wall of his palace room where his great round shield hung above his throwing spears and sword. He stared at them for a moment, and then shut his eyes tightly against the still-flashing images of his nightmare.

It had been some years since his father's horrible death when his own horses tore him to pieces after Pelias' funeral games, and yet the images kept coming back to him in the darkness of night. He had not been there when it happened, but he was made to revisit his father's end over, and over.

Bellerophon felt his jaw tighten and went over to the stone wall where two handprints darkened the whitewash. He squared off before the wall, placed his trembling hands upon it, and pushed with all of his might. He focussed on the strain in every part of his muscular body - arms, shoulders, legs and torso - and forced the tension to still his mind, and provide some focus. When he felt calm, he stepped back from the wall. The surface had cracked where he had been pushing for so long, and yet the wall still stood.

Taking a leather thong from the small wooden table beside his bed, he tied his long, dark hair back and went through an open door that led out onto a small terrace overlooking the clay rooftops of the palace and battlements beyond. He breathed deeply of the fresh Spring air and watched the servants moving about the palace like ants about a mound of dirt. Some carried water into the palace from the spring outside the walls, and others headed out into the fields of olive and orange to begin their toils.

In the courtyard below, he could see a slave preparing a chariot for his brother, Deliades, to go out hunting, while another saddled horses for his other two brothers.

Bellerophon did not care for his siblings. He never had, and the feeling was mutual. He had never felt that he was a part of that family, and with the death of his father, the link that had kept them all civil toward each other had been broken. Some people whispered in the dark corridors of the palace that Bellerophon had not been the son of Glaucus, but rather was the result of an indiscretion between his mother, Eurymede, and Horse-Taming Poseidon. Whether or not that was the reason for his siblings' dislike or fear of him, he had never cared. He was an outcast in his family, and preferred his own company anyhow.

He chose to spend his days alone, training with sword, spear and shield for a life he did not have. His mother chided him sometimes for his lack of ambition, even for not being possessed of the cunning and ingenuity of his grandfather, Sisyphus, never mind that those 'qualities' had landed the latter in the darkest depths of Tartarus.

Corinthos was a prison to be sure, but where else could Bellerophon go? His father had had few friends, and it was rumoured that the goddess Aphrodite had hated Glaucus for preventing his mares from breeding. Even if there was a king or lord who would have wanted to take Bellerophon into their household, they would not have wanted to risk the goddess' wrath.

The sun was rising quickly now, the heat burning away the morning chill over the plain.

Bellerophon put on his crimson tunic, strapped on his sandals, and then took down his bronze sword, shield, and a clutch of short throwing spears in their quiver off of the wall. He closed his chamber door and went down the fire-lit halls of the palace, still haunted by absence, to the kitchens where he took a skin of wine and a loaf of fresh bread from the servants before going out into the lower courtyard to leave.

"Bellerophon?" his mother, Queen Eurymede called to him. "Where are you going?"

"To train," he answered.

"You have a wild look in your eyes, my son." She approached him, her long, pale hair falling over her silk-covered shoulders. Her green eyes looked upon him with pity and, for once, a little kindness. "The servants heard you cry out this morning again. Are you unwell?"

"I'm fine, Mother. I'm a grown man now. You need not worry."

"A mother always worries."

Just not for me, he wanted to say, but held his tongue. "The Gods sent me another dream."

She was quiet, and he saw that she took a small step backward from him. "Sit. Tell me of this dream," she said, going over to the bench beneath a large olive tree in the middle of the courtyard.

Bellerophon watched her sit, but did not move. Instead, he stood there in the gathering light, his shield on his arm, and the spears slung over his shoulder. She had never spoken up for him when it came to the others, nor tried with the council elders to gain him a seat since the crown was out of his reach. Now, years later, she pretended to care.

I don't want any of it anyway, he thought as he took a few steps forward, but did not sit.

Eurymede of Megara sat there looking up at her son expectantly. "Tell me," she said, placing her hands in her lap when she saw he would not sit.

"It is nothing," Bellerophon lied. "I dreamed of father's end. That is all."

She stared at her clasped hands in her lap and, for a moment, there was sadness there, more than he thought her capable of feeling.

It surprised him.

"Your father was ruled by fear of many things. He lived in your grandfather's shadow, and the end he too met still endures. Sisyphus built this great polis, and was married to the daughter of a Titan. Glaucus always compared his life to those before him, those around him. He was King of Corinthos, and he wanted to appear as such to his peers. And yet, he feared greatness and the punishments the Gods might mete out to him as they did to his father."

"I don't see what this has to do with my dream, Mother."

She pursed her lips, the long, golden earrings she wore dangling from her lobes. "That fear of appearing weak to others led him to treat his mares badly in the hopes that it would make them aggressive enough to win at Pelias' funeral games. He sowed his own doubt all his life, and in the end, it brought about his downfall. Now…while his father is tortured for all time in Tartarus, Glaucus' shade haunts the hippodrome of Isthmia."

Bellerophon lowered his shield arm as the weight of it began to strain.

"The problem was," Eurymede continued, "Sisyphus was not someone to aspire to. He was a trickster, and though he did found Corinthos, and fortify the mountain above us, his end is not to be envied."

She stood, walked over to her son, and looked up into his dark eyes. "I see the fear in your eyes, the anger… And I know that I have not done enough for you since Glaucus died. I am sorry for that." She placed her hands upon his broad shoulders. "Men need to aspire to their own deeds, Bellerophon. You need to overcome your own, individual fears and trials without looking to the past, or the deeds of other men. Envy and comparison only leads one to lose oneself." She searched his eyes for a moment, a glimmer of hope there, but even that was as fleeting as the feigned tenderness she now displayed in the palace courtyard. Eurymede stepped back.

"I must go now," he said to her as he hoisted his shield.

"Yes. Go. Train. Think on what I have said."

Without another word, Bellerophon turned and made his way out of the gate, the fear that had awoken him that morning now replaced with anger.

Standing in the swirling dust of the courtyard, Eurymede watched her son leave through the stone archway and make his way along the road that led to the Acrocorinthos. She turned and went back inside the palace.

Bellerophon walked briskly up the gently-sloping road that cut through the olive and orange groves that surrounded the base of the mountain. He was in no rush, for outside of the palace, away from his mother and siblings, he felt at last like he could breathe.

He did not see the point of his mother's words. It angered

him how she thought she knew him. She was always a bit sad, speaking only dark words to him. *She has had her own trials, I suppose.* But that darkness had seeped into him since he was a child.

The dream of the previous night flashed once again in his mind, and he gripped his shield more tightly and removed one of the spears from the quiver. He paused in the middle of the road, his eyes searching the surrounding trees where the sound of cicadas was settling in.

A few stray workers moved about the trees, pruning, but none else that he could see. But his dream stretched through the veil it seemed, for the sound of that roaring, and the sight of gnashing horses, seemed to be all around him.

Bellerophon shook his head, as if shaking away a flurry of flies, and looked up at the Acrocorinthos built by his grandfather.

Clutching his shield and weapons, he continued up the road that led to the sun-baked crown of the mountain.

CHAPTER 3

A MONSTER EMERGES

It was a long climb to the end of the road and the path that led onto the top of the mountain, and Bellerophon was sweating by the time he got there.

During times of war, the guard tower would normally be manned, and the fortifications dotted with sentries, but it was a time of peace, and so the high fortress was devoid of men. Only a few stray goats jumped from rock to rock across the surface of the mountain as Bellerophon made his way past the great spring to the high plateau. There, he set down his weapons and turned his head to the sky with his eyes closed, taking slow, deep breaths. Then, he walked to the nearest cliff edge and looked out over the world.

Despite the dizzying height of his vantage point, and the stabbing panic that rose in his chest every time he stood there, Bellerophon forced himself to look, to gaze down the jagged walls of the mountain to his grandfather's city set among olive and orange. He took in the turquoise mass of the sea and allowed his eyes to wander along the shore to Isthmia and the gulf of poor King Saron beyond where it stretched away into the distance to lands he had never seen.

The world seemed to be throbbing with colour and light, more than ever before, and he wondered at this, whether he was falling into a dream again, just as he always felt from those heights that he would tumble out of the sky. He hated the heights, but he had never admitted as much to anyone. Strangely, Bellerophon had found it necessary to go up there every day, to challenge himself, to train in the sky where only the Gods could see him.

After a few moments, he stepped back from the edge and went back to where he had left his weapons. The large, dead tree trunk he usually practiced on was set about fifty paces away. Bellerophon unwrapped the throwing spears he favoured, and began to throw.

One, two, three… His spears plunged into the dead wood, sending splinters into the air each time as they gathered together in a group. Four, five, six, seven… In rapid succession he threw, never missing, always accounting for the gusting wind in that high place.

When he finished throwing, he ran about the surface of the plateau, as agile as any goat there present, running and leaping from one boulder to the next, avoiding the basking serpents that usually stretched out up there, again, tempting his fears, his dreams of beasts and striking teeth and fangs.

Toward midday, when the sun was hot upon the mountain, Helios lighting his temple there, Bellerophon sat to drink some of the wine from the skin, and to tear into the bread he had brought with him.

He leaned back to look up at the sky, and felt the calm settle over him at last. Martial pursuits always calmed him, helped to clear his mind after the long nights.

"Goddess Athena..." he said, reaching out to the daughter of Zeus in his mind. "Grant me wisdom of action and thought. Guide me, oh Goddess, for I feel lost in this world." He looked at the gorgon head upon his shield, reminiscent of the Aegis carried by the goddess into battle. "Take me away from this place, away from the long shadows of the past..."

There was a flash of light then, blinding and hot, but when Bellerophon stood and looked around, he saw nothing but the wind in the grass, and the nodding heads of thistle and poppies upon the mountaintop.

Then, voices broke into his hearing, harsh and angry.

Bellerophon recognized the voices of some of the men from the city, and realized they must have followed him.

They were as jackals searching for the one lion cast out of the pride. The leader of the group was Belleros, the eldest son of his cousin, Thoas, whose father Ornytion was Glaucus' brother. Ever since the death of Glaucus, Thoas' family had been making attempts to take full control of Corinthos, and Belleros had been the most active in those efforts.

The group walked up the rocky slope toward Bellerophon, pointing in his direction. They began to spread out as they approached, until they formed a wide circle about him. Belleros stood facing Bellerophon.

Belleros was about ten years younger than Bellerophon, but the latter knew he should not underestimate him. Belleros was fast, and quick with a bronze dagger. He was not so strong as Bellerophon, but still, there were four of them.

Bellerophon checked that his dagger was tucked into his belt, and then bent to pick up and sling his quiver of throwing spears across his back, making no pretence about it. He glanced to see that the grips of his shield were facing up beside him.

"Run away from the palace again, Cousin?" Belleros said, chuckling as he pushed back his blond hair. "What are you training for? You pretending to kill the horses that ate your father? We all know how vicious horses can be!" he laughed, and his fellows joined him, their voices echoing around Bellerophon who could tell they were inching closer.

"What do you want, Belleros?" Bellerophon asked, but in that moment he could not help but see the vibrancy of the colour around him, feel an energy in the air that made his fingers and muscles tingle. His awareness was unusually acute, even as he saw Belleros draw his blade and point it at him. "I would put that away."

"Or what? What are you going to do? We've tolerated your family for long enough. Why should your brother rule, or your whore mother have a say in the ruling of the city? My father is the rightful king of Corinthos!"

"You speak of things I care little for," Bellerophon said, holding his cousin's gaze as he adjusted his grip on the spear shaft, holding it near the butt end. "Go home."

"I will. But not before your body lies here for the carrion crows," Belleros growled.

There was a tense pause, as if the four attackers were holding their breath collectively before they struck.

Then, Belleros rushed forward as quickly as he could, his blade out to kill.

Bellerophon parried his cousin's arm with his spear shaft and kicked hard, sending Belleros backward down the slope. Without wasting a moment, he spun, slashing the spear tip across the neck of the man who had been rushing him from behind.

Blood sprayed from the wound, and slowed the attack of the other two who were rushing over the rocks on either side.

Bellerophon bent quickly to pick up his shield with his left arm and turned again to loose the spear at one of the men, but the attacker was already crashing into him.

The man cried out as the spear tip found his gut and blood poured over Bellerophon as the wounded man wiggled like a harpooned fish out of water.

Bellerophon tried to gain his feet, but another attack came from his other side and he raised his shield just in time to deflect a dagger thrust. He pushed out and hit the man in the nose, sending him backward screaming.

Belleros rushed again, and Bellerophon turned and made for the high plateau where it was flatter.

"Get him!" Belleros yelled to his one, surviving fellow, and together they rushed after him.

When Bellerophon reached the top, he turned to see them rushing up the rocky path, spreading out. In that moment, he felt nothing but disgust and disappointment, with his entire family, with Corinthos, with his world in general. He could see the hate in Belleros' eyes, even though he had never done anything to the younger man or his friends.

And yet, all they wanted to do in that moment, was to kill him.

Bellerophon reached for a spear and, more quickly that they could have anticipated, he loosed it so that it shot down the slope to slam into the other man's throat, sending his body rolling back down the rocky path.

Belleros stopped, breathless, his dagger shaking in his hand as he pointed it at Bellerophon.

"Don't do this, Belleros."

"Put down your spears, coward!"

Bellerophon could tell with absolute certainty that his cousin would not stop. "Your father wouldn't want this."

Belleros laughed. "You idiot! He's the one who sent me!"

Bellerophon's anger rose at that, but he forced himself to stay focussed. He slid the quiver of spears off of his back and laid it on the ground beside his shield. Then, he drew his own, gleaming bronze blade. "Just remember," he said. "I gave you a choice to stop, and you wouldn't."

"You'll dine in Hades tonight!" Belleros yelled as he leapt at Bellerophon, his blade diving in and out like a viper's darting head.

Bellerophon parried wildly, dodged left and right, and stabbed out trying to lame his cousin, but Belleros was too fast, pressing him backward more and more with his attack.

Then, a moment came when Belleros thought he could deal his death blow and drew his arm over his head for a final death-dealing thrust.

Bellerophon lunged and kicked him square in the gut, winding him and sending his blade clanging on the rocks nearby.

Belleros screamed with fury and rushed with flailing fists, seeing that Bellerophon was near the precipice. He landed a blow, and then a second on Bellerophon's jaw, but then Bellerophon spun to get behind him, and Belleros teetered on the edge of the cliff, his arms waving as he tried to regain his balance.

Bellerophon's fist struck out and he grabbed hold of his cousin's tunic to keep him from falling to his death.

"Why did you have to do this?" Bellerophon yelled at him, his angry voice breaking out in the rising wind. "I've done nothing to any of you!"

Belleros spat in his face. "You breathe." Then, a second dagger whipped out from behind him.

Bellerophon swept his arm across to parry Belleros' arm, making him spin, and then he kicked out as hard as he could.

Belleros' body tumbled over into the air from that high Acrocorinthos, and he fell like a young vulture, too soon pushed out of the nest.

Bellerophon fell to his knees on the rocks to watch as his cousin fell to his death, his body cracking on the cliff face a couple of times before landing on the sloping earth of the olive groves outside the city.

Screams echoed up the mountain as the slaves gathered around the body, their voices rising up to Bellerophon's ears.

"Damn you, Belleros!" Bellerophon cursed, but as his eyes strayed from the groves to the rooftops of the city beyond, he knew that it was he who was damned.

Bellerophon slept uneasily that night.

Outside, the night sky was lashed by lightning strikes that echoed over the city, as if Zeus's fist pounded the rocky mountain above. Horses cried wildly from within the palace stables, and in the groves, sheep and goats bleated incessantly, running about the walls as if Corinthos were in the midst of a great maelstrom.

Bellerophon found himself on the top of the mountain again, surrounded by slavering jaws and red eyes. In the darkness beyond, there was roaring…hissing…and fire. The sound of shod hooves was all around him, and an angry neighing accented the night.

He spun, launching spears into the darkness around him, but the eyes, those horrid sounds, still closed in, pushing him more and more until he found himself on the cliff's edge.

From out of the darkness came Belleros, his body broken

and bloody. He reached out, and before Bellerophon could block him, he kicked.

Bellerophon felt himself falling wildly through the air, the dark earth rushing up to meet him, his final thought... *This is the end...*

CHAPTER 4

QUEEN OF SPITE

"AHHH!"

Bellerophon sat bolt upright in his bed. Sweat dripped from his brow and his body shook.

The pounding upon his chamber door echoed in his head and, disoriented, he looked about the room which was already filling with morning sunlight. On the floor, he could see his spears and shield, the blood still caked upon them where they lay beside his bloody and torn tunic.

"Open up, Bellerophon!" his brother Deliades said from beyond the olive wood door.

"What is it?" Bellerophon answered, though he knew in his heart what it was.

"You know what!"

Bellerophon stood and went slowly to the basin of water that stood upon a tripod near the window. His brother continued to pound upon the door, but he did not rush, did not care. He splashed his face with water and looked up at the risen sun through the refracted light of his wet eyes. "Gods… do with me what you will. I no longer care."

He dried his face and turned to dress, his ribs sore from the fight the day before. He pulled a clean, crimson tunic over his head, belted it, and strapped on his sandals. For a moment, he thought to take his dagger, but then he knew it was pointless, that Deliades would not have come alone.

He walked to the door and unbolted it.

Deliades, his older brother, stood there scowling at him with two armed palace guards beyond his shoulder. "What have you done?"

"They attacked me, Brother," Bellerophon answered.

"Four men are dead, and one of them our royal cousin! They city is in an uproar!"

"What are you doing here?"

"You're summoned to the bouleuterion. The council has assembled. I'm to bring you before them."

Bellerophon looked at the two guards behind. They gripped their long spears tightly, and stared at him from beneath the brims of their boar's tusk helmets.

"Don't make this difficult," Deliades said. "Please. Let's get this over with."

"Of course," Bellerophon answered. "We wouldn't want you to be late for your hunting." And with that, he pushed past his brother and the guards, and marched down the fire-lit corridor to go to the council house outside the palace walls.

Deliades and the guards followed closely behind him, their weapons pointed at his back.

The morning was clear, clean, and bright after the storms the previous night. The air smelled of damp earth and juniper.

As Bellerophon marched out of the palace toward the bouleuterion, stray dogs ran across his path, barking at him in passing. Silent citizens stared at him with dismay, some with hate, from the dark doorways of their dwellings.

He ignored them all as he went, numb to the outside world, and yet, he marvelled at the brilliance of colour and light around him. It was as though he walked through a dream.

But his dream ceased the moment he passed beneath the soaring columns of the council house and into the crowded chamber. The seats were packed with faces, including his other brothers and sister, his cousins, the scowling, aged men of the council, and even his mother, the only one who would not meet his eyes.

Bellerophon stood in their midst, the guards at his back as Deliades took his seat beside their mother.

Then, his cousin Thoas, Belleros' father, stood.

If there had been hatred in Belleros' eyes when they had fought, there was now purest malice in the eyes of his father as he gazed upon his son's killer.

"Bellerophon..." Thoas began, "you are accused of...of the murder of my son, your own cousin...Belleros."

Bellerophon did not speak immediately. He stared into his Thoas' eyes. "I did kill him."

There were gasps and accusations from the seats.

"So you admit it?" Thoas said, his feigned tears quickly drying up.

"I admit that I defended myself against attack. Belleros and his three friends attacked me."

"Lies," Thoas said.

"At your order, Cousin." Bellerophon pointed at Thoas.

But Thoas was unfazed. "More lies!"

Bellerophon looked from his cousin to his own family, his brothers, sister, and his mother, and none of them met his gaze. None of them wanted to be there. None of them cared.

He shrugged. "It seems that there is no justice in this chamber."

"There is always justice," Thoas said.

"What is the council's decision?" Bellerophon asked plainly.

"Death!" someone barked from behind Thoas.

"Death!" cried another.

In that moment, Eurymede jumped to her feet. "No!" Her eyes at last met her son's. Then, she turned to face the council. "Please, wise elders. You cannot execute Bellerophon, the grandson of Sisyphus."

"He is a murderer!" Thoas' voice echoed over the chamber, the lengths of his long grey hair shuddering like his jowls.

"Please," Eurymede said. "Not death. Let it be banishment for all time from Corinthos. The Gods will smile on you for it, for your just decision. It was well-known that Belleros hated my son."

"But he killed them all!" Thoas said.

"Yes," Eurymede conceded. "So let him be banished, never to return here."

Thoas continued to stare at Eurymede before turning his eyes on Bellerophon. He could see his cousin had no ambition, that he did not care for Corinthos, nor care for the throne like his older brother Deliades did. *I can deal with Deliades later,* he told himself.

"The council must vote!" Thoas proclaimed. "All those in favour of execution?"

Several hands went up behind him.

"And those in favour of banishment?" Thoas asked.

Even more hands were raised, including those of Bellerophon's own brothers.

"Banishment it is!" Thoas declared, stepping forward to

face Bellerophon. "Bellerophon... You are hereby banished from Corinthos and all its lands for the remainder of your lifetime. Return here only on pain of death. Do you understand?"

"Yes," Bellerophon answered. "You've got your wish, Cousin."

"My wish was to see you dead," Thoas whispered. "But this is a fine alternative." Thoas cleared his throat and spoke once again so all could hear. "You must be gone from Corinthos by nightfall!"

Bellerophon looked at his family then, and only his mother met his eyes. He nodded resignedly, turned, and left the chamber.

"Follow him!" Thoas said to the guards. "Make sure he leaves."

The guards nodded, and went after Bellerophon.

That afternoon, Bellerophon stood in the courtyard with his newly-cleaned spears and shield slung over his shoulders, and his sword and dagger hanging from his belt. He carried a satchel filled with his few possessions - a cloak, some food, and a tinder box - and stood waiting to see if his family would come to bid him farewell under the watchful eyes of the guards.

None but his mother came.

Eurymede emerged from the shadows of one of the corridors off of the courtyard. She was cowled, but her eyes were dry and unfeeling.

Bellerophon looked upon her, the woman who had born him, and he felt little besides a long-simmering resentment, and a void between them that had stretched wider and wider over the years since his father's death. He forced himself to be calm, however, for he knew that he would not see her again in that lifetime. And he could accept that.

"Thank you for staying the execution, Mother," Bellerophon said.

She stopped a few feet from him and pushed back her cowl. "Whatever distance there may be between us, you are still my son. You are still the child whom I bore for many moons."

"What have I ever done to you?"

She looked confused by his question, but she knew she had never been affectionate with him. In truth, she did not know why exactly, only that, unlike her other children, she had a constant feeling that he was not entirely hers to mother.

"You never did anything."

The answer confounded him, but he simply shrugged. He had stopped trying to win her favour long ago.

"Be careful of Thoas, Mother," Bellerophon warned. "He will stop at nothing to eliminate my brothers, as he tried to eliminate me."

"I know," she said, looking at the weapons he held in his hands and on his person. Then, she looked up. "My son. I know not what the Gods have in store for you, but know that you are a man of great strength and skill, and the battle upon the mountain yesterday only proves it. Wherever you go, I pray that the Gods protect you better than I have."

"They will do with me what they will," he answered, and he found that he cared less and less. He shrugged. "I only have to pick a road."

"There, I can help you," she said, stepping closer to him. She reached inside her cloak and pulled out a small bee's wax tablet which she handed to him discreetly. "Put this in your satchel now."

Bellerophon wanted to look at it, but he saw the guards eyeing them. "What is it?"

"A letter of introduction to King Proetus of Tiryns. I had the scribe write it out for me. Proetus knew your father, and though they were not great friends, they were not enemies either. Go there. Take the road southwest, past high-walled Mycenae, and then go south into the kingdom of Argos."

"You are sure that is the way?" he asked, never having travelled beyond the confines of Corinthos' borders.

"Yes. Your father and I travelled that way long ago. But do not stop at Mycenae. There are rumours of the harshness of the new Atreidai kings who rule there."

That was it. She had nothing more to say.

Bellerophon nodded and stared at her for a few, uncomfortable moments, waiting to see if she would step closer to kiss his brow, or even lay a hand upon him in farewell, but she did nothing.

"Thank you for the letter," he said, hoisting his shield and spears. "May the Gods give you what you want, Mother, you and my brothers and sister."

"And may the Gods protect and guide you better than I have, my son."

For a moment, he thought she might embrace him tightly, for once in his lifetime, but she only backed away a step as she pulled up her hood, and turned to go quietly back into the darkness of the palace.

Bellerophon glanced at the guards who had stepped closer. "I'm going," he said as he turned. He then walked beneath the great stone lintel of the palace to join the track that led around the Acrocorinthos to the main road.

.   .   .

The days grew increasingly hot as time and the road wore on. It seemed to Bellerophon that the road constantly sloped downward as he went, though he knew that was not the case. The arid mountains sloped up to either side of him and the sky, a radiant and pulsing blue accented by occasional clouds, seemed to stretch into infinity all around.

In some ways, Bellerophon felt that he could breathe at last, and he wondered how it was that he had never left Corinthos, never thought of wanting more, of wanting a family of his own, of seeing the wonders he had only heard of. Truthfully, he was not sure he cared anyway, for he felt still that he was a spinning leaf on the wind. But the brief glimpse that had already been captured by his eyes had sparked a minor curiosity.

After some days upon the road in which he spotted only a few scattered shepherds upon the stark mountainsides, Bellerophon passed into the rich lands of Mycenae.

Groves of olive and orange stretched out before him, and soon patrolling groups of warriors in bronze began to appear. They were pulled by teams of stomping stallions harnessed to sharp-wheeled chariots which hovered around the fortress' high walls like bees about a hive.

The men of Mycenae had always been lions and, if Bellerophon was honest, he was curious to meet them. But he did not need to add further accusations of murder to his deeds, and so when the patrols appeared, he hid himself deep in the olive groves until they passed.

From a distance, he could see the high, thick and warlike walls of Mycenae's citadel, but that was enough. And so, he carried on his course, turning south toward the kingdom of Argos.

At night, he lay beneath a canopy of brilliant stars and

wondered at the glittering forms those heavenly lights created. It was a script of the Gods' making, and if anything made him feel small in his life, it was the vastness of those heavens.

If only I could soar up to those heights and touch them! He thought as he lay beside his fire, his sword, shield and spears close by him.

The next morning, as the mist rolled around his sleeping form, Bellerophon's eyes opened slowly. He was surprised not to have dreamed that night, but rather to have slept soundly, unusually so. The sounds about him were different from the palace at Corinthos, the smells too, and all of that newness brought a hint of wonder.

He sat up suddenly when he saw a pair of eyes staring at him from behind the broad trunk of an aged olive tree. He reached for his sword and held it out at his observer.

"What are you doing?" Bellerophon asked. "Come out from there!" He stood, his limbs suddenly alert, ready to pounce.

"There is no need for your weapon," said a vaguely timid voice. "I belong to these groves. I play my flute, and the trees grow."

The satyr stepped out from behind the tree, his hooves clicking on the hard ground, his arms out, showing the expanse of his lean, hairy chest. He smiled, and the horns upon his head seemed to stretch with the action. In his hand he held a reed flute.

"Why are you watching me?" Bellerophon demanded.

"You are not from around here, are you?" the satyr asked, moving to a boulder to sit slowly.

"I am Bellerophon of Corinthos. I'm on my way to Tiryns to see King Proetus."

"For killing a man?"

Bellerophon's sword came up again quickly, and he stepped toward the satyr. "How do you know that?"

"We have our ways…whispers on the wind, music in the air…the trees flutter and tell."

Bellerophon was not sure what to make of the creature, whether he was lying or not.

"Why would you go to Tiryns?" the satyr asked. "There are kinder places to go."

"My mother knows the king."

The satyr shook his horned head. "A king in name only, holed up behind his high walls. He does not go out to roam the land."

"I don't really care what he does."

"You should."

"I don't much care. But I would be grateful if you put me on the correct road."

The satyr was silent a moment, then smiled. "Of course I can. Once you rejoin the road, turn south. Soon, you will reach a fork in the road, before you arrive at the walls of Argos. Take the road on your right."

"You are sure?" Bellerophon looked doubtful.

"You do not wish to walk, armed, through the city of Acrisius. They will imprison you."

"I see." Bellerophon bent to pack his satchel and gather his weapons as the satyr watched closely. "Where do I go after I pass Argos?"

"Go east along the edge of the sea, and you will come to Tiryns. Past Argos, if you reach the swamps of Lerna, you have gone too far."

"How will I know?"

"You will know from the putrid air." The satyr cocked his head suddenly and turned to leave. "I must go now. Farewell, Bellerophon of Corinthos!" he said, chuckling as he disappeared into the misty grove.

Bellerophon looked about, suddenly aware of the deep quiet all around him, and the feeling of growing menace that began to take hold of him. In the distance, on the road, horses neighed and he gripped his sword. He made his way to the road cautiously, and looked in either direction for travellers approaching him. To the south, a chariot sped away and the sound of horses faded.

He stepped onto the dirt track and began to walk in the direction of Argos, where smoke hung in the air.

Just as the satyr said, the road forked with the one on the right climbing up slightly around the city. The closer he had got to the city, the more people he saw - foreign-looking men from across the sea, traders, farmers, and some warriors - but he tried to ignore them all.

Bellerophon took the path the satyr had suggested, and carried on his way, glancing occasionally at the rooftops of Argos in the distance where it was set among groves like a dirty jewel among emerald leaves. It was larger than Corinthos, and yet seemed to be more scattered and haphazard in its design.

He walked on, his eyes drawn to the turquoise gulf in the distance. The road climbed up and he found himself among the sloping olive groves of another mountain. After some time, he emerged onto an open area with a view toward the sea. There, on a great flat space, stood a pyramid of thick stone, and outside of the pyramid, stood a chariot with two horses hitched to it.

Bellerophon froze at the sight of the horses, and the spears leaning against the outer wall of the pyramid.

The sound of the cicadas was loud, and he wondered if he should go back the way he had come, but as he turned, he was met with the point of a bronze blade.

"Who are you, stranger?" a warrior in bronze said, his dark brow creased and angry-looking.

Bellerophon put his hands out to the side. "A traveller. I'm headed to see King Proetus of Tiryns."

"You're going the wrong way," the guard said, straightening. "This road leads into the mountains."

Satyrs! Bellerophon thought, angry with himself for being so naive.

"Is the king expecting you?" the guard asked as he looked over Bellerophon's weapons.

"No. But I have a letter of introduction."

"From who?"

"My mother, Eurymede of Megara, Queen of Corinthos." Bellerophon stepped back a little, wary of the blade still in the guard's hand. "I am Bellerophon, son of Glaucus."

The guard lowered his weapon and sheathed it. "I have heard of your father."

Bellerophon wondered if the man would say anything about his father's fate as others had, but he did not.

"What are you doing so far south?" the guard asked. "And why seek King Proetus?"

"I needed to leave Corinthos. That is all." Bellerophon's eyes strayed to the horses warily, and the other soldier who had just emerged from the pyramidical guard house.

"Who's this then?" the other guard took one of the long

spears from beside the entrance to the guard house and approached them.

"He's fine," the first guard told him. "This is Bellerophon of Corinthos. He's here to see King Proetus."

"He's in the wrong place," the other guard laughed, leaning on his spear shaft.

"Can you show me the way to Tiryns?" Bellerophon asked the first, more friendly guard.

"I'll do better than that. I'll take you in my chariot. I was just about to return there anyway."

Bellerophon looked from the warrior to the horses yoked to the chariot, and shook his head. "I prefer to walk."

"You certain? You won't arrive there until dusk."

Flashes of bloody, gnashing teeth ripped through Bellerophon's mind and he shook his head. "I'm sure."

The guard saw Bellerophon glancing at the horses. "Very well," he said, remembering the stories of Glaucus' end. "Cut through the olive groves below the guard house," he pointed, "and make straight for the sea. Once you reach the water, follow the coastline and you will arrive at the walls of Tiryns. The guards there will question you, but tell them that Ampyx already spoke with you."

"Who is Ampyx?" Bellerophon asked.

"Me. They won't be rough with you if they know we've spoken." He paused and observed Bellerophon again. "You sure I can't take you in the chariot? My horses are tame."

"No. Thank you." Bellerophon nodded and began to make his way down, through the olive groves as directed.

"I'll see you in Tiryns!" Ampyx called after him.

.   .   .

The smell of brine and rotting seaweed got stronger as Bellerophon neared the coastline. It was a far cry from the dry, floral scents of the fields about Corinthos, but he was glad for the sea's breath coming off of the waves to his right where the water lapped at the long, curving shoreline.

In the blue gulf, just barely visible in the haze before the mountains rising to the southeast, Bellerophon could see the sails of various merchant ships coming and going from the port of Tiryns.

In the distance, mountains rose into the sky, and he wondered which gods had their abode in those high places.

He stopped suddenly, for he had a feeling he was being watched, but all he saw was the swaying of the long shore grasses in the hot breeze. He drew one of his throwing spears, adjusted the grip on his shield, and continued on along the stretched shore.

The closer he got to Tiryns, the larger and more imposing it appeared. It was not as grand as Mycenae, from what he could tell, but its walls were high and wrought of great stones. Smoke hovered around its crown where buildings were clustered, but the latter disappeared as he came close to the walls.

It was then that he put his spear back in his quiver and walked slowly toward the citadel, for all along the walls, he could see the heads of soldiers' boar tusk helmets, and glinting, bronze-tipped spears. They formed a strange halo about the battlements which ensured there was no mistaking that Tiryns was used to a war-time footing.

Bellerophon continued on his way toward the port where ships bobbed at berth, their rigging creaking gently while gulls cried over their heads and atop their masts. He approached an old, lone fisherman who sat in the sun mending his nets with weathered hands.

"Hello," Bellerophon said as he approached the fisherman.

The man did not look up, but a strange smile did form on the lips hidden beneath his beard. "I'm busy, can't you see?"

Bellerophon stopped and looked back at the fortress walls where the guards still had their eyes on him. He wiped his sweating brow and turned back to the fisherman, noting the tattoo of a trident on his dark forearm. "I'm a stranger, here to see King Proetus. How does one get into the palace?"

The man looked up from beneath his bushy eyebrows. "You want to go in there?"

Bellerophon shrugged. "Yes. Why not?"

"Cause you might not come out, is why."

"Just tell me, old man. That is all I ask." Bellerophon was ready to ask someone else when the man put down his net.

"You can't trust kings, you know," he whispered. "Especially that one."

"The laws of Zeus protect travellers and guests, do they not?" Bellerophon answered.

The man nodded. "They do, but only so far as a king will honour those laws." The fisherman sighed. "I see you are determined, so I will tell you. Continue down the road beside us until you get to the other side of the fortress. The main gate is on the eastern side."

"Thank you," Bellerophon replied and left right away. He did not notice the glow of the trident upon the man's arm.

The man smiled and went back to his mending. "And so it begins," he muttered.

Bellerophon felt his heart racing a little as he walked along the road, around the eastern side of the fortress and up to where the main gate was located. The air smelled of orange blossoms from the grove nearby, and there was a buzzing of bees from the fields about. His every step was observed, but no one addressed him until he came to the main entrance of the citadel.

There, two guards stood on either side of a wide gate propped up by two enormous stones.

"Hold!" one of the guards said. "State your business!"

"I am Bellerophon of Corinthos. Son of Glaucus. I am here to see King Proetus." To his right, he noted the chariot parked beneath a pair of olive trees.

The other guard turned to the one who had spoken. "He's the one Ampyx told us to expect."

They both turned back to Bellerophon. "You can make your way up. You'll need to leave your weapons in the court before entering the propylon."

Bellerophon nodded, and passed between the guards.

The walls were high on either side of him as he turned left up a long ramp. It was confining, especially with soldiers looking down on him from above, their spears at the ready.

He walked slowly up to a great gate comprised of two enormous wooden doors covered in hammered bronze sheets that glinted in the sunlight. There, two more guards crossed their spears before him, and he repeated his name and purpose.

The warlike men unbarred his way, and rapped on the doors.

On the other side, a bar was removed and the gate groaned open, as if it were a sleeping titan just waking in the morning.

Bellerophon then passed into a roofed corridor, lit only by a few torches, that led to another double door, this one smaller than the previous one. He paused and looked around for the eyes that were no doubt following his every move, but he saw nothing. He felt uncomfortable now, as if he were going deeper and deeper into the belly of a great beast, and he longed for the fresh mountain air once more.

Then, the doors swung inward and he stepped over the threshold into a trapezoidal court that was open to the sky and surrounded by brightly painted columns.

"You made it, son of Glaucus!"

Bellerophon looked to his right to see Ampyx standing with some other guards and walked over to him.

"I did," Bellerophon tried to sound casual, and at ease, but in truth he sweat a great deal as he had passed through the corridor, half-expecting to have to fight his way in. "I've never seen a fortress like this."

"Few have," Ampyx said.

Bellerophon looked around the court at all of the men staring at him, some armed, others not. There were some rooms where weapons were stored, and a stairway leading down at the south end of the court, lit by a single torch in the stone wall. To the right was the great propylon gate that led into the palace complex.

"How do I get an audience with the king?" Bellerophon asked.

"I have already sent word that you are coming," Ampyx said.

"Thank you for that."

"But you need to leave your weapons here." Ampyx pointed to a niche in the wall.

Bellerophon went over to the niche and, however reluctantly, set down his shield with the gorgon head upon it. Beside it, he laid his sword and dagger, and his quiver of throwing spears.

"Your satchel too," said another of the guards.

Ampyx nodded that it was all right to Bellerophon.

Bellerophon removed the letter of introduction and set the satchel upon the ground.

"I will present you to the king," Ampyx told him.

Bellerophon handed the tablet over and followed Ampyx between the soaring columns of the great propylon into the outer court.

It was quiet in the palace, peaceful within the surrounding columns of pale red accented by the blue and pink of the dusky sky above.

Around the fringes of the court, slaves were lighting fires in bronze tripods, but Ampyx paid them no heed as he led Bellerophon through another propylon into the smaller, central court of the palace. Here, the columns were more ornate, decorated with geometrical patterns. The smell of incense wafted from the circular altar in the middle, the smoke weaving about the columns and the cedar roof beams that covered the perimeter and provided shade during the heated days.

They crossed the court, passed between two more columns and through the middle of a triad of open doors. They crossed a room, the walls of which were decorated with a fresco of two women driving a chariot.

Bellerophon looked at the beautiful paintings and felt like the wheels of the chariot were turning as he walked past. On the other side of the room, they ascended a short staircase of red and green limestone until they passed through another guarded doorway into the great megaron of Tiryns, the king's throne room.

They stepped into a broad, sprawling room, the roof of which was supported by four thick, ochre columns that were narrow at the bottom and thick and ornate at the top. In the middle of the room was a hearth fire that was constantly kept burning.

On the right, across a floor that was decorated with myriad tiles of painted octopi and dolphins, was a raised dais where the king sat, slightly obscured to Bellerophon's sight from where he stood just inside the entrance.

Several people were gathered around the fringes of the megaron, some foreign-looking, others oily and officious. A group of women were gathered there as well, to the left of the throne, their backs turned to Bellerophon, their long, colourful robes touching the floor so that one had the impression that they were tall lotus flowers sprouting up out of the earth.

Above the murmur in the megaron, Bellerophon could hear Ampyx addressing the king, and a moment later, the guard returned to him.

"You may address the king," Ampyx said, and led Bellerophon to the side of the hearth fire opposite the king's throne.

All eyes were upon him now, and he cleared his throat before speaking.

"A cup of water for our guest," the king said before any words were spoken.

Bellerophon took a clay cup from a slave, drank and handed it back. When he looked across the hearth fire, he saw King Proetus sitting upon his stone throne as a tall woman, who was obscured from Bellerophon's view, whispered something to the king before stepping aside.

"By the laws of Zeus Xenios, Bellerophon, son of Glaucus, I welcome you beneath my roof."

King Proetus was older than Bellerophon had expected. His hair and beard were grey but thick and carefully oiled. He was still muscular however, betraying his many years at war, mainly with his own brother, King Acrisius of Argos. His eyes were keen and bright as they took in Bellerophon, waiting for the younger man to reply.

Bellerophon bowed slightly and spoke. "I thank you for welcoming me into your home, King Proetus."

"You are welcome to Tiryns, Bellerophon, son of Glaucus, by the laws of Zeus Xenios, Protector of Guests and Strangers, but also by my command." The king narrowed his eyes, taking in the man before him. "You have travelled a long distance alone and on foot." He noted the tablet in Bellerophon's hand. "Can you tell me what brings you into my kingdom?"

Bellerophon held up the tablet with his mother's letter. "My mother, Eurymede of Megara, sends greetings, and this letter, King Proetus."

The king held out his hand and Bellerophon stepped around the wide hearth fire to hand it to him.

King Proetus read the missive slowly, the room silent and watchful as he did so. The fire crackled and burned, the smoke rising up to the square vent in the roof above. When the king finished reading, he looked up, his face contorted in a frown. "You are banished from Corinthos for murder?"

"By the wise goddess, Athena, I did not seek to murder, King Proetus. My cousin, Thoas, sent his son and three others to murder me. I defended myself in battle."

Everyone looked askance at Bellerophon, curious and wary of the dark, handsome Corinthian.

"If my deeds are distasteful," Bellerophon began, "or if they cause offence to you, King Proetus, then I will trouble you no more, and continue on my travels."

The king closed the tablet and leaned back in his throne. He looked to his side at the taller of the women to his left, and there was a quick, silent exchange between them before he turned back to Bellerophon. "Your mother speaks of your deed, and of how you are innocent of murder. I accept that." He turned to his right and handed the tablet to his steward. "The Gods also know that family can be the most tiresome adversary, for I have warred with my brother Acrisius for many years."

The king stood and descended the dais to stand before Bellerophon. "I greet you as a friend, protected by the laws of Xenia. And while you are beneath my roof, none shall harm you."

King Proetus then took Bellerophon by the shoulders and kissed him in friendship on the cheeks.

"Thank you," Bellerophon said, bowing slightly again.

"You shall meet the people of the court and the rest of my guard soon enough, but for now, may I introduce you to my queen, Stheneboea..."

From the middle of the small group of women, one of them turned to come to the king's side.

She was tall, with long, dark, oiled tresses that fell from the crown of her head to her waist. She wore a long, dress of geometric patterns and waves, alternating in colours of red, yellow, blue and white that fitted closely, and was cinched at the waist. Her breasts were firm, and exposed, giving her the countenance of a priestess, rather than a queen, but it was her blue eyes that struck Bellerophon and made him not a little uncomfortable.

"You are most welcome to Tiryns, Bellerophon of Corinthos," she said, a thin smile on her face as her eyes bored into him. "You need not fear injustice here. You are safe and welcome. The Gods have declared it to me."

Bellerophon looked confused, but King Proetus spoke.

"Stheneboea was a priestess in Lykia before we married. She is quite gifted."

She held out her hand to Bellerophon who took it awkwardly and bowed to touch his forehead to it.

Then, King Proetus turned to all of the other courtiers and guards. "We welcome Bellerophon into our home as an honoured guest. Treat him well, and as one of us!"

There was clapping then, and Bellerophon felt awkward.

"Beginning tomorrow, let there be three days of feasting to welcome him!"

More clapping, before the king turned to Ampyx. "Captain, I want you to show Bellerophon to one of the palace chambers where he may clean himself from the road and rest. Have food brought to him as well, and return to him his weapons. We trust him."

"Yes, my king!" Ampyx bowed low and stepped to Bellerophon's side.

"Thank you, King Proetus," Bellerophon said bowing to him and to Queen Stheneboea beside him.

"Until tomorrow," the king said before turning to go back up the dais.

Bellerophon followed Ampyx out of the megaron, but he could feel the queen's eyes on him still as she took in his broad back on the way out. When they were alone in the central court, Ampyx turned to him, his face serious.

"The king likes you. I can tell."

"He is very kind," Bellerophon answered, wary of the change in the guard.

"The queen also likes you..." Ampyx said, his eyes betraying something. "Be careful there."

Bellerophon nodded, but in that moment he felt a chill as he looked up at the now starry night sky and followed Ampyx back through the maze of the palace to get his weapons.

. . .

The room that was given over to Bellerophon was located on the west side of the palace across the corridor that surrounded the great megaron. It was near the palace baths and was reached by a small staircase that led up from the corridor. The room was not large, but it was clean and well ventilated from high windows that let light and air in from the sky above.

Once Bellerophon was alone in the room, with the servant assigned to him waiting outside his door, he sighed and wondered how long he would be there. He realized that he felt terribly dirty from the road and asked the servant to take him to the baths on the level below.

The baths were not large either, but made use of fresh water that came out of one wall to land in a small pool and then overflow across the sloping, stone floor to go into the drain on the other side.

Bellerophon was given oil, a bronze scraper and sea sponges to wash. As he did so, he observed the painted scenes of river reeds, lotus flowers, and priestesses adorning the walls. The water echoed off of the bath walls as Bellerophon splashed and scrubbed himself clean. At one point, he paused in his washing to stare at the walls, a sudden feeling that he was being watched coming over him. But all he saw were the painted reads and priestesses' eyes. He went back to his task, and when he was done, the servant brought him a blue chiton hemmed with meander in gold while his crimson tunic was taken away to be washed.

The servant, a younger man, attended him silently and with purpose, never meeting his eye, never replying, only carrying out the tasks he was assigned by the queen who had sent him to care for Bellerophon.

Once he was clean and back in his room, Bellerophon found that a platter of food had been placed upon a small table beside his bed. He dismissed the servant and sat down to eat. The fresh bread and goat's cheese tasted good, and the wine he had been given was welcome, but as he ate, a sense of loneliness came over him that he had not experienced during those nights on the open road beneath the stars.

Bellerophon knew the laws of Zeus protected him as a guest, but he found it difficult to trust after all that he had experienced. He knew the king had welcomed him, but still… there was something amiss.

He decided to sleep and see what the morrow brought.

The following two days, Bellerophon awoke to the sound of gulls soaring in a blue and rose, dawn-painted sky. Food and drink were always brought to his room by the servant attending him, and he was free to roam the entire palace and explore the streets and stalls of the lower citadel as he chose.

Every guard along Tiryns' high walls, and at every gate, knew him and greeted him warmly wherever he went, and there was never a sign of distrust. In fact, Bellerophon quickly began to settle into the place, and even began to envision a new life for himself there, perhaps as one of the king's guards.

During the days, he roamed the corridors of the palace and the lower citadel, and observed the ships berthed in the harbour. In the evenings, King Proetus feasted with him as a true guest-friend.

It surprised Bellerophon, how friendly King Proetus was, but then again, he had never had much experience of kings beyond his father and older brother.

At the banquet, Bellerophon sat on the king's right side, while the queen sat to his left, and though they spoke little, Bellerophon felt the queen's eyes constantly upon him.

He had taken Ampyx's warning to heart, and had avoided the queen as much as possible, but she often appeared out of nowhere, familiar as she was with the hidden passages within the palace walls, those ways in which she and he women could move freely without the soldiers' gazes following them.

As they feasted, King Proetus asked Bellerophon of his experience in war and with horses.

Bellerophon stopped eating and turned to the king to speak earnestly. "To be honest, King Proetus, I have never been to war, but I have trained almost everyday of my life with spear, sword and shield."

"I've no doubt," the king answered. "If you could defeat four attackers, then you must have some skill. And what of horses? You must know much about them since your father was such a keen horseman and charioteer? Tomorrow, I can give you a tour of my stables. We have beautiful mounts!"

Bellerophon stiffened. "Forgive me, but I dislike and distrust the creatures."

The king's eyes widened, but then he realized his mistake. "Of course. Forgive me my forgetfulness… Your father's end was terrible and tragic. I do not blame you for distrusting horses, though, in truth, not all horses are the same."

Bellerophon tried not to think of the bloody dreams that still harassed him and had followed him to Tiryns.

It was the queen's voice that interrupted his thoughts as she leaned to look around the king at Bellerophon.

"They are sacred to Poseidon, Bellerophon, and worthy of high regard," she said softly.

"I realize that, lady, I do. But I cannot abide the beasts. That is why I walked to Tiryns."

"Perhaps you have just not ridden the right mount?" she

said, and her eyes widened as she stared at him from behind the king's shoulder.

"It is no use, lady. Horses and I shall never be friends," he said.

The king sighed. "It is a pity, but I understand your reticence, Bellerophon." He continued eating as a troupe of dancers filed into the great megaron to entertain them.

As the music started, all eyes turned to the dancers who twirled and tumbled around each other in an intricate choreography, all eyes that is, except for the queen's, for hers were locked upon Bellerophon.

That night, Bellerophon barred his door, for he could feel himself upon another precipice.

Queen Stheneboea was young and beautiful, it was true, but her silent attentions discomfited him greatly. As much as he would have enjoyed laying with her, he knew that to do so would offend the Gods and the laws of Zeus, for guests too were bound by those laws.

The next day, wherever Bellerophon went in the palace, he kept a wary eye out. To be safe, he decided to explore the more remote passages of the palace, possessed as he was of his grandfather Sisyphus' curiosity for engineering.

Toward the hottest time of day, when many were tucked away in the shaded corners of the palace chambers, Bellerophon found his way back through the great propylon gate into the court where the guards were gathered.

"How goes it, Bellerophon?" Ampyx's voice echoed from the shaded portico around the court where he stood with a few of the guards.

Bellerophon smiled and walked over to him. "Well enough.

I'm just exploring. I can't sleep at midday." He looked to his right where he spotted a staircase going down, then turned back to Ampyx. "Where have you been? I haven't seen you around the last couple of days."

"I've been at the guard tower up the mountain. The one where we met."

"Any trouble from Argos?"

"No, thank the Gods. The peace holds," Ampyx said, just as the other two men with him took their leave to make their round of the walls. Ampyx lowered his voice. "And how has your peace been here? Any trouble?"

"I've avoided trouble," Bellerophon said.

"Good. Keep to that."

"I find myself restless though. I can only roam the palace and lower citadel so many times. The only place I've not been is down there." He pointed to the staircase.

"Feel free to explore as the king said," Ampyx answered. "Down there is the galaria and storage rooms. If you're thirsty," he winked, "that is where the wine is kept."

"I am rather thirsty!" Bellerophon laughed.

"Then go," Ampyx said. "I'll keep watch!" he slapped Bellerophon on the back and sent him in the direction of the stairs.

Though it was broad daylight without, on the staircase, it was dark, lit only by the occasional torch. The walls here were painted with scenes of hounds pursuing wild boar, and the animals seemed to run with Bellerophon as he descended the short steps.

When he arrived at the bottom, he came to a long gallery of arched stone that went on for some distance directly ahead of him. He had never seen such a construction, the stones so expertly fitted together and peaking above his head.

As he walked down the corridor, he passed storage rooms on his right, the first filled with amphorae of grain, the next with precious olive oil made with olives from the king's own lands around Tiryns. Another storage room held game and salted meats, and another stored fruit and nuts in the deep darkness where no sunlight penetrated. The last two rooms were filled with wine, and with wheels of cheese, made from the herds and flocks that the queen had brought to the marriage with the king.

Bellerophon stopped in front of the wine storage, only able to see a little from the torch in a bracket on the wall behind him. He was about to step in when a voice surprised him in the dim light.

"I thought I would find you here."

Bellerophon turned quickly to see Queen Stheneboea standing directly before him, filling the entrance to the storage room, blocking his way. He bowed quickly, his heart beating wildly at the surprise.

"Queen Stheneboea! You startled me."

She moved closer, her exposed breasts rising and falling slowly as her long skirt dragged upon the stone floor. "I thought you might be here. It is the only part of the palace you have not explored in recent days."

"The captain in the court said it was all right to come down and get a drink of wine." Bellerophon stepped back a little, but was stopped by a stack of amphorae.

"Of course it is," the queen smiled, her kohl-lined eyes wide and bright, even in the torchlight. "We would not be very good hosts if we did not grant you the delights of Dionysos' nectar. Here, let me serve you."

Queen Stheneboea stepped forward, her shoulder and arm brushing Bellerophon's chest as she reached for a ladle upon a tall pedestal table where a few clay cups rested. She then removed a cloth that lay over the lid of the only open amphora, and dipped the ladle in before filling one, and then a second cup.

"Will we not add water?" Bellerophon asked, his thirst suddenly gone.

"It is best drunk in its purest form, so that we may experience all of its pleasures." She set the ladle down, replaced the cloth, and then handed Bellerophon a cup.

He took it reluctantly, conscious of her proximity and dark allure. She was beautiful, but there was also something he did not trust in her. She was like a beautiful panther, lovely to behold, but dangerous if one got too comfortable or close.

And he felt far too close to her.

She was about to drink, and reached out to raise his cup to his lips for him when he spoke.

"To the Gods," he said, pausing and tipping a little upon the ground between them.

She did not back up, but smiled and did likewise, the wine splashing his sandaled feet.

He found it hard to breathe in the cellar, but could not have left if he wanted to.

They drank, she slowly, and Bellerophon but very little at first, before gulping it down.

Queen Stheneboea's lips lingered on the rim of the cup, even redder from the nectar upon them as her blue eyes looked at him. She then set her cup down, her arms reaching out to rest upon his hips.

"The Gods have brought you here, Bellerophon. I knew it

the moment you entered the megaron. And I have been watching you ever since."

Bellerophon attempted to move, but she had him cornered, her grip firm and unwavering. Her breasts were now nearly pressed against his chest and her cedar and clove scent filled his nostrils above the wine. "My lady, King Proetus has welcomed me under the laws of Xenia into your home. This is not proper."

"You are honourable too. I like that. But you are also strong… My husband is old, Bellerophon, and I am still young. Am I not beautiful to you?"

"You are very beautiful," his voice was raspy and the wine was already clouding his head.

"You were meant to come to Tiryns, I know it. And you could…rule…in this place."

"My lady?"

"The people of the court are loyal to me. They tolerate King Proetus. You are young, beautiful and strong, Bellerophon. You come from the blood of Titans. If you were to slay Proetus, we could rule in Tiryns together. My father's army in Lykia would back us, and we could take Argos too."

Bellerophon began to panic, realizing only then that she was even more dangerous than he had imagined. "My lady, despite my reasons for coming here, I am not a murderer. I could not betray my host in such a way."

She paused, but then continued. "He is cruel to me. He neglects me. Would you have me live in such a state?"

"I am sorry to hear that, lady," he said, doubtful it was true.

"I could give you sons, Bellerophon. And then daughters." She grabbed his hands and placed them upon her flat tummy, her hips pressing forward very slightly. "Lie with me tonight, and I will show you the secretes of Aphrodite's realm."

She pressed her lips to his, and it was a supreme struggle for him not to kiss her back, however little or reluctantly. She tasted of wine, fresh herbs and honey. It was dizzying, but he clung to his reason in that dark cellar.

"Please lady, not here," he said.

She pulled back, her lips wet in the firelight. "You are right. We must honour Aphrodite properly. Come to my chamber tonight after the feast. I will make sure I am alone and that my servants are not there." She leaned forward to kiss him again. "You will see, Bellerophon. We can make a greater world together."

And as quietly as she had appeared out of the darkness, she disappeared.

Bellerophon stood there, dumb for a moment, his heart racing in his chest. He stepped quickly to the doorway to watch her leaving, but she was nowhere in the long corridor. He looked both ways, and along the walls for another door, but there were none that he could tell.

Suddenly, he had quite a chill of dread. It shot through him like a bolt of lightning, for he only then fully realized what the queen had proposed to him. Not only had she offered herself, but also the entire kingdom, and he knew that should even a whisper of that reach anyone else's ears, he would be dead before the following morning.

The thought harried him the rest of the day.

That night, King Proetus threw an even more lavish banquet in the great megaron of Tiryns. The tables groaned with food and kraters of wine, and the shadows of the guests danced upon the elaborately painted walls and across the ornate floor.

The entire time, Bellerophon found it difficult to focus on

his conversation with the king, for he was aware of every look and word of the queen's. He was grateful that the king sat between them, but he knew that would not stop her for long.

"If it were not for King Iobates of Lykia, then I may not have won the war against my brother Acrisius. Stheneboea, however, can be very persuasive, and convinced her father to send an army," the king said to Bellerophon.

"Was it a bloody conflict?" Bellerophon asked, trying to train his mind to the conversation.

King Proetus paused. He looked sad as he took a sip of his wine. "Acrisius is my brother. Yes, it was bloody and bitter. There is a lot of bad blood now between the people of Tiryns and of Argos, and still there are occasional acts of violence, despite our mutual decrees against it. Farms and families between here and Argos were ravaged for years." He sighed. "It is no easy thing to ignore Ares' battle cry when it sounds in your ears. The drums of war beckon to men like no other sound."

"We have had peace in Corinthos for some time now, but I wonder if it will last," Bellerophon said, realizing then that he would never have to go back there or worry about it again.

King Proetus noticed this and laid his bejewelled hand upon his arm. "When war is absent, the fighting starts from within. It is best you are not there."

"Perhaps," Bellerophon said, seeing the queen stand just then as many of the guests began to file out or fall asleep in their cups around the megaron, exhausted and well-feasted.

Stheneboea leaned down to kiss her husband's cheek. "My lord, I will retire for the night now. I am tired and in need of rest."

"I shall come to you later," the king whispered.

But she shook her head. "I am feeling ill, and weak. Perhaps you can tomorrow?"

"Very well, my dear. Rest. Feel better." The king kissed her hand and she turned to leave, but not without first glancing back at Bellerophon who quickly looked away.

Queen Stheneboea smiled to herself at his discomfort, and left through the corridor at the back of the megaron.

"My queen tolerates an old man very well. She keeps me young!" King Proetus laughed and held out his golden cup to his wine server to be refilled. "Now, Bellerophon. Let us talk of your future here," the king said, smiling at the younger man.

On the eastern side of the palace, just behind the small megaron reserved for the queen and her attendants, Stheneboea lay alone in her chambers waiting for Bellerophon, her thoughts bent upon his touch and smell. She was naked beneath a thin sheet, her body stretched out, relaxed and feline as she smiled to herself. She felt the chill of the night air come in at the high window to caress the soft hairs upon her arms and neck as she watched the smoke from her offerings to Aphrodite smoulder from a nearby tripod, and the dance of the firelight upon the painted walls where dolphins dove in the sea.

She waited for some time, standing at one point to pace before lying down again. She gazed at the daggers she had laid out upon her table, blades she believed she and Bellerophon could use to slay Proetus in the night, after they had enjoyed each other.

With a cup of wine in her hand, she entertained the prospect of her new life with a younger, virile king beside her. But as the hours wore on, and the palace servants stilled in the surrounding corridors to sleep where they would, she began to realize that Bellerophon was not coming, that he had scorned her.

It was then that her lust turned to anger and hate, and a new plot entered into her mind.

She rose quickly from her bed and went to her table to take up the bronze mirror that lay beside the daggers. She gazed at her reflection for a moment, partially hating herself, but mostly hating Bellerophon. She then slapped her face with her other hand, once, twice, three times. Over and over she did so, and then she raked her nails across the soft curves of her chest until she could bear it no more.

Eventually, she lay upon her bed and wept herself to sleep with curses upon her swelling lips.

Bellerophon slept little that night, for he could sense that his sojourn in Tiryns would soon be at an end. As he lay awake in his bed, gazing at the twinkling stars he could only just see out of the high window, he thought that he would try to make amends with the queen, to try and explain how much he honoured her husband for his kindness and how he would stay and serve her as a champion, but nothing more.

As the cock crowed, however, early the next morning, just as Bellerophon had drifted off to sleep, there was a loud rapping upon the door of his chamber.

The door burst open suddenly and in came the guard, Ampyx, and two others with their swords drawn.

"Arrest him!" Ampyx said, his face no longer affable as it had been. He saw Bellerophon look to his weapons and stepped between them and him. "Don't even think about it, Corinthian!"

"Ampyx? What is this about?" Bellerophon asked.

"Get dressed!" Ampyx growled, and the two bronze-armoured guards moved closer, their blades levelled.

Bellerophon put on his newly-cleaned, crimson tunic and laced up his sandals. He then stood, and before he could gather his things he felt the tip of a dagger in his ribs, pushing him toward the door.

"One false move, and you'll regret it!" Ampyx said.

"What is going on?" Bellerophon said as he was forced out into the corridor that led to the great megaron.

"Only lies come from your lips, son of Glaucus. I should have known!"

Before Bellerophon could say more, they entered the great megaron which was filled with people, mostly guards. The king sat upon his throne, staring at the fire, one hand gripping his wife's where she stood beside him, surrounded by her women.

Queen Stheneboea's face was bruised and scratched, and she hung her head low in shame.

As she looked up at Bellerophon, a feeling of dread came upon him, for he saw a glint of deep anger there which he had not expected, not even from her.

"Stand here!" Ampyx barked as he stopped Bellerophon before King Proetus.

When the king looked up at his guest, his face was haggard. He let go of the queen's hand slowly, and stood to look down at Bellerophon.

"King Proetus," Bellerophon said. "Why have I been woken and arrested?"

"How dare you!" the king shouted, and all murmurs around the megaron halted.

Bellerophon was confused for a moment, but as he stood there, looking at the king and the faces of the courtiers around him, the guards, and the queen's, the mystery began to reveal itself, and he began to suspect what had happened.

"King Proetus. As your guest, I ask to know exactly what I am accused of to be treated so harshly beneath your roof." Bellerophon stood straight and stared directly at the king.

The king looked at his wife, and she nodded meekly.

"Bellerophon, son of Glaucus of Corinthos, you are accused of attempting to rape Queen Stheneboea this past night, and of beating her when she refused your advances!" The king's fists clenched and unclenched as he spoke. He stepped down quickly to pull the queen forward and rip off the cloak that covered her, to fully reveal the scratches across her breasts, neck and face for the accused and all others there to see.

There were gasps around the megaron.

"Execute him, Lord!" someone shouted.

"The Corinthian has defiled our queen!" another accused.

Bellerophon looked away from the queen in disgust, worry setting in, for they were like a group of rabid dogs about him now, wanting nothing but his death.

"What have you to say for yourself?" King Proetus demanded, his voice soaring and angry above the others.

When the voices faded around Bellerophon, he spoke directly to the king, his eyes never waving from the older man's.

"King Proetus. You have welcomed me beneath your roof, and under the laws of Xenia, those sacred laws of Almighty Zeus, you have treated me with kindness, as is right...until now."

"Liar!" Queen Stheneboea cried out, standing tall now for all to see. "You attacked me!"

Bellerophon did not look at her, but held the king's gaze. "I did not, lord. Yesterday, in the wine cellar, the queen came to me and offered herself, and your kingdom, to me…if I should slay you. She told me to come to her last night, but I never went. After you and I feasted into the night, I returned to my chamber and never left the whole of the night."

"More lies!" Stheneboea cried. "He tried to ravage me!"

"I did not," Bellerophon answered plainly. "And I swear by Zeus Xenios and the goddess Athena that I was not near the queen last night, but for the banquet, and that I never even considered her proposal to overthrow you, King Proetus. The laws of Xenia go two ways, and I respect the ways of the Gods!" Now, he looked directly at the queen, and back to King Proetus. "Can the same be said of you?"

The king's face reddened, his anger rising, but there was also doubt behind his tired eyes.

There were some whispers behind Bellerophon, and then Ampyx stepped forward to whisper something in the king's ear.

The king scowled, his eyes looking for someone in the crowd behind Bellerophon, before he looked doubtfully at the accused. "Your assigned servant has said that you were in your chamber the whole of the night."

"The servant lies!" Stheneboea said, her hands grasping the king's arm. "We all know how false slaves are!"

"But the laws of Zeus are not!" Bellerophon added quickly. "Nor is my oath to the Gods that I did not do this thing I am accused of."

"My King!" Stheneboea growled. "He must die!"

"Silence!" King Proetus cried out, turning to his queen. "You are the one who told me to welcome him beneath our roof and honour the laws of Xenia, are you not?"

The queen stepped back.

"Be silent then, and let me speak!" King Proetus turned back to Bellerophon, his mind reeling as he thought about what to do. He looked from his wife to the accused, back and forth, and then settled upon something. He cleared his throat and drank water from a golden cup before speaking.

"The laws of Zeus Xenios are sacred, and as such they must be honoured!" King Proetus declared for all to hear. "However, our queen's dignity has been attacked and marred, and that cannot go unpunished."

Bellerophon's heart pounded more rapidly as he waited to hear what his punishment would be.

The king stood and looked down on him. "Bellerophon of Corinthos," King Proetus said. "You are banished for all time from the Kingdom of Tiryns, to return on pain of death. But you shall live, for the laws of Father Zeus must be honoured. Therefore! We shall send you on a ship this day to King Iobates of Lykia. I will give you a letter of introduction."

"And does King Iobates respect the laws of Zeus?" Bellerophon asked, annoyed that they should seek to send him to the queen's father.

"King Iobates is just, and honours the Gods. That should be enough for you!"

Bellerophon looked around him at the hate-filled eyes of the king, the queen, the guard and the rest of the court. *This is no place for me, for I will never be treated justly.* "I agree," he said to the king, refusing to look at the queen. "I entrust myself to the Gods' care!" he declared. *For I no longer care what happens to me,* he thought.

"Captain!" the king addressed Ampyx. "Take this man back to his chamber to collect his things, and see that he boards the ship that leaves this very morning for Lykia. I want him out of my sight!"

"Yes, my king!" Ampyx said, and then pulled roughly at Bellerophon's shoulder to march him out of the megaron with the other two guards in tow.

Bellerophon took one last look at the king and queen, before exiting the hall.

King Proetus turned to his wife as those about them began to gather in groups to talk of what had just happened.

"You should have killed him," the queen said to her husband, pulling her cloak back over her shoulders and chest.

"And incur the wrath of Zeus Xenios for sacrilege?" King Proetus answered. "There are other ways to see Bellerophon punished."

"How so?"

The king stared at his wife. "Your father will know all that has happened here, and so I will ask him to see to Bellerophon himself. He would not want Tiryns endangered by slaying a prince of Corinthos. But he will not want his daughter's attacker to go unpunished."

The queen smiled, and the king placed his hand upon hers.

"Summon my scribe!" the king said. "I must write a letter to King Iobates!"

An hour later, Ampyx and the guards were marching Bellerophon down the long staircase of the western side of the palace, to the harbour outside of Tiryns' walls. The heat of the morning sun blinded Bellerophon, and when his eyes adjusted, he saw that they were standing beside a rubbish heap.

"By the Gods!" Bellerophon cried as he spotted the body of the servant who had been assigned to him, who had spoken up for him in the megaron. "Is this how King Proetus rewards honesty among his servants?" he said to Ampyx.

"Shut up!" Ampyx said, shaking his head as he too stared at the young slave's corpse. "This is all your fault! You did this!"

Bellerophon shook his head and turned to the captain. "I did not, and you would do well to remember that. You even warned me about the queen."

Ampyx looked at the other guards for an uncomfortable moment.

"What I said in there was true," Bellerophon told him, sighing. "But it makes no matter." He hefted his shield upon his shoulder, along with his spears and satchel. "Which ship is it?" he asked, nodding toward the nearby harbour.

"The ship with the lion upon its sail," Ampyx said, his voice less angry and accusing than it had been that day. "The captain has been told to await you and welcome you aboard."

"Fine. Farewell then," Bellerophon said, and without another glance at Ampyx or the walls of Tiryns, he marched off toward the bobbing ships in the blue harbour.

From the ramparts of Tiryns, Queen Stheneboea watched Bellerophon board her father's ship and smiled to herself.

"Father…" she whispered to the wind and crying gulls, "… make Bellerophon suffer!"

HYMN II

TAMING THE BEAST

CHAPTER 5

SEA OF DREAMS

A voyage upon the sea has a way of playing with the mind, of cleansing, and of helping to forget the past. However, for Bellerophon, as he sat near the prow of the foam-cutting ship bound for Lykia, the last thing he could do was forget.

As the mountains of the Argolida faded into the hazy distance behind him, he still clung to the thought that no matter what he did, nor where he went, he would still find betrayal. He decided that mortals were inherently dishonest, and that wherever the road led him, he would not be caught unawares again.

He knew that he could not trust the welcome that awaited him in Lykia. He would have been a fool to do so. He decided to trust in the Gods, and though the pressure of the unknown weighed heavily upon his heart and mind, he gave himself over to their will.

Do with me what you will, divine Olympians. I will let myself drift upon the sea, for I do not care anymore what fate befalls me!

Hopelessness is a poor travel companion, upon the road, and upon the trial of this mortal life, but it was Bellerophon's and not even the cleansing sea could remove it from his side.

For three nights, Bellerophon slept upon the deck of that bobbing ship, gazing up at the stars' lights until he drifted into a sleep made deeper by his resignation and lack of care.

It was between the islands of Crete and Rhodos, with the dark outline of Carpathos' mountains far to the port side, that Bellerophon finally felt a measure of wonder at the world about him. The deep dark of the sea at night, mingled with the soaring songs of Poseidon's subjects, rose up out of the deep to surround Bellerophon and touch the stars.

In the sky above, the great Herdsman laboured in the heavens, and Orion drew his bow on the hunt. The Pleiades sang in the great echoing chamber of the heavens, and the Hyades turned and danced together, mesmerizing Bellerophon where he lay upon his back on the deck. Over them all, Sirius, the Dog Star, illuminated the eyes of the beholder, a beacon for all.

The ship's rigging creaked and the waves gave way easily to the prow with its great, painted eyes watching the way ahead. In the distance, from the shores of the rocky island, a conch shell sounded in the night and a deep silence fell upon the ship and its crew.

"Beautiful, is it not?"

Bellerophon turned quickly to see a woman sitting upon the railing of the ship. She was dressed in a long peplos that shimmered in the moonlight, and her long, dark hair poured out and down her back from beneath a finely wrought helmet with moving scenes of battle, which rested upon her noble crown. But it was her light-infused eyes, all-knowing, all-seeing, stern and yet caring, that drew his attention.

He turned immediately onto his knees and bent before her.

"Divine Goddess Athena!" he said, his voice but a whisper, filled with awe. "Forgive me. I did not see you there." He dared to look up then, and she smiled.

"You see me when I wish you to see me, Bellerophon, son of Glaucus."

Bellerophon looked at the scattered crewmen about the deck of the ship.

"Do no worry. They are all deep in Morpheus' spell. Only we two are truly *here*." She looked up to the sky once more and then back at Bellerophon. "Stand now."

He stood, as did the goddess, and he found himself looking up at her, his heart calm, his soul still as her light touched him.

"Divine and Wise Athena..." he began, "...why do you come to me? Am I to be punished at last?"

The goddess shook her head slowly. "Punished? For what? For defending yourself? For speaking truth? No. There is no punishment coming to you from the halls of Olympus. But it does come from those whose envy of you is like a poison in their veins, and in their minds. No, Bellerophon. I do not come to punish you, but rather to warn you of the danger into which you now go, and of the trials ahead."

"What trials?" he asked, wondering what awaited him in Lykia such that the goddess saw the need to warn him.

"As you know, King Proetus and Queen Stheneboea cannot be trusted. As such, the intent of the letter you carry is dire."

"I guessed as much," he nodded gravely.

"But this letter, which you must give into the hands of King Iobates, will set you on the proper path to your destiny."

In the distance, the conch horn sounded again, and

Bellerophon thought he could hear the distant, deep breathing of another god upon the shore of the island.

Athena held his gaze and reached out to take him by the shoulders. "It is important that you let events play out as they will, and that you know that I am with you. You are not alone upon this road, Bellerophon."

The goddess' beauty and strength filled Bellerophon's eyes, his heart, his mind, and he felt her strength reinforce his defences, make him aware of his own power and skill.

Athena smiled. "You are ready." She lowered her hands but her eyes remained locked upon his. "You must remember that you are a guest in Lykia, and that you continue to be protected under the laws of Xenia by Zeus. Invoke this protection at the court of King Iobates in Xanthos when you arrive."

"I will do all that you say, Divine Goddess," Bellerophon said, bowing his head.

"I know you will." Her smile was fleeting, however, and there was concern now upon her heavenly features. "You will need all of your strength and skill in the time to come, Bellerophon. Make no mistake. And there are things you must do without the aid of Olympus. Such is the way of things."

"I understand," he said.

She observed him for a long moment, and in his mind, he could hear the roar of lions, and the deafening cries of horses. The clash of great battles was added to the chorus of terror then too, and Bellerophon shut his eyes against all of it.

"I am not afraid," he told himself.

"You will be," Athena said, "but such is the way of the trials that fear is an ever-present possibility. However, I have no doubt that you will meet the coming challenges with honour." She leaned forward then, and kissed his brow. "Go now...sleep...rest..."

Bellerophon did as the goddess bid, and laid himself down upon the deck beside his weapons and few possessions.

The conch horn sounded a third, lingering note, and Athena turned upon the deck to look to the distant shore where a rock jut out into the sea.

From that rocky seat, Poseidon looked to his niece and nodded.

The Wheel of Fate is in full motion now, the God of the Sea thought.

Yes, it is, Athena replied.

You must be ready for Death to take him, he said, the tip of his trident aglow in the darkness, reflecting upon the still surface of the sleeping sea.

I am ready for that...as is he... And with a flash of light, Athena departed Bellerophon's side for the heights of Olympus while Poseidon watched the ship coast by on its way to Helios' island, and thence to Lykia.

A couple of days later, the ship finally came within sight of the broad Lykian coast. A long, sandy beach stretched into the hazy distance, its water-lapped dunes soft and pale in the early morning sunshine.

Bellerophon stood at the prow observing the terrain of this new land, and wondered what beauty or terrors he might find therein. The turquoise sea and sand were welcoming, but beyond that initial greeting, the land and sky fell away to a world of green groves and dry mountains beyond. It was not dissimilar to his homeland, but the unfamiliarity of the place, and the uncertainty of the greeting he should receive, lent it a sense of menace.

It was peaceful, however, until a great roar echoed in the

distance, unlike anything Bellerophon had ever heard. The crew on the deck froze momentarily in the midst of their anchoring tasks.

The captain appeared at Bellerophon's side, staring out at the landscape.

"What was that?" Bellerophon asked.

The captain looked at him for a quick moment, his eyes wide, but then he looked away to where a pillar of smoke was rising in the distant mountains. "It is nothing," he said.

"It didn't sound like 'nothing'," Bellerophon said.

"It is nothing," the captain repeated.

Bellerophon shrugged, and turned to see some of the crewmen lowering a skiff into the water beside the ship. "Where is the king's palace?"

"King Iobates is in Xanthos, just upriver from here." He pointed to where a river poured into the sea.

"How long will it take to get there?" Bellerophon asked.

"Not long," the captain replied before shouting to some of the men. "Careful with those amphorae! That's the king's Nemean wine!"

The crewmen looked up, sweating as they bent their backs to their work.

The captain turned back to Bellerophon. "You can walk with the wagon train," he nodded toward a few gathered wagons just cresting the ridge behind the beach, "or a couple of my men can take you upriver in the skiff to the palace walls."

Bellerophon shrugged. "I'll walk with the wagons," he answered. "After so many days at sea, I could use it."

"Very well," the captain said, nodding. "Gather your things and get into the skiff to go ashore."

Bellerophon belted on his sword and dagger and then bent

to pick up his satchel and quiver of throwing spears. Once his cloak was on, he picked up his shield and made his way to the edge of the ship where he lowered himself carefully into the waiting skiff beside a few amphorae.

It was a short distance to the beach, and the water below was clear and blue until the waves gathered the skiff in the white surf and sent it skidding onto the sandy shore.

It felt strange to set foot in a new land, but as Bellerophon climbed the dunes to where the wagons were gathered and being loaded, he felt that he was where he was meant to be.

He remembered his dream of the goddess Athena, and threw up a silent prayer to her, and to Earth-Shaking Poseidon for bringing him safely to the shores of Lykia.

It was like a dream, his journey, and now his arrival in that strange land. What had the Gods warned him of? What awaited him in the halls of bitter Queen Stheneboea's father?

For a moment, his mind began to race, but then he slowed it, resigned to his current situation. He trusted in wise Athena's words, the image of that goddess still lingering in his mind, behind the lids of his eyes.

I will trust in you, Goddess...

After some time unloading the ship, the crew settled for a rest upon the beach while the wagon train departed.

The armed men around Bellerophon who marched alongside the wagons and their cargo to protect it from marauders, observed the stranger in their midst in silent distrust. The captain had told them Bellerophon was to be a guest of King Iobates at the palace and that he would travel alongside them. They observed the armed, dark and long-haired Corinthian from beneath the brims of their broad rimmed hats, their fingers playing upon the shafts of the long spears they carried.

Bellerophon could see that he made them all nervous, that if he made a wrong move, they would not hesitate to run him through, and so he minded his own business as they wove their way up from the coast to King Iobates' Xanthian capital.

The plain grew hot very quickly as they travelled in parallel to the river on their left. The cicadas whirred deafeningly among the swaying field grasses and bitter laurels that sprang up in splashes of white and pink. Farmers toiled in their groves, and slaves heaved dirt as they dug new irrigation ditches for the crops that no doubt went to feed the palace of the king.

It was a rich land, there was no doubt, but there was something troubling in the eyes of every person that Bellerophon looked at closely. It was as if they could not rest, as if they were expecting something at any moment that caused them a permanent discomfort.

He wondered if the Lykians were at war, and thought about asking one of the soldiers guarding the wagons. But he decided against it, that he would wait to ask the king himself. He walked on, his eyes scanning the distant mountains, and taking in the dry-smelling air of that increasingly mesmerizing land, despite the hidden dangers he suspected lurked in the distance.

The Lykian capital of Xanthos was located on a high acropolis, overlooking the river below, and was visible from all directions. It was a jewel set in the crown of Lykia, surrounded by low, rocky hills covered with scrub and olive groves, sweet-scented pine, and towering cypresses.

As they travelled the road toward the hazy acropolis, the

river reached to its walls, tree-shaded, and lithe like a serpent stretched out in the sun.

To the northeast of the acropolis, among a scattering of small hills, various monuments of the necropolis dotted the landscape, some carved out of the very rock. Before the city gates, outside the great, layered cyclopean walls, altars and monuments to the Gods stood sentry, offerings from that morning still smouldering silently to scent the air.

The flow of traffic increased all around them as farmers and traders came in from the surrounding countryside to set up shop in the agora. There was everything from olives, wine and cheese, to weapons, linens, and even colourful birds, the likes of which Bellerophon had never seen in Corinthos.

The wagon train eventually came to a stop before the broad-linteled gate of Xanthos where several soldiers approached the confer with the train's head guard.

One of the soldiers, a man with a high, crested helmet of bronze and a breastplate with a lion upon it, spoke with the captain leading the wagons. They whispered for a few moments before turning their eyes upon Bellerophon.

The Xanthian soldier then approached the newcomer.

"State your business, stranger," he said.

"My name is Bellerophon, son of Glaucus of Corinthos. I have been sent here to accept King Iobates' hospitality at the request of his son-in-law, King Proetus of Tiryns."

"King Proetus sent you?" the guard asked.

"Yes. And I have a letter of introduction from him," Bellerophon said, suddenly distrusting the contents of the letter.

"May I see the letter?" the guard asked.

"I would hand it directly to the king, as instructed by King Proetus."

The guard looked doubtful, but he would not dare question the king's son-in-law. "Very well, Bellerophon, son of Glaucus." He relaxed and glanced at the wagons passing through the gate. "My name is Milyas. I'm captain of King Iobates' palace guard. Welcome to Xanthos."

Bellerophon inclined his head. He liked the man, but he reminded himself that had also been the case with Ampyx in Tiryns, who had no trouble turning on him, despite his innocence. *Trust no one,* he told himself.

"Come. I'll take you to the king," Milyas said before giving instructions to his men, and then leading Bellerophon through the gates into the city.

The streets were crowded, and the sound of the marketplace buzzed everywhere one went. The flow of traffic was certainly headed toward the agora on the acropolis, but there were also smaller laneways where humble dwellings were located, their occupants standing upon their thresholds, speaking with neighbours, or watching children play. They all glanced at the strange Corinthian as he passed, led by the captain of the guard.

People were everywhere, right up to the walls of the palace, which was located on the southwestern corner of the acropolis and abutted the steep cliffs that rose up from the river far below.

Captain Milyas greeted locals as he passed, and Bellerophon noted that he seemed respected, though not through fear.

But the air seemed to grow more serious once they passed through the great cedar and enamelled gate of the palace. It was quiet as the sound of the marketing crowds without died away and their footsteps echoed off of the high, rampart-crowned walls.

Soldiers in thick, linen armour with long spears watched from above as their captain led the strange, armed Corinthian through the streets, past a temple, to the king's megaron and residence.

The courtyard where they stopped was floored with stone, broad and hot in the midday sun. There was a scent of frankincense coming from an altar in the middle of the courtyard which was surrounded by a portico where guards stood at equal intervals.

Captain Milyas turned to Bellerophon and removed his helmet. His smile was gone now, as if he were relieved to have stopped forcing it as they had plied their way through the crowds, and his green eyes settled on Bellerophon.

"The markets are busy today," he said, sighing and wiping his brow before tucking his helmet beneath his left arm. "I don't know why you are here, son of Glaucus, but I suppose that letter you hold will explain everything to the king."

"I have not read it," Bellerophon said, "but that is what King Proetus told me. I am to hand it directly to King Iobates."

Milyas looked a little suspicious. "Very well. But… As you are a stranger here, I am going to have to ask you to leave all of your weapons behind. They will be safe. No one will touch them."

Bellerophon nodded, and felt the presence of the guards behind him grow nearer. "I understand, of course." First, he set his shield down to lean against the wall, the gorgon head staring up at him, and he prayed silently to Athena that she stay with him. He then laid down his quiver of throwing spears, and his belt with his sword and dagger.

"The satchel?" Milyas pointed.

Bellerophon dug inside to remove the tablet from King Proetus, and then set the satchel with his belongings beside his shield.

"Thank you," the captain said. "Follow me." Without another word, he turned and walked across the courtyard to the propylon on the other side which led into the megaron of King Iobates.

They passed through a wide corridor, the walls of which were covered in reliefs of battle between gods and beasts, including the battle between Apollo and Python. There were also images of great lion hunts, but the image that struck Bellerophon most as he passed was one of a strange-looking lion whose giant claws tore through fallen warriors and seemed to set all ablaze.

Captain Milyas saw Bellerophon slow down to look. "Come. The king is within."

Bellerophon caught up and was just behind Milyas when he rapped upon the tall wooden doors of the megaron. The doors swung open and they entered a great square hall, much larger than that of King Proetus in Tiryns.

Thick columns rose up like trees to support a cedar roof painted with stars about an opening where rays of sunlight and moonbeams could reach into the megaron at any time. There were painted reliefs everywhere, of charioteers and dancers, and of what appeared to be harpies over them all, as if to ensure their good behaviour with constant menace. Eyes watched from every wall and corner, such that if one were the only person in the throne room, one would not feel alone.

There were small groups of people gathered in various quarters of the megaron, some quite official-looking, dressed in plain robes and carrying armloads of tablets. Several scribes waited nearby too. Other groups appeared to be nobles, dressed in colourful silk gowns that clashed with their long, curled and oiled, black beards. Their dark eyes locked onto Bellerophon as he was brought before the king.

King Iobates sat upon his raised throne and was busy speaking with one of his courtiers. This gave Bellerophon a chance to observe him more closely. He was close in age to King Proetus, but not a warrior himself, though he was tall and might have been formidable if armed. His eyes were shaded with kohl, almost the same as some women, but it did not detract from his masculine look. His hair was also dark and oiled, and held in place by a golden circlet about his brow; it fell to his waist and was knotted with tiny golden lions, as if he carried protectors wherever he went. A great gold and lapis eye hung about his neck as if to observe all before him.

Then, the king's grey eyes turned upon Bellerophon, and he smiled.

"Welcome to Lykia..." the king began, looking to his captain.

"My king," Milyas said, stepping forward. "May I present Bellerophon of Corinthos, son of Glaucus. He arrived here by way of Tiryns at the behest of King Proetus and Queen Stheneboea. He was with the ship when it arrived this morning from Argolida."

The king's smile faded at that, but he regained his composure as he stood to welcome Bellerophon. "You are most welcome to Xanthos, and by the laws of Xenia I welcome you with open arms." The king descended the steps to stand before Bellerophon, took him by the shoulders, and kissed him upon both cheeks. "I remember your father, Glaucus. He was most skilled in horsemanship, and a fine warrior."

"Thank you, King Iobates," Bellerophon answered.

"Such an early and tragic end to what could have been a

magnificent life." The king sighed, his eyes locked onto Bellerophon's, such that it was disconcerting for the newcomer.

"Sire, I bring a letter from your daughter and son-in-law in Tiryns." Bellerophon held out the sealed tablet to the king who looked at it with some disdain, though he did accept it.

King Iobates turned to one of his scribes and handed it to him. "I will read this missive of King Proetus' later." He leaned closer to Bellerophon and whispered. "My daughter, Queen Stheneboea, depresses me, and I do not want to cast a shadow over your timely visit." He then returned to his throne and sat again.

"Timely, King Iobates?" Bellerophon could not help but ask.

"Yes," the king smiled. "The seers told me just this morning that Apollo declared that a great warrior would join us this very day from across the sea."

There was silence around the throne room, and Bellerophon looked around him, confused.

"Forgive me, sire, but I am no warrior. Perhaps some other man has landed in Lykia this day?"

"Perhaps," the king said, looking over Bellerophon. "Do you not have weapons? Rarely have I seen an unarmed Corinthian."

"I do."

"My king," Milyas stepped forward, "I had him leave his weapons in the courtyard."

"You may return them to him immediately. No one in Xanthos goes about unarmed."

The words were ominous, and as another silence fell on those gathered, Bellerophon looked around to see that every man there carried a dagger in his belt, and some swords or spears, even if they were courtiers. He thought that King Iobates must trust his people a great deal to allow such a thing.

The king suddenly stood up and cast his eyes over everyone in the megaron. "I declare that we shall have ten days of feasting in honour of Bellerophon, the son of mighty Glaucus!" He turned then to Bellerophon. "After that, I shall read my daughter and son-in-law's no doubt spiteful and demanding letter." He smiled. "In the meantime, you may roam about Xanthos as you wish. I only warn you that there are dangers in the surrounding countryside, and so you should not wander far from the city walls."

"I...I understand, King Iobates. I thank you for your hospitality to a weary traveller, which is pleasing to the eyes and ears of Zeus Xenios."

"Hail Zeus!" King Iobates said, and the words were echoed around the megaron. "Captain Milyas."

"Yes, my king?"

"You shall be Bellerophon's escort wherever he should choose to go. I want him given a suite of rooms in the west wing of the palace, and servants to attend upon him."

"It shall be done, my king." Milyas bowed low and backed away.

"I will see you this night for the feast, son of Glaucus."

"I thank you for welcoming me," Bellerophon said before turning and going to follow Captain Milyas out of the megaron.

When they were gone, one of the young priests of Apollo approached the king slowly, his long white robes swirling about him as a breeze swept through the throne room. His staff, which helped him with his failed eyesight, found the edge of the king's throne.

"Is he the one you spoke of? He is not a warrior," the king said, disappointment in his voice.

The priest bent low so that only the king could hear him. His prematurely-rheumy eyes sought his lord. "My king. I feel certain that he is, though he be not a warrior. Apollo was not a warrior when he first slew the great Python. But I shall make offerings and consult the Gods again on your behalf."

"Yes. Do that, Polyidus, and tell me what the Gods say."

Milyas led Bellerophon through the brightly-lit corridors of the palace to the aforementioned suite of rooms in the west wing. As they walked, having first gathered Bellerophon's things, Bellerophon noted more carvings upon the walls depicting great hunts, and he remembered what the king had said about carrying weapons. He decided to question Milyas about it.

"Captain, what did the king mean when he said that no one goes about Xanthos unarmed? Is that not dangerous for him?"

Milyas' step slowed noticeably, but he carried on without turning. "King Iobates does not need to worry about a threat from his own people… But all people worry about threats from without."

That was all he said for the moment and before long they were entering a suite of rooms through a pair of polished cedar doors at the end of the corridor. The three servants who had prepared the rooms came filing out, each of them dressed in acanthus-embroidered tunics, their heads bowed as the two men stood before them.

"These three boys will serve you while you are here, son of Glaucus," Milyas said, pausing before them.

"I really don't require servants," Bellerophon answered

preferring not to have someone looking over his shoulder at all times”

“It is the king’s wish. They can bathe you, if you like, or just bring you food when you are hungry. They sleep in the servants’ quarters on the other side of the palace.” He turned to the older of the three servants. “Are the rooms prepared for the king’s guest?”

“Yes, Captain Milyas. All is prepared,” the young man said.

“Good. Remain here should our guest require anything. The king is throwing a banquet tonight in his honour. See that he has clean clothes and a basin for washing.”

The servant nodded, and Milyas led Bellerophon through the rooms which were painted in hues of red and blue that echoed the sky. Except for a wide bed, a cedar chest at the foot, and an olive wood table and stools, there was little else in the way of furniture. At the far end, another set of double doors led onto a broad terrace where a tripod stood open to the sky. In the middle of the room, beneath a high vent, a round hearth fire burned, the flames like tiny Bacchae in a ritual dance.

“Is everything to your liking?” Milyas turned and asked Bellerophon.

“Of course. It’s more than enough for me. My tastes are quite simple. But you did not answer my question, Captain. Why must everyone go about armed?”

“Xanthos is surrounded by enemies who pose a constant threat to the kingdom.”

“Other tribes?” Bellerophon asked.

Milyas did not answer right away. “In part. The Solymi for one.”

“Who are the others?”

Milyas began to walk toward the door. "I must get back to my post, son of Glaucus. A guest should not worry about such things."

"But I should go armed to the banquet?"

"You should go armed everywhere."

Before Bellerophon could utter another word, the captain was gone, his crested helmet cutting its way down the long corridor.

"What is your name?" he asked the older of the servants.

The young man entered the room, his head still bowed. "I am Phoebos."

"Can you bring water for washing?"

Phoebos looked up and walked to a far corner of the room where a table sat with a basin upon it and sea sponges beside. Rose petals floated in the water.

"I see," Bellerophon said. "What else do you have to show me?"

Phoebos turned to point at another room where there were tunics hanging, cloaks, various belts and sizes of sandals.

"The king is very hospitable," Bellerophon said. He was, admittedly, a little suspicious of the welcome after his experience in Tiryns, but he would just deal with things as they came. "And food?"

"On the terrace, there is fruit, water and wine. There is also incense and sacred herbs should you wish to make offerings to the Gods." The slave pointed to the tripod at the end of the terrace.

"Good." Bellerophon eyed the servant. "Tell me something, Phoebos... What is the great threat that requires everyone to carry weapons?"

The slave's head bent lower, as if he were trying to hide himself to avoid questioning. Bellerophon noticed he began to shake, and that his fists were clenched together before him, whether in prayer or restraint, he could not tell.

"No matter. You may go now," Bellerophon said, and the slave quickly made his exit, closing the doors behind him.

Alone now, and trying to set aside his discomfort at the reaction his questions had elicited, Bellerophon set his weapons down and roamed about the room, his eyes searching the walls for any holes from which he might be observed. There were none that he could see.

Perhaps King Iobates pays more honour to Zeus Xenios than King Proetus did?

He looked at himself and saw how dirty he was from his travels. He knew he could not attend the banquet in such a state, and so he removed his tunic and sandals and went to that corner of the room where the basin of water was. In the ground at his feet were holes where the water could drain away, and as he splashed his face and washed with the sponges and scented water, the filth drifted away beneath the stone floor. Once he was clean and oiled, Bellerophon tied his long dark hair back and went to the dressing room where he chose a long red tunic bordered with a painted black meander pattern, and a thick, black leather belt to match. He put his own sandals back on and walked out onto the terrace.

The air outside was dry and hot, and smelled sweetly with a faint hint of perfume. Bellerophon could see the terraces of the palace rising up above him, designed such that none were visible from the lower vantage point, offering privacy to those higher up. At the highest level, he thought he spied a head of reddish hair peering over the edge, but whoever it was quickly disappeared.

He turned to see a woven basket of offerings and bent to pick up the tinder box and a heavy chunk of incense.

The bronze tripod, at the end of the terrace which jutted out over the river far below like the prow of a ship at sea, was thick and heavy, its broad bowl supported by three muscular lion's legs. Inside were newly-placed wood shavings which Bellerophon set alight and then placed the incense atop.

Soon, the scented smoke was rising into the air and he raised his hands to the sky.

Father Zeus, Protector of Travellers... Thank you for bringing me safely to this far off land... Lord Poseidon, I thank you for granting me passage upon your great kingdom that I may arrive here in Lykia. He breathed deeply, in and out, feeling the calm wash over him now that he was alone. *Goddess Athena, I hold your words to my heart, and will be prepared for whatever lies upon the road ahead of me. Guide me and protect me, Divine Goddess...*

It was then, for the first time in a long while, that Bellerophon began to hold to some form of hope for himself and his life, to believe that perhaps all was not lost for him, that he had some purpose. Only what that purpose was, he could not tell. He still felt adrift, and wondered at the strange lurking danger he could sense all around him.

Certainly, the letter he knew the king would eventually read was a matter of concern, but there was nothing he could do about that. All he could do was deal openly and honestly with King Iobates, and then speak truth when he was questioned about the no-doubt damning contents of that letter.

He decided not to think on that any longer, and sat beneath the silk awning on the terrace to eat, drink, and then doze in the shade.

.   .   .

Some hours later, still sleeping off the exhaustion that he had felt from his journey, Bellerophon woke suddenly to hesitant hands upon his thick shoulder.

He opened his eyes quickly, his hand upon his dagger only to be faced by the terrified visage of the servant, Phoebos, staring at him.

"F…for…forgive me, Lord, but I was sent to rouse you for the banquet which has already begun."

Bellerophon set the dagger back in his belt and rubbed his eyes, unsure of how long he had slept. He felt more rested than he had in a long while. He looked up at the servant. "I didn't mean to frighten you. I was having a bad dream."

This made the slave look more concerned.

"Will you show me the way back to the megaron?" Bellerophon asked.

"Captain Milyas will take you. He is waiting in the corridor outside."

Bellerophon stood and stretched and saw that the sky was darkening into deeper blues and purples, the sun having already dipped into the West. He went back into the room to a clay pot set behind a curtain to relieve himself, and then emerged to splash water upon his face once more. He looked to his weapons and thought about taking them, but decided the dagger was enough. "Will you wash my travel clothes?" he asked Phoebos.

"It is already done," the servant answered, bowing.

"Very well. I will see you later." Bellerophon turned and went out the double doors to find Captain Milyas standing there waiting with his helmet tucked beneath his arm.

"Ah, there you are, son of Glaucus!" Milyas said, his smile returned. "You must have been tired from your voyage."

They began to walk together. "Yes. I was, but I am rested now. This land casts a spell."

The captain said nothing to that. After a few moments, as they turned down another corridor that led to the court before the megaron, he spoke again. "The king has commanded ten days of feasting in your honour."

"Why such generosity?" Bellerophon asked. "I am no king. I am of no importance, really."

"King Iobates takes the laws of Xenia very seriously, and he hopes that-" Milyas stopped himself quickly.

"Hopes that what?" Bellerophon asked.

"He hopes that your visit will secure trade ties between Corinthos and Lykia."

Bellerophon laughed. "I think the king will be disappointed, Captain. I have no ties to Corinthos any longer. I have been banished."

The captain stopped and turned toward Bellerophon. "Why?"

Bellerophon thought about lying, but then decided against it. "For murder."

"Murder?" Milyas' hand went slowly to the handle of his sword.

"My own cousin sent his son and others to slay me whilst I trained. I defended myself. They lost."

Milyas relaxed visibly. "So you defended yourself in battle?"

"Yes. That is how I see it."

"Then you are falsely accused," Milyas said matter-of-factly.

"I'm glad that you see it that way too," Bellerophon said as they continued to walk. "But have no fear, I shall relay this to the king myself."

"He appreciates honesty, to be sure." They arrived at the propylon before the megaron. "So you train?"

"Yes, but I have never been to war."

"You have seen battle though, else you would not be here." Milyas smiled. "Perhaps we can train together in the coming days?"

"I would like that." Bellerophon looked through the open doors of the megaron and his eyes were met with a scene of light and colour, his nostrils with the sweet scent of spiced and roasted meats.

"Come," Milyas said. "Let me take you to the king."

They entered the megaron and immediately all eyes turned to them.

Musicians played upon the cythara and aulos from one corner, and in the middle of the megaron, tumblers performed acrobatics for the men and women of the king's court.

The king himself sat at a wide table with his attendants behind him. To his right was an empty seat with the seer, Polyidus, on the other side, and to the king's left was another empty seat, this one ornately decorated in a fashion after the king's own throne.

"Ah! Bellerophon, son of Glaucus! Join us!" King Iobates said aloud, and there was a general murmur around the diners as Bellerophon took his seat to the king's right.

"Please forgive my tardiness, King Iobates. I was overtired from my journey."

"There is nothing to forgive. It is a long way from Tiryns to Lykia. Sit with me, drink of the Nemean wine that accompanied you on your journey."

Bellerophon accepted a golden cup from a servant behind him and spilled some to the Gods before drinking with the king.

Almost immediately, fresh platters of roasted boar and goat were set before him, along with steaming flat breads, bowls of olives and plates of cheese.

They ate for a time without speaking, the king wanting his guest to eat his fill before they spoke.

When it appeared that Bellerophon's appetite was sated, and he settled into his cup of watered wine, King Iobates turned to speak with him. The rest of the guests continued their conversations and their laughter, and enjoyed the entertainment.

"So, tell me, Bellerophon, son of Glaucus. What brings you to the shores of Lykia? Why are you not in Corinthos, helping manage your family's kingdom? Should you not be leading Corinthos' armies while your older brother rules?"

Bellerophon's eyes stopped looking about the room, and he turned in his seat to look upon the king. There was genuine curiosity in the man's eyes, perhaps even a little concern, but Bellerophon knew better than to fully trust anyone, especially a king. However, he decided to tell the truth of what happened in Corinthos. *Goddess Athena, grant me wise words...*

"I was never given much of a role to play at court in Corinthos, King Iobates."

"That is certainly strange, especially for someone as fit and strong as yourself. Certainly, even though you were not a first son, you should have been given some responsibility, especially after your father's passing?"

Bellerophon shook his head. "I asked my mother and older brother if there was anything, and was constantly put off until years passed." He shrugged. "I saw to myself, training every day to pass the time."

"And yet, you have not seen war?" the king asked.

"No. At least, not war involving armies. But in Corinthos'

streets and goat paths, I often encountered men who sought to harm me, men sent by my cousin."

"Your cousin?" The king shook his head and sipped his wine. "I have never understood family turning on each other in such a way, especially when there are so many threats from neighbouring kingdoms. This is why I was reluctant at first to aid Proetus against Acrisius. Were it not for my daughter..."

Bellerophon pressed on, wishing to avoid talk of Stheneboea. "In Corinthos, perhaps it was because we were not under threat for so long that things began to go awry inside?" Bellerophon emptied his cup and a slave immediately refilled it. "My cousin seeks the throne. He always has. And he knew that if he made a move upon my brother or mother, I would be a problem for him. So, one day, while I was training upon the mountain, he sent his son and three others to kill me."

Understanding began to dawn upon the king's face, and something of relief. "They tried and failed, I assume."

Bellerophon was quiet. He could still see Belleros falling through the air, so far, to his death. He felt the king's hand upon his arm.

"It is no easy thing for a good man to kill, Bellerophon. I can see that what happened distresses you. But you defended yourself, correct?"

"I did." Bellerophon nodded.

"And you slew them all? On your own?"

"Yes."

King Iobates sat straight and nodded. "You did nothing wrong. And you proved yourself a strong warrior. Some men do not even kill one enemy in a pitched battle, but you slew four with your own hands."

"And I am not proud of it."

"The more honour to you for saying so," the king added,

and before Bellerophon could say more, King Iobates stood and raised his cup.

The room grew silent immediately as all the other guests turned their attention to their king.

"I drink to Bellerophon, son of Glaucus, a man of great courage, honesty, and honour. By Zeus Xenios, we are honoured to welcome him to our halls for as long as he need stay! Bellerophon!"

"Bellerophon!" the guests echoed and drank with the king.

Bellerophon felt his face grow hot, but found the grace to incline his head in humility and drink along with them. To his right, he felt the seer, Polyidus, lean in to speak to him for the first time.

The seer's eyes were veiled with white cataracts, but Bellerophon got the sense that the man - who was not as old as one might expect - could see more than he let on. In truth, seers made Bellerophon uncomfortable, for they had communion with the Gods on a completely different level to most men.

Polyidus' blue robes rustled as he made to speak. "I could not help but hear your story, son of Glaucus. Truly, I think the Gods have a different purpose for you. They have protected you thus for so long."

"I honour the Gods, as is fit and right," Bellerophon answered, leaning away from the seer in his chair.

Polyidus smiled kindly and nodded. "Have they approached you of late? Especially she of the Bright Eyes?" He whispered this so low that Bellerophon wondered if he had even spoken, but then he realized Polyidus' meaning.

"A man's converse with the Gods is his own," Bellerophon answered.

Polyidus nodded. "True enough, unless you are a king's

seer." He winked with his pale eyes and went back to his meal, his hands finding things upon his platter with precision.

Bellerophon noticed King Iobates listening to them as well, and then looked beyond the king to the empty seat on his left.

"King Iobates, I see an empty seat to your left. Is your queen not joining us?"

King Iobates' face darkened and he looked down. "My wife was taken from me many years ago, in an attack by the Solymi tribe. They slew her and many others she was trying to protect."

"How terrible for you."

King Iobates said nothing, but the dark look that overtook his features said much. "I will never forgive those people, and I will not rest until they are wiped out." They drank again. "My people lost their queen that day, a queen they loved. I lost my wife, and my young daughters their mother."

"You have more than one daughter?"

"All I have left here is my younger daughter, Philonoe. The Gods never sought to give me sons." King Iobates seemed to retreat at that moment, his mind elsewhere. "Philonoe was not feeling well this night, else she would have been here to receive you as our guest. Tomorrow, you shall meet her."

Bellerophon nodded. He understood why the seat beside the king was empty, but he suspected there was more to what the king had said about his lost queen. *Another daughter?* he worried. *If she is at all like Queen Stheneboea, I will leave Lykia as soon as I can.*

Bellerophon slept deeply that night, more so than he had in a long time, and when he awoke the next morning, it was to warm breeze coming in at the curtained doorway to the terrace of his rooms. The scent of dew-covered jasmine tickled his senses, and he could hear mourning doves cooing on the terraces of the palace above him. When he opened his eyes, it was to the sun's faint light where it cast a soft glow onto the altar that jut out over the river far below.

Bellerophon rose from his bed and rubbed his eyes before going to relieve himself and wash in the basin of fresh water which, apparently, the slaves had refreshed while he still slept. When he finished, he went outside to find the table filled once more with fresh fruit, cheeses, and honeyed breads. The sight made him hungry, but first he took up the tinder box and a sprig of herbs from the basket near the doorway and went directly to the altar.

Bellerophon knelt upon the stone floor, lit the herbs which began to smoulder and burn, and raised his hands to the sky.

Goddess Athena, thank you for protecting me and guiding my words...

He felt a breeze upon his face and opened his eyes to see the goddess standing on the other side of the altar. Her eyes pierced him and he struggled not to look away.

Do not fall under the spell of this palace or of King Iobates, the goddess commanded. *Remember what I told you, son of Glaucus.*

I do, oh Goddess, Bellerophon responded in his mind.

There is a rot in Lykia, Athena warned, *but there is also a great goodness. Seek it out and protect it.*

Bellerophon looked up from the smoking offering again, but the goddess was gone once more. He stood, suddenly feeling quite cold, and stepped around the altar to look at the spot where the goddess had stood. He gazed down the cliffs to the swift-flowing river far below and stepped quickly back from the edge, recoiling from the great height. When he turned however, he was made more uncomfortable by the sight of the seer, Polyidus, looking in his direction from one of the higher terraces.

Beyond the seer also was the outline of another whose clothing was only just set alight by the sun's rising rays.

Bellerophon could not tear his eyes away for a few moments, and then the apparition was gone, leaving only the seer looking down on him. Bellerophon waved back, though he doubted the man saw the gesture, and went immediately to sit beneath the awning to eat.

The palace was quiet in the west wing, but he had the impression that there were indeed eyes everywhere, and he did not enjoy the feeling.

Bellerophon remained in his rooms the whole of that day, preferring to keep to himself and rest as the king was apparently busy with his advisors and the business of running the kingdom.

King Iobates had sent word to him by way of Captain Milyas that he would see him at the banquet that night.

The day passed quickly enough as Bellerophon rested and trained on his own with sword and shield in the spacious rooms where he dwelled. A part of him wanted to explore the city, but something inside him said he should not venture out just yet. But the time he had alone was accented with moments of worry, for he wondered if the king had decided to open the letter from King Proetus. He half expected the guards to burst into his rooms to arrest him at any moment, but they never came.

When the sun set that evening, and the braziers were lit around the palace, Captain Milyas arrived to bring Bellerophon to the feast once more. He was in a jovial mood, and gave no hint of anger or aggression.

"You must be tired from your journey to Lykia?" Milyas asked as they walked. "Did you sleep the whole day?"

Bellerophon shook his head. "I am well rested now. I spent some time training in my rooms."

"Training?" Milyas said. "There is not the space to train in there!"

"There is enough," Bellerophon answered.

"Perhaps tomorrow you may wish to accompany me to the training grounds outside the eastern wall? I would like to see how you use your throwing spears."

Bellerophon looked at the captain and saw no hint of malice there. "We can do that," he said cautiously.

"That is, if we don't drink too much this night!" Milyas laughed and slapped him on the back as the two of them entered the megaron.

There were fewer guests that night, and when Bellerophon looked, he could see the same empty seats to either side of King Iobates. There were no tumblers or acrobats this time, as the gathering was more civilized and sedate. A single musician played the aulos whilst a young woman in flowing, sheer robes danced, moving about the hearth fire like a nymph at a midsummer celebration.

The other guests acknowledged Bellerophon as he made his way to his seat between the king and Polyidus once more.

"I trust you had a restful day, Bellerophon?" the king asked, smiling at him.

"I did. Thank you, King Iobates. The mornings here are most peaceful."

"I am glad to hear it, but you should venture out into the markets at some point. You will be amazed by the wares you see. I wonder if our markets outdo those of Corinthos?" the king smiled.

"I can tell you now, Lord, they do. From what little I saw when I arrived, you have trade from far and wide." Bellerophon poured some of his wine onto the floor and drank before taking food from the platters of vegetables, cheeses and breads that had just been set out before them. "I will accompany your captain to the training grounds tomorrow," he added.

King Iobates did not answer for a moment. "Excellent. I should like to see your skills for myself. Would you not also, Polyidus?"

"Yes, my king," the seer answered as he picked at a hunk of bread.

They ate in silence for a time, but after a while, Bellerophon could not wait any longer. "King Iobates..."

"Yes, Bellerophon?" the king responded, still smiling.

"Have you read the letter from King Proetus yet?"

King Iobates set his food on his plate and wiped his fingers on a cloth napkin which lay to the side. He turned to look at Bellerophon.

This is it, Bellerophon thought. *I will not be welcome for long.*

"From what you have told me of your life in Corinthos, of your family after your father's passing, they are not trustworthy. Indeed, they seem to have used you, put you out as bait for your cousin to take. Perhaps as a gauge of his loyalty?"

"I...I have never thought of it in that way. I thought they simply did not care." The realization hit Bellerophon hard in the moment.

"I am only guessing, but from what you told me last night,

they certainly did care, only it was for themselves and not for you."

The feeling of loneliness in that moment was supreme and overwhelming, but the king's hand upon Bellerophon's arm brought him back.

"Forgive me. I do not mean to upset you after all that you have been through. Kings have ways of seeing things where more innocent men do not. But I say this because it is the same with my daughter, Queen Stheneboea, and King Proetus. They do not care for me or Lykia. They care for themselves. My daughter pulled me into a war - a family squabble - in which I should not have been involved. True, we gained some trade from the agreement, but let us be frank. There is not much in Argolida which we cannot get from our own lands and allies to the East." The king sat back in his chair and held his cup up to Bellerophon. "As I said when you arrived, my eldest daughter depresses me with her Stygian moods, and I have no wish to taint my duties as host with her news. You have told me the reasons you left Corinthos, and I believe you. That is enough for me, Bellerophon. I will read her missive at a later date, when I am ready."

"I thank you for your confidence, King Iobates," Bellerophon said.

"Think nothing of it," the king said waving his hand.

It was in that moment that the room grew silent and all stood, except for the king, Polyidus, and Bellerophon, for behind the three, Princess Philonoe had entered the megaron and approached her seat to her father's left.

"Good evening, Father," she said with a voice as soft and clear as the aulos being played on the other side of the hall.

Bellerophon stood up immediately and turned to greet the princess who stepped to her seat beside her father, but not before turning and smiling at the other guests for them to take their seats.

She also smiled shyly at Bellerophon, and that simple, slightly curious look gave the Corinthian pause.

Princess Philonoe was not at all what Bellerophon had expected as a daughter of King Iobates and sister of Stheneboea, for they were both dark of complexion and hair. The princess who stood before Bellerophon was pale-skinned, though not at all sickly. In fact, her face had a scattering of faint freckles that came with time in the sunshine. These orbited her green eyes in a way that was mesmerizing and drew one in. Her hair was of a fiery red in the light cast by the hearth, and it was tied back in a long single tress with golden ribbons. She wore a thin golden circlet about her crown to match her father's. Her body, from what one could see, was unexpectedly athletic, with long, lithe and muscular limbs. She too carried a dagger, but she carried it in a way that was more natural to her, not with the required awkwardness with which most of the courtiers carried theirs.

When Princess Philonoe sat, Bellerophon retook his own seat.

"Bellerophon of Corinthos, I present my younger daughter, Princess Philonoe," King Iobates said, looking from his daughter to Bellerophon.

"Princess," Bellerophon said, inclining his head.

"Son of Glaucus, you are most welcome to Xanthos," she said graciously, with a smile that made one want to study her more.

Careful, Bellerophon told himself. *Remember the beast her sister was.*

The truth was, however, that his initial feeling from Philonoe was in no way similar to how he had felt upon meeting her older sister. Still, Bellerophon decided he would be slightly distant, though not uncouth. He needed to exercise caution in his precarious position.

"Thank you, Princess Philonoe," he said, trying not to lock onto her eyes.

"My father has told me about your journeys and the reasons you left Corinthos-"

"Daughter!" the king protested at the breach of confidence.

"It is all right, my lord," Bellerophon said. "I accept the trials the Gods have put before me."

He did not see the king glance across at Polyidus.

Bellerophon looked to the princess again. "I am grateful that my path has led me to Xanthos, no matter the torment I endured in my homeland. Your father truly does honour to Zeus Xenios."

"My father is true to the Gods and their laws," Philonoe said, placing her hand upon her father's arm and making him smile.

But the king frowned when he looked at her face. "You have been too much in the sun, Daughter. It mars your features."

Rather than be silenced or angry, Philonoe smiled and kissed her father's cheek. "Oh, Father. Helios' rays bless us every day and bring health and vitality to mortals as well as to crops. Worry not."

Bellerophon tried not to smile at the way this young girl dismissed a king's chiding with such kindness.

Philonoe leaned forward to see Bellerophon as she took a sip of her watered wine from a golden cup. "Tell me, Bellerophon of Corinthos... What do you think of our kingdom thus far?"

Bellerophon set down his cup and turned in his seat to look

at her across the king. "In all honesty, lady, I have seen only the road from the sea, and the interior of this palace. But from the little I have seen, it is most striking and beautiful."

She smiled at that, though he was not sure he had meant the words to come out of his mouth in such a way. "Then you must see more of it. I can accompany you if the king allows it."

King Iobates was not happy, and turned to his daughter with silent displeasure. "I'm afraid that is out of the question." He turned to Bellerophon. "Not because of you, son of Glaucus, but rather because of the dangers posed to the princess." He turned back to his daughter. "You know of what I speak, Daughter."

Bellerophon could see that Philonoe wanted to challenge her father's decision, but she chose not to. The eyes of several people about the megaron were also on the princess and king, evidently straining to hear what the king would say, or what she would say.

"Then perhaps Captain Milyas will show you the city?" She looked down the table to her left to see the captain in his seat where he had been granted occasion to eat with them. "Captain? Will you show the son of Glaucus our fair city tomorrow. He must go beyond the palace walls at some point, devout as he is in his offerings to the Gods." She smiled at Bellerophon then, and he knew that it was she whom he had seen looking down on him from the higher terrace of the palace.

"Of course, my lady!" Milyas said. "In fact, we have plans to train together on the morrow."

"Excellent!" King Iobates said, clapping his hands once before the next course of food was brought out.

The rest of the evening was spent in polite conversation,

but Bellerophon found that he had to constantly restrain himself from looking across the king at Philonoe, especially as the king wanted to know more about his weapons of choice, and the seer on his other side about the customs in Corinthos.

The entire time, however, the flame of Philonoe's strength, her kindness toward the other guests with whom she conversed most eloquently, drew Bellerophon in like a moth. Despite every warning in his mind, he hoped for just one glance from her direction.

Over the next few days, Captain Milyas took Bellerophon to the training grounds to the southeast of the city walls where the palace guard underwent a strict regimen of strength training and weapons practice.

At first, Bellerophon expected the men of Lykia to see him as an upstart outsider, and that they would want nothing more than to throw him down in the dust. In fact, some did try, but he made short work of them, earning more respect with each small victory.

Milyas was, by far, the most skilled among the warriors of Xanthos, and it took Bellerophon several bouts to prove that they were a match for each other, each one coming to a close draw whether in wrestling, boxing, or running.

The troops watching cheered the two men when they were finished.

"Come," Milyas said, breathing heavily after their exertions. "Are you sure you've not been to war, Bellerophon? By the Gods, you're a strong man!"

"I had nothing to do with my days growing up but train. I suppose it paid off," Bellerophon laughed, also breathing heavily as he poured a ladle of water over his face from a bucket beside them.

"One thing you've not shown me yet is how you use those throwing spears of yours. Do you mind?" Milyas asked. "I can have the men set a target up over there."

"Why not? I need the practice anyway," Bellerophon said.

Milyas nodded to two of the men who ran to take up one of the straw targets and set it somewhere over fifty paces away. "I'll go first," Milyas said, stepping onto the dirt of the stadium and taking aim with his doru, the long spear used by their hoplites in battle. After sighting along the shaft, he took a running start and hurled it.

The spear flew in a high arc, soaring against the blue of the sky before landing in the middle of the target with a distant thump.

"By Ares, that was a great throw!" Bellerophon said.

Milyas turned to him, smiling as his men cheered. "Your turn. Show us what you can do with those throwing spears."

Bellerophon stood and picked up his quiver of throwing spears which were less than half the length of Milyas' doru. He took six of them out of the quiver and gripped them in his left hand, with one in his right. "Ready?" he asked, looking at Milyas.

Milyas nodded expectantly. "Go!"

Bellerophon threw one spear and it struck the bullseye beside the doru, but then he began to run zig zagging back and forth, throwing from every which angle at the target until each one of his spears was thrown.

It happened quickly, and when he stopped to look at the Lykians watching him, he saw their blank, awed expressions.

"Was that not good?" he asked.

There was a moment of stunned silence, and then Milyas jumped into the air, yipping like a giddy child.

"By the Gods! That was incredible!" Milyas yelled and he and the other men ran to the target to get a close look.

Bellerophon's spears had grouped tightly all around the point of Milyas' doru, and the men gathered around to marvel at it.

"How did you manage to do that?" one of the soldiers asked Bellerophon.

"Constant practice. In Corinthos, I would set up various targets and run in every direction, throwing as I went. I eventually got good at it."

"Good?" Milyas said, turning to face Bellerophon. "Outstanding! I've never seen anything like it!"

It was at that moment that the soldier who had just praised Bellerophon, all smiles and awe, pitched forward in an explosion of blood, a spear through his neck.

"What in Hades?" Bellerophon said, but before he realized what had happened, the soldiers all around were rushing to their weapons.

After a stunned second, Bellerophon's eyes saw that it was not an attack by many men but rather by a single warrior perched on the rocks in the distance.

As Milyas and his men gathered their weapons, Bellerophon ripped three of his spears from the target and bolted after the attacker, his bare feet padding across the stadium.

"Bellerophon! Wait!" Milyas called after him.

Bellerophon had no idea what had got into him as he ran. He only saw the image of the friendly soldier's neck being blown out, and only thought of planting a spear in the attacker's back.

The attacker - a man seemingly dressed as a shepherd, was climbing the steep rock formations in an attempt to get away, and this gave Bellerophon time to reach the bottom, following him so as to get a clear shot. He threw one spear and it missed, and then a second and that missed too.

When the man reached the peak and was about to get disappear, Bellerophon hurled his last spear and it soared into the sky to take the man in the lower back.

There was a garbled cry from on high, and then the man fell backward through the air to slam with a deafening crack in the dirt near to where Bellerophon stood.

Meanwhile, Milyas' men had reached him and were scrambling up the rocks to search for more attackers.

"Excellent throw!" Milyas said as he watched his men go up, and then he turned to look at the body of the man Bellerophon had slain. "Damned Solymi!"

"Is he from that neighbouring tribe?" Bellerophon asked.

"Yes," Milyas nodded gravely. "And he just sent one of my best new recruits to the Underworld!"

"I am sorry," Bellerophon said, bending to rip his spear out of the attacker's body. "He doesn't look like a warrior. More like a goatherd."

Milyas spat at the corpse. "They are bandits. Not warriors. But they are many."

"A scout?" Bellerophon asked.

"Perhaps, but more likely a lone rogue looking for target practice. They do this often, the cowards."

Bellerophon looked up to see the Lykian warriors combing the rocks for any more attackers before they climbed back down.

One man approached him and handed him back his two spears.

Bellerophon thanked him, and watched as they dragged the body of the man he had slain back to the middle of the stadium.

"Put his body on a spike as a warning!" Milyas said. "Anything to dissuade the bastards from trying that again. "Back to the city. We must lock down the palace!"

"Yes, sir!" the men said as they took up their things and put the body of their fallen brother upon a cart.

"I will have to visit his parents tomorrow. Good people. Olive growers on the other side of the river."

"Do you want me to come with you?" Bellerophon asked.

Milyas shook his head. "No. This happens more often than you would think. Come. You'll be late for the night's banquet."

On that fifth night of feasting, the air in the megaron was more somber, for word had spread of the attack at the stadium, and the people were wary of another offensive by the neighbouring Solymi.

"Captain Milyas told me how you slew the attacker at the stadium, Bellerophon. It was impressive work," King Iobates said.

"I only wish I had seen him before he slew the young recruit," Bellerophon said.

"It happens frequently," Polyidus added on Bellerophon's other side.

"Will you attack them?" Bellerophon asked the king.

King Iobates shook his head. "No. For one slain man, the cost would be too great. We would lose far more trying to attack them in their rocky home. They do not fight with honour, but like animals from trees, hiding behind rocks in secret. I regret the death of the young soldier, of course, but I cannot risk the lives of so many. You slew the attacker, and that is sufficient punishment. He was obviously a skilled killer, so that will hurt them.”

Bellerophon could see the sadness in Princess Philonoe's face. “I am sorry to discuss this before you, lady.”

She turned to him and shook her head. “It is not that. I am used to such talk. I was just thinking of how it was not always like this. From what I have been told, in the days before my father ruled, such attacks did not happen. They choose to burden him with this aggression.”

“What was different then?” Bellerophon asked.

“Much,” the king said, cutting him off.

“It is not only the danger from the Solymi, but from others as well,” Philonoe said. “And then there is the constant threat from the Chi-“

“That's enough!” the king shouted, his composure cracking.

Philonoe grew silent, her eyes staring directly into her father's as the entire megaron grew silent.

“I do not wish to speak of this any longer,” the king said, more calmly, before taking a gulp of his wine.

“My apologies, King Iobates,” Bellerophon said. “I ask too many questions.”

“It is not you, Bellerophon. My daughter knows better than to discuss such things.”

Philonoe sat back in her chair then and ate in silence for the rest of the feast, as did the other guests there present.

The next day, Bellerophon remained within the palace walls as much of the city was locked down in case of another attack. But another attack did not come.

That night, at the next feast, Bellerophon arrived to find the king absent but Philonoe already seated and speaking in hushed tones with Polyidus. They both looked to Bellerophon when he entered the megaron on his own.

"Is the king unwell?" Bellerophon asked them when he arrived.

"The king is meeting with representatives from the trade guild about the dangers they face in the kingdom," Polyidus said. "He will be along shortly."

Bellerophon smiled at Philonoe and sat in his usual seat. "The danger posed by the Solymi, you mean?" he asked Polyidus.

The seer shook his head. "A more serious and constant threat."

"More serious?" Bellerophon asked, surprised. He could not imagine living in such a way. "I had not realized how peaceful life was in Corinthos until now." He could see that Polyidus did not want to speak more of the dangers they faced, and so he let it be.

"Do you miss your homeland?" Philonoe asked on his other side. With the king absent, she had turned fully in her seat to face Bellerophon, and the sight of her stopped his heart.

It took a moment for him to answer, but he came around to it. "No, lady. I do not. I was never wanted or welcome in Corinthos. To my mind, I have no home."

"How very sad," she said, and there was true feeling in how she said it. "Your mother did not care for you?"

"No. She did not. For some reason, I was a disappointment, though I shall never know why." Feeling awkward, Bellerophon took a gulp of his wine and leaned back in his chair, looking sideways at the princess.

"How upsetting to have had your mother, and yet feel so

distant from her." She was quiet a moment. "I never really knew my mother, but from what I have been told, she was extremely brave and kind."

"Having met you, lady, I can understand that," Bellerophon said, though he looked away when he did so.

Philonoe's eyes locked onto him, and she smiled very slightly. "The people of Lykia and the surrounding lands loved her very much."

"Perhaps that is why there were no troubles then?" Bellerophon ventured. "But your father is a great king. Surely the surrounding lands would welcome such a strong ally?"

"I do not understand it myself," Philonoe said.

"Nor would the king wish you to, Princess," Polyidus interrupted, his eyes glancing at the door through which the king could come at any second. "My lady, please leave talk of Queen Pasandra for the moment."

Bellerophon turned back to Philonoe. "'Pasandra'? That was your mother's name?"

"Yes. It was," Philonoe said.

"Do you remember her at all?" he asked, ignoring the worried looks from the seer beside him.

"I remember feelings of love. I remember her soft but strong voice, and the songs she used to sing to me. But that is all. My father tells me that I look very much like her."

"I can believe that," Bellerophon said. "Your sister, Queen Stheneboea, and King Iobates look very similar."

"It is true," Philonoe said, then she looked at Bellerophon intently. "You met my sister?"

"Yes...I did," he answered cautiously.

"Was she kind and welcoming to you in Tiryns?"

"King Proetus and Queen Stheneboea welcomed me for a

short time. And they were kind enough to grant me passage here."

"You do not regret coming here then?" Philonoe asked. "Even after the attack?"

"For one day, I have had to deal with the dangers I hear so much about in Xanthos, lady. For you, it has been a lifetime."

"It is much easier to endure in the company of friends, Bellerophon."

There was such tenderness in her look and the lilt of her voice, that Bellerophon was taken aback. He had never experienced such sincerity and good will, and he fought that part of himself which said he should not trust her.

They ate in comfortable silence for at time, and then settled into conversation about Corinthos' lands and neighbours.

Polyidus too was a part of the conversation, and it became clear to Bellerophon that the seer was quite protective of Philonoe, that he cared for her welfare even above that of the king's.

King Iobates did not appear that evening.

That night, Bellerophon dreamed of home, of the empty corridors and pitying looks that had haunted his childhood like a recurring dream that left one bereft of joy in the morning.

When he awoke, the sun was already high in the blue canopy of the world. His thoughts lingered sadly on the father he had lost too soon, and the mother who had remained behind, removed, uncaring, and as cold as winter wind down out of the mountains of Arcadia.

Bellerophon had long ago decided the world was not his friend, that he was meant to lead a lonely existence. He had accepted that. He knew that he was not an easy person to love or care for, not like Philonoe.

He had dreamed of her too that night as he tread the pathways of Morpheus' realm.

He had been surrounded by darkness. The Goddess Athena was behind him, urging him forward into the dark as the terrible sounds of roaring and hissing and rushing flame came at him from out of the deep, sightless distance.

And then she had appeared. Philonoe. Standing still as a statue, tall and strong and radiant. She was not afraid, though menace was all around them. She did not speak, though her eyes held him fast. She simply stood there, the wind playing at her peplos and hair, moving them in a strangely slow motion.

In looking upon her he felt a calm come over him, but the sounds of terror beyond her became louder and Bellerophon rushed to her side, his spears and shield at the ready for an attack. The rush of anger upon the wind was deafening, and then the darkness spoke.

I am waiting for you! Come to die!

Bellerophon did not venture out that morning, though he longed to glimpse the princess, to speak with her and see her smile. However, he did not want to mar her day with the darkness that had beset him the previous night, a darkness that seemed to follow him wherever he or his thoughts wandered.

He heaped offerings upon the altar on the terrace that day, and the smoke rose up into the air in all directions as if the winds were as undecided as he was. Sitting beneath the fluttering canopy on the terrace, hoping Helios' sunlight would cleanse him of the shadow of his adherent mood, he fought with all of his might against the hopeless feeling of being adrift, not only in the living breathing world, but more so upon that sea of tortured dreams on which the Gods seemed intent he remain.

As his eyes took in the broad landscape, the rising palace behind him, and the distant monuments to past glories, he wondered what it would be like to have such a home. He found himself admiring King Iobates for his courage in the face of so many dangers, so much adversity, and the fact that he still found it in himself to care deeply for his daughter.

By the later afternoon, when most were indoors sleeping off the day's high heat, Bellerophon finally ventured out of his rooms, along the carved and painted corridors of Xanthos' palace, until he came to the great court before the megaron.

A couple of guards stood at attention and he greeted them as he passed. They returned the greeting, well aware of who he was and the skills he possessed.

It is strange how slaying one man can earn one such respect, he thought. He knew it was only chance and circumstance that had earned him the respect the troops showed him, and so he did not linger in that adulation.

He made his way up to the northern ramparts where he could glimpse the agora and those parts of Xanthos that lay outside of the high-walled precinct of the palace. In the distance, mountains rose higher and higher, as if they were a sort of staircase to the heavens. Crops of olive radiated around the city, and the silver line of the river was lost among the trees lining its shore to the left. The sky was blue overhead, falling slowly to evening indigo as the sun's chariot sped away with fire in its wake.

"It is beautiful, isn't it?"

Bellerophon turned to see Philonoe coming toward him, accompanied by Captain Milyas who remained behind, farther down the ramparts, to speak with the men on duty. He waved to Bellerophon and then turned to his men.

The princess came to stand beside Bellerophon, leaning on the wall with him to gaze out at the undulating and rocky landscape of her father's Lykian kingdom.

He smiled at her. "It is indeed a beautiful land, Princess. You are fortunate to live in such a place as this."

"Do you mean Lykia, or the palace?" she asked.

"Both." He was silent, and she waited for him to say more.

Philonoe could tell that Bellerophon had much on his mind, for the spark that was in his eyes the previous night was slightly dimmed by clouds of worry. She reached out to grip his arm. "What is wrong, Bellerophon?"

It was a simple question, and yet one without a simple answer.

He turned to look upon her, his dark hair falling over his shoulder to be blown by the rising wind. He was not usually wont to trust others, but in her, in Philonoe, he felt there was not an ounce of betrayal. He longed to share, to speak to her, to say what was in his heart and let the Gods, and her, decide if he was worth a spared thought.

"Tell me," she urged.

He worked his jaw, clearly uncomfortable. "To be honest, Princess... I feel adrift in this life. I have no purpose at all, though I do not shun the idea of having one. The Gods torture me with such dreams - they always have - and there is not a morning in which I do not wake drowning in hopelessness."

"Perhaps the Gods have been preparing you for something?" she suggested. "I too have had a lifetime of lapses into despair, mostly for the loss of my mother, but also for the dangers that constantly lurk about our kingdom."

"And yet, you are strong, Princess. I see it in you. You

have a strength that few men or women possess, despite the threats you face." He looked at her and she blushed, but she did not turn away. She was not one to turn away. "I admire you for it, your strength and courage."

"And I admire you, Bellerophon. I see such courage in you, honour, strength and truth." She turned to fully face him. "Do not fear or worry, for the Gods often show us the way, and then our hearts confirm it."

"What if the Gods wish only to torment us, or worse, what if they do not care enough to even look our way?"

She smiled. "The Gods will never look away from a good man, Bellerophon. And you *are* a good man. I can see that as plainly as I see those mountains in the distance." Here she gripped his hands, and looked him in the eyes. "No matter what happens, I am glad that the Gods brought you here."

"My lady!" Captain Milyas called from down the ramparts.

Philonoe let go of Bellerophon's hands and they both turned to face him.

"Yes, Captain?" she said, unashamed of her closeness to Bellerophon.

"The king is at table. You are both to go in now!" Milyas' eyes lingered suspiciously on Bellerophon for a moment before he turned back to the soldiers with him.

"Come," Philonoe said. "Let us go into the feast and enjoy a few moments of music and wine so that you may leave your dreams aside for a time." She smiled again and went to join the captain.

Bellerophon followed, even more in awe of her than he had already been.

. . .

It was well into the deep dark of night, as the stars lit the sky's ceiling with their light, that Bellerophon stepped onto the terrace of his rooms to make his offerings to the Gods.

Athena... Goddess... I honour you, and I pray to you for wisdom and direction, for I feel I have none. My thoughts are awhirl in this land, and this palace weaves a spell over me. Why could I not have grown to manhood in a place such as this?

The smoke of the offerings rose up thick and scented of cedar and pine, and when the night's breeze carried it off, the Bright-Eyed Athena stood before Bellerophon.

Because you were not meant to, son of Glaucus, the goddess said.

Bellerophon looked up and saw the brilliance in her Olympian eyes, the absolute certainty. He sighed. *I am grateful that you have always helped me, Goddess, even though you were the only one who ever cared.*

Careful of your words, Bellerophon. You cannot see it, but there are others who care for you, who have watched you and given you silent aid when you did not suspect it. You are not alone, though you feel storm-tossed every day of your life.

He hung his head in shame, but Athena leaned down and pulled him to his feet. *You have been brought to Lykia for a reason. Do not forget that.*

For Philonoe?

Your heart betrays you, Athena said, her voice sterner than he would have wished. She shook her head slowly. *Not for the princess, though she is the only good in this place.*

Why am I here then, oh Goddess? he asked. *Is it to help the king?*

Athena seemed to grow angry, but her wrath was not directed at Bellerophon. *King Iobates is not deserving of your friendship, or much else, let alone such a daughter as Philo-noe. Remember my warning about him. Do not be too trusting, and do not let your guard down. From this day on, you must be prepared for whatever may come. Do you hear me?*

I do, Goddess, though it fills me with fear to hear you speak in such a way.

You should be afraid, Bellerophon, for the trials that await you are nothing to your past traumas. Athena then bent over and kissed him upon the crown of his head. *Prepare,* she said softly.

And then, she was gone.

Ten days after his guest arrived in Xanthos, King Iobates sat alone at the broad table in his private chambers by the light of several oil lamps. He had been unable to sleep much, especially since the attack by the Solymi scout several days before.

He had been impressed with Bellerophon, his skills, and his respect of his daughter. The troops respected him as well, and Polyidus seemed more and more certain that the son of Glaucus was the one the Gods had spoken of, the one who had finally come to aid his ravaged and beset kingdom.

Iobates forced himself to look up at the painted walls of his broad chamber. The images of marching warriors haunted him, but not more than the central image of the great beast. His eyes lingered on the creature that tormented him day and night, in his dreams and waking days. That bringer of death to many had caused his people more pain than he could ever have imagined. It kept him from taking his place as the ruler he had always wanted to be.

And it was all his fault.

From the day of his great sin, when he had desecrated the

traditions of that ancient land, the beast had appeared in a shower of violence and blood, a punishment that would not end, an enemy which he could not overcome.

He tore his eyes away from that dreaded form upon the wall, and looked at the piles of missives upon his table. There were many, but one in particular he could not put off any longer.

King Iobates sighed and picked up the tablet with the seal of Tiryns upon it. It might be from King Proetus, but he knew that the words belonged to his eldest daughter. They always did.

Iobates broke the seal, leaned toward the nearest lamp, and began to read.

CHAPTER 6

A DARK MISSIVE

When the misty morning arrived, King Iobates was sitting in the middle of his private garden on the upper terrace of the palace. He lay upon a gilded couch beneath the broad olive tree which he had planted there long ago. In his hand, he still clutched the tablet from Tiryns, having read, and re-read the missive.

He had been turning in a maelstrom of opposites the whole of the night as he lay there - anger and deep sadness, aggression and conciliation, duty and faith - and he hoped that it was simply a bad dream or misunderstanding that had brought him to this.

Oh, Stheneboea... he thought of his eldest, her pride, her strength, and he hoped that she was not hurt by what had happened. However, it did occur to him that she was made of stern matter, as though forged by Hephaestos himself. "What has happened?" he wondered aloud, wishing he had the power of the Gods to look back in time to see.

King Iobates looked around the gardens, the colourful blooms all about him that were still closed from the dewy night, the gently shivering olive boughs above him, and the bougainvillaea climbing the wall to the rooftop, splashing colour along the way. He remembered the days when he and Pasandra used to lay in that very place, undisturbed in times of peace. That memory however, always ended up like a dagger to his heart, and a mountain of regret.

Were Pasandra still here, Stheneboea would never have gone across the sea, he told himself, *and I would not be in this predicament.*

But he was indeed in a terrible position, and he needed to act.

I am a king!

The serpent of doubt in his mind, however, would not go away. Bellerophon had seemed, to all of them, a man of honour, but Iobates did wonder if he was capable of what Stheneboea and Proetus accused him of. *He is a man, and men are capable or terrible things. I know this myself.*

The laws of Zeus Xenios were clear, however. Iobates could not harm a guest he had welcomed into his home. If he broke the laws of Xenia, then he risked the wrath of Olympus, and he could not afford to do that again. He also might require Tiryns' aid in the future, should the Solymi decide on a full-scale attack on Xanthos. He knew this all too well.

King Iobates turned to the slave who slept in the shadows of the garden. "Bring me Polyidus!" he demanded, and the slave roused himself quickly and stumbled out of the garden to go and find the seer.

King Iobates stood and went to the altar in the middle of the garden and there lit a bundle of rosemary from a basket and placed it in the bowl of the altar. He raised his hands to the sky, his eyes searching the clouds.

"Oh great Zeus Xenios, guide me in what I must do. I wish

to honour your wishes, but I wish also to keep faith with my family. What should a king do under such circumstances?"

Iobates' eyes searched the sky for answers, for any sign from Zeus, but he was met only with silence, even as the smoke from his offering was taken by the wind.

"My king?" Polyidus cleared his throat as he entered the garden.

Iobates turned to his seer and went to the couch. "Sit and listen. Advise me on what course of action will not anger the Gods and defy the laws of Xenia."

Polyidus' milky eyes looked confused, but he sat, leaned upon his walking staff, and cocked his ear as the king began to read.

"'King Iobates, my friend and ally. I write to you about a grave matter concerning the man who brings you this letter. Bellerophon, son of Glaucus of Corinthos, is not what he seems...'"

"Quickly now," Polyidus said to the slave who led him down the stairs and corridor to the princess' rooms. "I must speak with Philonoe! The king commands it!"

Polyidus' heart beat wildly in his chest, for all that they had been pinning their hopes upon was now under grave threat. He could not betray the king's confidence and warn Philonoe of what had happened - the slaves were always listening - but he knew the willful spite of Stheneboea, as did Philonoe.

All of a sudden, they were at the princess' chambers and the slave was rapping upon the cedar door.

Philonoe opened the door herself and it was as if she knew something was wrong immediately. "What is it, Polyidus?"

The seer caught his breath and reached out for her hands.

"My lady, the letter from Tiryns… You father has finally read it." He squeezed her hands very subtly then. "The king commands you to fetch Bellerophon and bring him to the megaron."

"Me? Why?" She was, of course, happy to do so, but the way in which Polyidus was speaking and behaving gave her a dark warning. "What has happened?"

"I cannot say, Princess. It is the king's wish." He bowed his head low, not in obeisance but rather in shame, a further warning.

"Very well," she said. "I shall go immediately to get Bellerophon and bring him to the megaron. I will see you there."

"The king only wishes for you to bring him there, not to remain."

She shook her head, though he could not see it. "I will remain there."

Polyidus smiled. "Yes, my lady."

Philonoe's thoughts raced as she made her way down the narrow staircases to the lower terrace where Bellerophon's rooms were located. She wondered what could be in the letter from Tiryns that would cause such an uproar and sudden action.

"I must speak with Bellerophon of Corinthos," she said to the slaves who were sitting outside of the suite of rooms.

"Yes, Princess!" said the one named Phoebos as he jumped to his feet, bowed, and opened the doors. "Master, Bellerophon!"

Bellerophon's voice came from farther in the rooms. "I told you, Phoebos, you don't need to call me 'master'."

"But sir…the lady Philonoe is here to see you."

Bellerophon came into view, a broad smile across his face as he tied his wet hair back and straightened his crimson tunic. His smile faded quickly when he saw the urgency upon her features. "What is wrong, Princess?"

Philonoe stepped forward slowly, her eyes never leaving his, and the slave disappeared back into the corridor. "Did something happen in Tiryns that you have not told me?"

Bellerophon felt the floor drop from under him. *The king has read the letter.* "Yes. I will not lie to you. Something did happen."

"What?" she demanded, and as she did so, she rose to her full, proud height. But there was no menace in how she asked, and that was a relief to Bellerophon.

"Have you read the letter from King Proetus?"

"No. I have only been told to bring you directly to the megaron."

He stepped forward but did not take her hands or plead. "Then I will go with you now."

"Tell me what happened, Bellerophon. As my friend…"

He shook his head. "If I tell you now, before you have heard what is in the letter, you will think I have tried to play you false, to cast doubt on the words which I believe it contains."

"I know you could not play me false," she said, this time grasping his hand tightly.

"And I pray to the Gods that you continue to know that after we hear what was in that letter."

She let go of his hand and nodded. "Then let us go together to the megaron."

Bellerophon turned to look at the rooms, his things there, including his dagger. He thought about grabbing it before leaving, but decided against it. *I will go unarmed. I have been down this path before, and daggers are of no use. I don't care anymore.*

The megaron was crowded with people - the courtiers, priests, and some of the soldiers whom Bellerophon had befriended - with the king seated upon his throne and Polyidus standing beside him.

"Daughter," the king said when Philonoe and Bellerophon entered the megaron. "Thank you for bringing Bellerophon to us. You may leave now."

"I will stay, Father," she said, her voice clear and certain in the silent room. She could see the king was angry at this, but he said nothing in reply, and so she made her way to her seat to his left.

Bellerophon stepped forward to face King Iobates. "You asked for me?"

"I did indeed, Bellerophon, son of Glaucus."

Bellerophon could see that the king looked very tired, as though he had not slept. Dark circles that could not be fully hidden by pigments had gathered beneath his eyes.

I have been here before, Bellerophon thought, and he knew he could have been back in Tiryns, under interrogation once more, were it not for Philonoe.

"What is this about, Father?" Philonoe asked, her abruptness causing some of the courtiers to gasp.

Without a word to his daughter, he handed her the letter from Tiryns for her to read.

Bellerophon tried to catch her gaze before she did so, but she was already reading the deadly symbols upon the tablet, shaking her head as she did so, her eyes growing glassy.

"I have read the letter from King Proetus of Tiryns which you brought, Bellerophon of Corinthos."

"Yes, King Iobates. I see that."

"Do you know what it says?" the king demanded.

It was at that moment that Philonoe looked up, horror upon her face.

Bellerophon found that he could not tell if the expressions of disappointment, fear, and anger upon the princess' face were directed at him, or at the accusations contained in the letter itself.

"I suspect so," Bellerophon said.

King Iobates began to shake with the rage that he found he could no longer contain. His fists gripped the arms of his throne as he stood and pointed at Bellerophon. "King Proetus says that you tried to rape my daughter, Queen Stheneboea!"

There were murmurs all about the megaron at that, at those dark accusations. People began to point at Bellerophon who stood in their midst.

Bellerophon met Philonoe's gaze and gave a slight shake of his head before turning to stare at the king. He could feel his own anger rising and he fought hard to keep it down.

"King Iobates... Under the laws of Zeus Xenios, you have welcomed me into your home and kingdom. I have fought beside your men and slain one of your enemies-"

"That is what murders do, is it not?" the king shouted.

"I see," Bellerophon said calmly, before turning in a slow circle to look at the members of the guard and court. "I tell you now, that the accusations against me that are contained in that letter are false. And the Gods know it!" He turned back to King Iobates. "By Zeus Xenios, I did not commit such an act."

"Of course you would say so, wouldn't you?" King Iobates

said, sitting back down on his throne. "Just admit you attacked my eldest daughter, Bellerophon. Do not make this difficult."

"I will not admit to something I did not do, King Iobates. You will have to decide what to do with me, before Zeus Xenios and all the Gods. As you have been a gracious host until now, I will accept whatever your decision is."

Bellerophon found that he could not be angry. Even with the accusations the king had levelled at him, and the humiliation he was now undergoing before all the court, for in Philonoe's eyes he could see that she did believe him. That was all that mattered to him in that moment. At last, he had an ally.

King Iobates was silent and torn, and he leaned over to listen to something Polyidus was saying before looking back to Bellerophon.

The entire court and guard watched the king closely.

"I will consult the Gods this night, and announce my decision as to your fate in the morning," the king said, ignoring his daughter's gaze beside him. "Until then, you are to remain in your chambers, under guard and without weapons. Captain Milyas?" The king turned to look at the captain who stood nearby. "Take the son of Glaucus away and set a guard upon his rooms."

Milyas bowed to the king and motioned for three of his men to join him. They surrounded Bellerophon who went with them silently, his eyes holding onto Philonoe's as he was marched away.

"The king is just, Bellerophon," Milyas said to him when they reached the chambers. "He will make the right decision."

Bellerophon turned and looked at the captain. "The king has already decided I am guilty."

"And are you?" Milyas asked him directly.

"No. I am not. Queen Stheneboea approached me, and I refused her."

Milyas shook his bowed head. "Then you had the courage to do what many of my men never did. The king's eldest daughter bedded half the men in my regiment."

"That is not a consolation, Captain," Bellerophon said, feeling the sting of betrayal yet again.

"I know," Milyas said, looking up. "But for what it is worth, I do believe you."

"Thank you for saying so, but it is the king who must believe me."

"That is in the hands of the Gods, my friend. For now, I must obey my king and take your weapons from you." He saw Bellerophon stiffen at the thought. "Don't worry. I will keep them safe and locked away."

Bellerophon went into the rooms and returned with the quiver of spears, his sword, dagger and shield. He handed the items over and backed into the room.

"This will all be over tomorrow," Milyas said before he closed the door and bolted it.

"One way or another, I suppose it will," Bellerophon said as the lock clicked.

The megaron was empty again as King Iobates sat upon his throne staring into the flames of the great hearth. The frescoed walls seemed to mock and taunt him where he sat as he tried to think of a decision that would satisfy King Proetus and his eldest daughter, but also honour the laws of Xenia.

There is no such solution, he told himself.

The truth was that he knew his eldest daughter's ways, the magnitude of her spite. And yet, how well did he truly know

Bellerophon, a man who was a stranger until just a few days before? Stheneboea, however flawed, was family, and King Proetus an ally who might be able to help him against his own enemies one day.

The king was about to leave when he heard the shuffling sound of Polyidus' walk and Philonoe's voice as they approached him.

Philonoe's eyes were wild and stormy, and Iobates noted that they looked the same as her mother's when he had upset her so greatly in years past.

"Father!" Philonoe said, leaving Polyidus' side to step forward quickly. "You cannot do this!"

The king took a deep breath before speaking. "You read the letter, my daughter. You heard what Bellerophon did to your sister."

"Allegedly," she said. "Father, you know Stheneboea's will. She is not kind."

"Perhaps she angered him, and that is why he attacked her?" Iobates said.

Philonoe shook her head. "He is not that kind of man, Father."

"Oh, daughter, you are young and inexperienced in the ways of men. Men are capable of terrible things."

"As are women," she replied, "and my sister is one of them!"

"You take the side of a stranger over family?" the king accused, pointing his finger at her.

"I take the side of truth!"

"But you do not know the truth, do you? You know what you want to believe. I know you see in him a brave and good man, but men are good at deception so that they can get what they want. Men use people."

"As do kings, it seems."

Polyidus listened intently to the king and his daughter argue back and forth, and as he did so, his mind was racing. The Gods had indicated that the kingdom of Lykia depended upon Bellerophon, but if the king executed him, they would be lost. He cleared his throat and raised his hand in the direction of the king's voice. "Sire, may I say something?"

"Yes, Polyidus, by all means! Say something reasonable."

"My king… I know that the accusations against the son of Glaucus are severe, and I agree that the honour of your house must be upheld. Such acts, especially toward a queen are heinous indeed. But we must tread carefully here. The laws of Xenia are very clear. That is, I believe, why King Proetus sent Bellerophon here to you. He did not want to betray Zeus' laws, and neither should you. It would ruin this kingdom and your reputation."

"As would letting such a villain go free," the king added.

"This is true," Polyidus said, hearing the exasperated exhalation of the princess beside him. *I hope she understands what I am trying to do.* "That said, I still do believe that Bellerophon of Corinthos is the one the Gods have shown me, the one who can help our beleaguered kingdom."

The fire in the hearth crackled loudly and one of the wooden logs split, sending sparks up to the ceiling.

The three of them were silent before the flames. "The action you take must, all at once, honour the Gods' laws, satisfy King Proetus, and give the son of Glaucus a fighting chance to prove himself."

"A fighting chance…" the king said to himself as he leaned forward and stared at the cracked and burning log in the hearth.

Philonoe shook her head as she observed the narrowing of

his eyes, and knew that the decision he was reaching would bring ruin on Bellerophon.

The next morning, the entire court gathered once more in the megaron of Xanthos' palace, only this time, there were more people than the day before. They crowded at the doors of the megaron, and strained to see the king, princess, and the king's seer seated before the hearth.

Iobates had been awake the whole of the night yet again and it showed in his face. Yet he had a determined and satisfied look in his eyes.

"Father, what is your decision going to be?" Philonoe asked him as they waited for Captain Milyas to bring Bellerophon.

"You will see," the king said angrily. "And if you gainsay me before the court, I will lock you up too. You are to remain silent or leave."

Philonoe had never been so angry with her father, and she did not understand why he was doing this. The night before, she had tried to sway Polyidus to convince the king to ignore the charges, but the seer had explained why that would not be good for the king either.

"All I can say, Princess," Polyidus had said, "is that the Gods favour Bellerophon. You must have faith in Them if anything."

That night, Philonoe had made offerings and prayed to Athena for wisdom for her father's judgement, hoping that the goddess would hear her prayers and help Bellerophon. *Help him now, oh Goddess!* she thought as she spotted Bellerophon being led into the megaron by Milyas and his soldiers.

The crowd, which was pressed up against the very walls of

the king's hall was abuzz with curiosity, but they fell silent when the king raised his hands.

"I have come to a decision regarding the fate of Bellerophon, son of Glaucus of Corinthos!"

Bellerophon looked up, but he did not look first to the king, but rather to Philonoe to confirm that she was still his friend and ally. The concern upon her face, the way she sat as far as she could from the king on her chair, told him all he needed to know. He looked to the king then.

King Iobates stood and looked at his people. "A king must make difficult decisions that affect not only himself, but his people as well. After all, a man's actions always affect others besides himself. The welfare of this kingdom is ever at the front of my mind. But I must also obey the laws of the Gods, of Almighty Zeus. Bellerophon, son of Glaucus, is a guest in my home, and as such, he is protected by the sacred laws of Xenia. However, if he has committed the crime levelled against him by the King of Tiryns and your former princess, then that is something that must not go unpunished." He stared at Bellerophon who looked back at him, his great shoulders back, his head high. This gave Iobates pause, but after a few heartbeats, he pressed on.

"As this decision concerns the Gods' laws, I say we let the Gods decide Bellerophon's fate!"

There were confused gasps and mumblings about the megaron, and Philonoe turned in her seat to look at her father.

"I shall set three tasks for Bellerophon, three trials that, if he should succeed, he will be deemed completely innocent of the crime for which he is accused. In fact, should he survive and succeed, he will be rewarded!"

Bellerophon stepped forward, his heart now pounding

quickly in his chest. "And what impossible tasks do you intend I should complete, King Iobates?" he demanded.

The court fell silent again.

"Your tasks are intended to protect this kingdom which has given you sanctuary. For the first task, you must fight and defeat the Solymi!"

Philonoe stood up quickly beside her father. "That's not justice! That is a death sentence!" she cried, her voice drowned out by the roar of the crowd in the megaron.

"Sit down!" the king barked at his daughter, before raising his hands for silence in the throne room again. "The Solymi have caused Lykians no end of trouble and pain with their atrocities. Indeed, we have *all* lost family and friends to them, have we not?"

The people roared their agreement, their anger at their enemy overwhelming any sense of justice that they might have harboured.

"Let the Gods decide his fate in battle!" someone yelled, and the king nodded when he heard that echoed around the megaron.

Iobates stared at Bellerophon, whose eyes were locked onto Philonoe's, and this made him more determined in his decision. "Bellerophon, son of Glaucus!" he called across the hearth fire. "You shall undertake your first trial tomorrow, before which you may go to our armoury to properly equip yourself for battle. Captain Milyas?"

"Yes, my king?" Milyas said, stepping forward, the stunned look still upon his face.

"You and a small company of men shall go with Bellerophon on this quest, but you shall *not* aid him. If he should choose to run, you will execute him on the spot!"

Captain Milyas bowed slightly. "Ye...yes...my king." He

looked at Bellerophon then, and in the man's eyes he saw resignation.

"No!" Philonoe cried above the din, but the king had two guards shuffle her quickly out of the throne room, her protestations lost in the voices of the haranguing crowd as Milyas and his men took Bellerophon out the opposite doors of the megaron.

CHAPTER 7

THE UNLEASHING

The night in Xanthos felt deep and quiet, especially in the guarded corridors of the palace of King Iobates.

Philonoe had tried to prevail upon her father to reverse his decision to send Bellerophon against the entire Solymi tribe, but whenever she approached his rooms in his wing of the palace, she was turned away by the guards.

"The king wishes to be alone, Princess," they told her. "He has commanded that none - not even yourself - should be allowed entry."

Frustrated, Philonoe had stormed off to find Polyidus where he sat upon a bench in the great courtyard, leaning against his walking stick. He was quiet, his eyes still and blank, but he knew when she approached.

"My lady...I tried to prevail upon the king-"

"How hard did you try, Polyidus?" she said angrily, standing over him. "Do you believe the charges laid against Bellerophon?"

Polyidus was quiet for a moment. He could tell that there was a sliver of doubt in her voice, but that she wanted more than anything to believe that the Corinthian was innocent. "My lady…it does not matter whether I believe it or not. The accusation was made, and publicly. It required a delicate decision, one that would seek justice, while at the same time not completely defy the laws of Xenia."

"Is my father not defying Zeus' laws by sending our guest to his death?"

Polyidus cocked his head to listen if there was anyone else nearby.

"We are alone," she whispered to him.

"Sit with me, my lady…" he answered, taking her hand. "You are correct. The king would have slain Bellerophon outright had I not told him what the Gods had told me."

"Which is what, Polyidus? Tell me!" Philonoe grasped his hand tightly.

He continued. "As always, the Gods are vague in their messages. It is for us to decipher them and understand their meaning and purpose… Before Bellerophon ever arrived in Xanthos, the Gods told me to expect him, a dark, lonely stranger from across the sea. This man was to help Lykia and its people in some way, and ensure the future of this kingdom."

"But how do you know it is Bellerophon they spoke of?"

"I don't know for certain. But, I know that he communes with the Gods. You have met him and spoken with him often, I know."

She lowered her head, but he did not see.

"There is no pretence in him. He is honest and true."

"Yes. He is," Philonoe said softly.

"And such men are often taken advantage of by those who are selfish and cunning."

"People like my sister," she added.

"I did not say that," Polyidus added quickly. "But I do say

that the Gods know the truth of it. If Bellerophon should succeed in this task, it means that the Gods are protecting him, that he is the one I saw in their divine messages."

Philonoe shook her head. "But how can one man defeat an entire people? It's impossible!" Only then did she feel like crying, now that her anger had ebbed away and the thought of the outcome of the following day appeared in brightly-painted strokes of crimson across her mind. She felt like running away with Bellerophon to fight at his side, no matter the cost.

"Have faith, my princess," Polyidus said gently. "For behind the curtain of fear and doubt, I feel that there is a beacon of hope that will burn away the clouds surrounding us all."

For much of the day, after King Iobates' declaration, Bellerophon sat upon the terrace of his prison suite, drinking and gazing up at the cloudy sky. He felt betrayed yet again, and wondered for a time why he carried on as a victim of the whims of others. He dozed in wine-soaked hopelessness for a time, but as night began to fall and the sun burned red in the distance before him, he felt a change inside.

Anger had its uses and, if harnessed, could give one strength in desperate situations.

Bellerophon began to look beyond his already-imagined death the next day. He stood in the setting sunlight and removed his tunic. He looked upon his arms, broad chest and thick legs and realized that the Gods had blessed him with strength and vitality, more so than any of his family.

For what purpose if not for this? he wondered. *I am no king, no leader of armies.* He lit a large chunk of incense and placed it upon the altar where he knelt and raised his hands to the heavens.

"Oh, Goddess Athena…" he whispered, his eyes closed as he tilted his head to the sky. "I know that you have been watching over me, and for that I am ever grateful. The time I believe you spoke of, has come, and tomorrow I go either to my death, or to victory." He paused and breathed deeply, pushing down the panic that threatened to rise in his gut and fill his chest. "Let it be victory, oh Goddess. Fill me with strength and the wits to overcome this enemy so that I may prove my innocence."

His eyes remained closed as he breathed slowly, in and out, upon his knees.

Be strong, Bellerophon. You have felt alone all of your life, but you are not alone now. Seek the bear's head, and see your trial blown to the winds…

Bellerophon's eyes fluttered open in time to see the goddess' helmeted head bending over to kiss his brow. Then, she was gone with the setting sun.

The next morning at dawn, Captain Milyas appeared at Bellerophon's rooms.

"Did you sleep at all?" Milyas asked. He was dressed in full armour, his helmet tucked beneath his left arm, his right resting on his sword hilt.

Bellerophon nodded. "Yes."

"Good," the captain said. It was obvious he did not relish the day's task, but he was careful not to gainsay his king, especially within the palace corridors.

"Do not worry, Captain," Bellerophon said. "I will not run or cause trouble. I am ready."

"Are you sure? This tribe…the Solymi…they have caused us nothing but grief."

"What good is it to bewail the situation? The Gods have decreed it."

"Do you wish to go to the temple and make offerings to them?"

"I have already made my offerings to the Gods, and They have received them." Bellerophon stepped out of the room. "Let's go."

"You need armour," Milyas said. "Come with me."

They walked along the corridors of the palace through the megaron and out of the propylon to the great courtyard, and as they went, Bellerophon looked about for a glimpse of Philonoe. When he saw no sign of her, he felt a pang of regret that he was not able to see her one last time.

"We have an array of weapons and armour down here," Milyas said as he unlocked a thick door on the south side of the courtyard. He then took a torch and led Bellerophon down a staircase. Once they were at the bottom, Milyas lit a tripod filled with oil and as the fire took hold, a vast room filled with swords, spears, shields and other weapons of war appeared like a mirage out of the darkness.

"The king said that you may take your pick of whatever you want." He pointed to the rows of armaments. "Choose."

Bellerophon took the torch and walked slowly along the rows of weapons and armour. He had never seen so much, and wondered if he had stepped into Ares' very own chamber. There were spears of varying lengths of shaft and blade, swords and daggers whose edges had never seen battle but whose oiled blades glistened in the firelight.

He wandered through the rows with Milyas following

closely behind him. "Tell me, Captain. How do the Solymi fight? What is their home terrain like?"

"The Solymi are animals!" Milyas growled. As I told you before, they do not fight with honour. They rely on surprise, and attack from afar. The only thing that makes them strong is their numbers. They are many, like wasps in a hive."

"Do they wear armour?"

"No. They dress like goatherds, in skins and pelts. Like the one you slew."

"So they are not invulnerable to arrows, spears, or even rocks?"

"Well…no," Milyas said, as if the answer were obvious. But he then realized that Bellerophon was working out the best way to prepare and attack.

"What weapons do they use?"

"Mostly sling stones and bows, which they use with great accuracy. They have no swordsmen, but they do carry daggers, as shepherds are wont to do."

Bellerophon nodded as he took down a bow and a quiver with several long-shafted arrows. He also took a quiver of relatively short spears. "I'll also need a few amphorae of oil. Will your men help carry all of this to the place of battle?"

"We have mules ready to go," Milyas said "But there is no one place of battle where we are going."

"What do you mean?" Bellerophon asked, turning to face him. "They have no capital?"

"It is not like Xanthos. Their kingdom is a scattering of small villages each with a head shepherd who leads fighting men."

"And their king?"

"Solimos. We have not seen him ever. They say he is a giant

of a man, armoured in bear fur. All the shepherds bow down to him. They offer up their wives and daughters to him as he commands. They live in fear of him, and in return he sends them out to harass us and die. They do his bidding without question."

"I see…" Bellerophon said, but his words stopped short as he came to the end of another row. There before him was a gleaming panoply of armour. He stepped forward to look more closely at the set.

"Where did that come from?" Milyas gasped. "I've never seen it before!"

The armour gleamed in the torchlight in hues of black bull's hide and bronze. There were matching greaves and arm guards, lined with bronze over the leather, and upon the breastplate, a great gorgon's head stared out menacingly at them.

Bellerophon peered closely at it and the face seemed to move, the mouth opening and closing, the serpents upon it writhing. He shook his head as if he were dizzy, and stood up to look upon the helmet which was unlike any other in the armoury. It was of the Corinthian style, with gorgon heads upon the cheek pieces and a great blue horsehair crest rising from the top.

"By the Gods, I don't now how this got here," Milyas said, "but it seems that this is meant for you. The king did say you could take anything from the armoury."

"Well," Bellerophon said, smiling. "We don't want to disobey the king."

Philonoe stood in the great courtyard as the morning sun was beginning to break through the clouds and heat the paving slabs at her feet. She had feared that she had missed

Bellerophon's departure, but when she arrived to see Milyas' ten armed men and three mules, she knew she had not.

Her father had not made an appearance, but there was no way she was not going to see Bellerophon before he departed. As she waited, she ran a long silk sash she had brought through her hands, her fingers playing with the golden suns and moons that had been woven into the fabric. It was one of her favourites, and she poured her prayers and hopes into it as she waited.

"Attention!" one of the soldiers called as Captain Milyas came out of the armoury doorway, followed by Bellerophon.

Silence fell over the courtyard as the son of Glaucus emerged, resplendent in his armour, carrying the weapons he would use against the enemy.

The armour came to life, catching the sunlight in a way that none of them had seen before. The bronze glimmered like fire, and the bull's hide shifted from deep blue to black. Some men even turned away at the sight of the gorgon's head upon Bellerophon's chest.

Bellerophon saw that his own weapons and shield were already on the back of one of the waiting mules, but when he saw that Philonoe was standing on the other side of the court-yard, he set down the new weapons he had obtained and turned to Milyas. "May I greet the princess?"

Milyas looked around for any sign of the king, and nodded when he saw that he was not there. "Go ahead. The men say she has been waiting for some time."

Bellerophon turned away from them and walked across the courtyard to meet Philonoe. "I am happy to see you," he said, unsure of how she felt about seeing him.

But she smiled, though sadly.

"I want you to know that-"

Philonoe put up her hand to stop him. "You don't need to proclaim your innocence to me. I know the truth, and I have prayed that you come through this ordeal. I believe you, Bellerophon."

He breathed deeply, and a sense of peace washed through him. "That is all I need to know."

She stepped forward and held out the sash. "Here. Wear this into battle. It will remind you of me and my belief in you."

She stood close to him, almost as tall, certainly as strong of will, and tied the dark sash tightly about his waist. "May the Gods protect you and grant you strength." She glanced at the soldiers waiting to accompany him. Each of them carried a bow and quiver of arrows, which was unlike what they normally used. "Are they going to help you?"

He smiled sadly, and looked at them. "No. The bows are if I decide to run."

"It's not fair!" she growled.

"It's the Gods' will, Philonoe. Do not worry, for I have never run from what the Gods determine for me."

"Come back to Xanthos, Bellerophon. Let all see that you are innocent, as I know you are."

She leaned in and kissed his cheek before he could answer, turned and disappeared through the propylon into the palace.

"Son of Glaucus!" Milyas called from the other side of the court. "Are you ready to march?"

Bellerophon put the helmet upon his head and turned to face the awaiting soldiers. "Let's go!"

The march was long and arduous, and the only thing to guide Bellerophon and the troops was the increasing feeling of being watched as they plodded over the rocky hills to the East of

Xanthos and then down toward the rolling, forested lands of the Solymi in the distance.

It was quiet as they went, and none but Milyas spoke to Bellerophon, and even he said little. The Lykian troops' eyes scanned the rocks and trees constantly, their ears cocked for a sound of goats and hence their attendant shepherds.

But there was not a sound except for the stirrings of cicadas as they shot from tree to tree like sling stones ahead of them.

The whole time, as the men looked out for the enemy, Bellerophon found himself falling deeper and deeper into the darkness of his thoughts. At first, he had just accepted King Iobates' decision, but now, the more he thought about it, how easily his word was dismissed, the more it made him angry.

The only thing that kept him from fully giving in to the resentment and rage that had begun to fill him was the memory of Philonoe's touch. He looked down at his waist to see the sash that she had tied about him. He touched it gently with his fingers and knew that there were better things in that world than the spite of others.

Goddess Athena, please get me through this day... he prayed as the sun beat down on them. He turned aside to look at Captain Milyas who marched beside him. "Tell me of the crimes these Solymi have committed against your people."

Milyas looked at him strangely. "Why? I do not wish to revisit them, for they are horrible and numerous."

"Tell me. I need to know," Bellerophon insisted.

Milyas sighed. "They regularly burn out crops, or raid our grain stores in the more remote areas. They are constantly attacking our people, slaying their sons and raping their wives and daughters. They do not take slaves, but rather leave them for dead, or to bear the bastards they leave them with."

Bellerophon could not help but remember the faces of the women and children in the streets of Xanthos then. True, he had grown up with little kindness in his life, but he had never been the victim of such acts. No matter the person that King Iobates was, his people were innocent. "What else?"

"Last year, they tied an entire farmer's family up in an oak tree and set it alight. As the family burned, the Solymi shepherds and their own families roasted meats in the very same fire, even as the farmer and his wife and children screamed."

"They make their children do such things?" Bellerophon asked, incredulous now.

Milyas nodded. "Yes. They train them to heartless cruelty from a young age. Earlier this year, they also burned down a temple dedicated to the goddess Athena which lay on our northeastern border. They say Solimos took the effigy of the goddess and now keeps it in his den so that the goddess can watch him abuse the women he takes."

"That's enough…" Bellerophon growled. The hate he began to feel then was acute. "How can they have gotten away with this for so long? The king has an army and they are shepherds!"

Milyas shook his head. "The Solymi are numerous and do not fight like an army." He looked up at the rising hills about them, beyond the soaring pine trees. "They will start a rock slide to wipe out an entire regiment."

Bellerophon could feel the other soldiers behind them growing skittish now. The feeling was palpable, and he scanned the trees. There was a hot wind blowing at their backs, and pine cones popped in the heat, making some men jump.

"King Iobates sent an entire army against them just once in the past - before my time - and apparently it ended in disaster."

"What happened?" Bellerophon asked.

Milyas shook his head. "No one knows, and those who are old enough to remember never speak of it by order of the king."

Something caught Bellerophon's eye in that very second and he reached out with his left arm and pushed Milyas back so that he stumbled into his men just as a spear whistled by and planted itself in a tree at the side of the road. "Attack!"

The men who had levelled their spears at Bellerophon now turned to the trees, only to see the shadow of a lone shepherd running for the road ahead as fast as he could go.

Before Milyas could rally his men, Bellerophon had grabbed his quiver of spears from the nearest mule and charged after the shepherd.

His legs carried him more quickly than he could ever have imagined, despite the armour he wore. He sighted the shepherd in the middle of the road far ahead of him, making for the hills, and he knew that if the young man reached his fellows they would be overrun.

The shepherd glanced back at his pursuer, and his eyes widened in fright at the sight of the brightly armoured warrior pursuing him and raising a spear above his head. He swerved to head for the trees to his right and just before he made it into the trees, he felt something tear through the back of his knee with such force that he crashed into the next tree over.

Bellerophon heard the crack of the man's skull as he ran, and when he arrived, he found the twisted body up against a tall pine tree, blood pouring from the head and knee to be sopped up by the bed of pine needles. He might have felt pity then for the shepherd, but for the stories that Milyas had just told him.

The others arrived just then and spread out to search for others.

"There will be more nearby," Milyas said. "They mute their flocks' bells with tufts of wool when they get near to the Lykian border.

Bellerophon pushed the helmet back on his head and looked around. "Is the terrain like this the entire way?"

"The hills get bigger and steeper, but yes, it is forested much of the way. Why?"

"Do you know where Solimos' dwelling is?" Bellerophon asked.

Milyas shook his head. "You can't be serious. It is madness!"

"This is the task your king has set for me. You can follow me if you like." Bellerophon bent down again to pick up a handful of dry pine needles and crushed them easily in his hands. He smiled to himself. "Captain… Do you have a tinder box in your supplies?"

"Several. Why?"

"We must get as close as possible to Solimos' dwelling."

They continued their march, but this time they left the narrow pathway and cut through the forest, making their way along a narrow ridgeback that gave them a view of the valleys to either side. The trees provided some cover, but still, they were exposed.

Which is how Bellerophon wanted it.

"We need them to see us as we approach, to come out of their hiding places. From this ridge, we have the high ground," he said, remembering the fight on the Acrocorinthos.

And he was correct, for as they went, they encountered lone shepherds all the way, taking some by surprise, and meeting others head-on. The Solymi were everywhere, and every time they rushed the lone warrior who marched ahead of the others, it was to meet the same fate, skewered on the end of a soaring spear.

It was as if a lion was clearing rats from the land, one after another without end. But the rats became more numerous and as angry as if they were cornered in an alleyway. Horns began to blow in the distant trees, and there were angry voices in the valleys to either side.

"We're done for!" one of the men yelled behind Bellerophon. "You've brought them down on us, Corinthian!"

Bellerophon jumped up on a boulder that stood on the narrow ridge and looked to either side. *They like fire?* he thought, thinking of the story of the farmer and his family. *I'll give them fire!*

"Captain! Bring me a tinder box, and one amphora of oil!" Bellerophon then went to one of the mules and took a recurve bow and two quivers of long-shafted arrows. "Quickly!"

"The king ordered that we not help you, Bellerophon!" Milyas said after a moment's pause.

Bellerophon turned and looked down him, the screams all about them growing louder and angrier. "I'm not asking you to fight! I'm asking you to light a fire!"

Milyas nodded and grabbed a tinder box, while another of the men brought the small amphora of oil.

"Light a small fire on the rock now!" Bellerophon ordered. "And open the oil jar and hold it for me!"

They did so, and the fire caught quickly with the dried brush that was all about. Another soldier held up the oil jar.

Immediately Bellerophon drew an arrow from the quiver he had, dipped it in the oil, and lit the point on fire. He then nocked the arrow to his bowstring and drew back.

The arrow soared to their left until it was lost in the

wooded slopes of the ridge. Nothing happened for a few moments, but then the angry cries that were rushing up the slopes changed.

There was terror now, and rage.

Bellerophon fired again and again to each side of the ridge. A loud crackling could be heard everywhere, and thick black smoke rose up into the sky as the pine forest lit up. He fired arrows farther along the ridge that led in the direction of the main village, and then jumped down from his rock to take up his throwing spears and more arrows. "Stand back!" he said as he pulled an arrow back and loosed.

The barb took the first Solymi shepherd in the neck, sending his body back down the flaming slope. Another arrow pinned two together as they rushed directly for Bellerophon.

He drew again and again, and every time his arrows found a mark, for the Solymi were everywhere as he turned, fleeing the flames in a panic, unaware of the warrior awaiting them upon the ridge they thought was their only hope.

There were screams all around them as men burned or had their throats torn out by Bellerophon's arrows, but they kept coming.

Seek the bear's head!

Athena's voice echoed in Bellerophon's mind, and he remembered the goddess' words, his eyes searching down the long ridge and the Solymi warriors gathering far ahead of them, blackened from the flaming forest.

After loosing several more arrows ahead and to the rear, Bellerophon tossed the bow and empty quiver to one of the soldiers and slipped the quiver of throwing spears over his shoulder. He took up his great gorgon-headed shield and drew his sword.

Breathe! He told himself. *Goddess, protect me!*

With one last glance at Milyas and the men, their eyes wide and panicked, Bellerophon charged down the ridge.

One of the men drew his bow to shoot at Bellerophon, but Milyas pushed his arrow aside, "Wait!" the captain said. "He's not running away! He's going for Solimos!" They watched as Bellerophon ran and slashed at every warrior that came up the slope at him, leaving their writhing or dead forms in his wake like so many piece of wheat beneath a scythe. "My gods," Milyas said. He turned to his men. "Come on! After him!"

Bellerophon felt blade after blade, and numerous arrows seek his death as he ran, but each time, they glanced off of the armour protecting his body. He ran and slashed, leaving death in his wake as he cut a swathe along the ridge and down the slope to the thatched rooftops of the distant village which was now in view.

Screams echoed down the valley and horns blew in the village as he and the fires he had lit sped toward Solimos' home. When Solymi shepherds rushed him from the flaming brush, their eyes shot wide at the sight of the warrior who bore down on them like an angry god, his blue crest and angry eyes wild and unmerciful.

Flocks of goats ran screaming and aflame, setting more of the forest alight as they went, bleating to their masters' homes, setting more villages aflame. Soon, smoke began to rise from the main village, and the blue of the sky became veiled with black smoke.

Bellerophon stopped, his breathing fast and deep. He coughed, the smoke now swirling about him, and looked back to see if the others were coming, but he could see nothing.

He then began to climb down the rocky slope where he

spied a path through the flames. Men came at him from different directions but not with purpose, for most were running away from the raging fires Bellerophon had brought with him.

At last he came to the part where the road emerged from the fires and led up a slope into the village. Bellerophon sheathed his blade and drew one of his throwing spears. With his shield raised on his left arm, he walked forward into the chaos ahead where Solymi men and women scattered in every direction, carrying children and ushering their animals away from the flames and the god they believed had just stepped into their midst.

"Solimos!" Bellerophon yelled, throwing a killing spear at a warrior who waited in the road ahead of him, and then drawing another. "Solimos! Come out and meet your death!"

As he walked, he clung to the images of slain Lykian women and children, of young boys robbed of youth and their families, and as the rage inside him peaked, he began to run.

Men came at him, half-heartedly or like crazed hyenas around a lion, but he cut them down, uncaring of the cuts he received as he went.

"Solimos!" he yelled again as he came before what appeared to be the largest round house where skulls adorned the threshold. *Bear skulls!* Bellerophon noticed. "Solimos! Come out here!"

There was a great bellow from somewhere around the smoking hovels and Bellerophon turned around to see Solymi shepherds in the skins, holding out daggers, spears, and staffs at him, but not making a move to attack. "Solimos, you coward! How many people must die for you?"

A sudden, heavy and fast crunching came at Bellerophon from the right, and he turned quickly with his shield out only to feel the full impact of the man running at him. He felt himself flying backward until he landed against one of the burning walls of a nearby hovel, and then fall to the ground.

He rolled to one side, slashing out with the spear he had been holding onto, and cut the throat of another Solymi man who had dared to attack.

But the giant of a man who had hit him was upon him again, grasping at Bellerophon with thick hands and throwing him back the way he had come.

Bellerophon rolled away and found his feet again before throwing his spear and taking the rushing man on the side of the cheek, sending a bear skin helmet falling to the ground.

It was then that Solimos stopped and rose to his full height, his great shoulders rising and falling with his angry breathing. His eyes were wild and white in the middle of the charcoal that had been spread over his face. Bear pelts fell from his shoulders and he drew a long, double-headed axe and pointed it at Bellerophon's arm. "You bleed!" He laughed, shaking his head. "You are no god," he growled, crouching into a fighting stance.

Bellerophon could see the shepherds closing in around him, waiting to see what their chieftain would do next.

Solimos straightened again for a moment, but then rushed with surprising speed, his great axe in a horizontal death blow that skimmed Bellerophon's crest as he ducked beneath it.

Bellerophon emerged behind Solimos, one spear loosed to plant itself in his bare thigh.

Solimos bellowed in pain, but ripped out the spear as if it were only a bee sting, and charged again, his battle-axe in a great sweeping motion from the ground up at Bellerophon's jaw.

The blow glanced off of the angled shield as Bellerophon

leapt backward, and the gorgon head then pushed forward quickly to slam into Solimos' face making him stumble back a step before another spear planted itself in his axe arm.

The axe fell to the ground with a thud as blood poured from Solimos' bicep, but the chieftain picked it up with his other hand and swung again and again, pushing Bellerophon back until he was almost with his back against the Solymi shepherds awaiting with their blades drawn.

Bellerophon slashed behind him, taking two in the throat before spinning toward Solimos' wounded arm and slashing with his last spear behind the knee.

"Arrggg!" Solimos screamed to the sky and he fell to one knee, turning his black head to Bellerophon and spitting in his direction.

It was in that moment that Bellerophon felt all of the anger and rage and resentment of the years come to a head, all of it focussed on that one barbarian who had caused so much suffering to Philonoe's people.

In that tiny lull of thought, Solimos launched himself from his good leg, his axe out. Bellerophon side-stepped it quickly, feeling the wind on his cheek, and drew his sword so that it swept down and took Solimos on the back of the neck.

The bear fell in the dust and his black head rolled away from his twitching corpse to be lost in the smoke that was closing in.

The shepherds were aghast, but they did not run. They growled and crouched and began to close in on Bellerophon, slowly but with purpose.

Bellerophon looked up at the sky and spread his arms wide. *Oh, Goddess Athena... I have tried,* he prayed, and in that moment barbed arrows came out of the fire and smoke to knock a dozen shepherds off of their feet.

A great silence fell over the Solymi then and, though they were many, they fell to their knees with their hands up for mercy, pleading to the sky and the bronze-clad god standing in their midst.

Bellerophon lowered his arms and turned slowly, looking at the people who lay prostrate before him. The blood of their chieftain dripped from the blade which he pointed at each of them.

"The Gods have punished Solimos for his crimes!" Bellerophon said to them. "If you do not stop attacking Lykia, the same fate awaits every one of you!"

The Solymi bent lower, unmoving, despite the burning homes at their backs, their faces in the dirt.

Bellerophon bent to pick up Solimos' head and the bear skull helmet the chieftain had worn. He held them aloft so that the shepherds could see clearly and then raised his face to the sky.

"Ahhhhhh!" he yelled, as if releasing all of his anger and pent-up rage. "Ahhhhhh!" he cried again, and this time thunder cracked in the sky above.

A moment later, it began to rain.

Bellerophon watched as the Solymi turned and ran from him, disappearing into the smoking forests about their village, eager to get away from the angry god in their midst. He, however, stood there for a moment, staring at the body of the man he had slain. *More death,* he thought, and with that thought came anger at King Iobates for sending him to do it. He held up Solimos' head and looked at the surprised eyes set deep in that heavy skull. *But you deserved it for all you have done.*

The Solymi had disappeared and Bellerophon walked out

of the village, alone and un-harassed, as it rained and the fires were doused.

When he emerged from the smoking village, he found Milyas and his men standing there with their bows drawn.

Bellerophon stopped and held up the head and bear pelt. "A gift for King Iobates," he said, tossing them at Milyas' feet.

Milyas looked at the head and pelt, and back at Bellerophon.

Bellerophon smiled. "I thought you weren't here to help me?" he said, nodding at the bows in the soldiers' hands.

Milyas shrugged. "I don't know what you're talking about, Bellerophon of Corinthos." He smiled. "We're only here to make sure you don't run away."

CHAPTER 8

THE DAUGHTERS OF ARES

Xanthos had been quiet for days, as if the entire population, having learned of what the son of Glaucus had been sent to do, was holding its collective breath. They had waited in fear, either for the Gods' wrath, or for the Solymi's retribution. Never did they expect to see the return of Bellerophon after he was sent alone to slay their kingdom's long-time enemy.

Philonoe was sitting upon the upper terrace of the palace, in her rooms, as she had been since Bellerophon left, when she heard the raucous cheers in the city streets far below. For days she had been praying to the Gods, fearing for Bellerophon, and as she ran through the corridors of the palace, she thought she might die from the anticipation. *Why are the people cheering so wildly?*

She burst into the megaron to find her father gathered with several courtiers and Polyidus beside him. She rushed to the latter's side. "Is it true? Have they returned?"

"Yes, my lady," the seer whispered. "But we do not know yet if-"

The megaron doors burst open with a loud thud and silence fell on the assembly as Bellerophon, armed and dirty, walked through the propylon with Milyas and the ten men, their weapons stowed.

"Son of Glaucus?" King Iobates said, unable to hide the surprise in his voice. "You have returned!"

"Yes, King Iobates!" Bellerophon said, glancing at the king and then bowing to Philonoe.

She smiled and saw that the sash was still about his waist. That was a comfort, but the look in Bellerophon's eyes was a source of distress, for in them she could see the detritus of battle and fury, the suffering that accompanies even victory.

"The Solymi will no longer attack Lykia or the city of Xanthos!" Bellerophon declared, and the entire court began to whisper in surprise.

"But how is this possible?" the king said. "I did not expect-
"

"You did not expect me to live?" Bellerophon added. "Well, I have, by the Gods who know my innocence!"

The king stared at Bellerophon intently, and then looked to the captain of his guard and the other soldiers there. "Captain Milyas? You and your men look as though you have been through a battle too. Did you fight also? Bellerophon was supposed to do this on his own, without aid."

Captain Milyas stepped forward and inclined his head, but very little. "My king, the son of Glaucus defeated the Solymi on his own with his wits, skill, and help from the Gods. He defeated the Solymi with fire and sword and wrested from them their oath that they should never again raise arms against Lykia."

"But what of Solimos?" Iobates demanded, his voice louder. "Did you let him live too?"

Bellerophon turned to one of the soldiers and took a bundled sack which had been tied to one of the mules. Here is Solimos!" Bellerophon said loudly and tossed the bundle at the base of the king's dais with a loud thud.

King Iobates stared at it for a moment, and then turned to one of the guards beside him.

The guard stepped forward and untied the bundle, and a moment later the face of Solimos was staring up at King Iobates.

The sound of flies became loud all of a sudden, and Philonoe turned, feeling her stomach lurch at the sight of the bloody, decaying head.

"He is dead," Iobates said to himself, and his fists clenched around the arms of his throne. "Take that out of here and throw it into the river!"

"Yes, sire," the soldier replied, tying up the bundle again and going out of the megaron.

"You have succeeded, Bellerophon," the king said. "And so we shall feast to your success tomorrow night. At that time, I will announce your second task."

Philonoe saw Bellerophon deflate a little at the words as he turned to go, and she felt great pity for him. She also felt anger toward her father, for he had used their guest terribly, no matter the accusations that needed to be addressed. "Why must you continue with this, Father?" she asked, turning to him.

"He has done it," the king said, more to himself. "By the Gods…what else can he do for me?"

"Father?" Philonoe repeated, but she received no response as the king went out of the megaron with his courtiers in tow. She did not like the greedy glint in her father's eyes in that moment, and feared for what he might demand of Bellerophon next. "I must go to Bellerophon!" Philonoe said to Polyidus, but the seer reached for her arm, shaking his head.

"Let him be alone for now, Princess. Though I could not see him, I could tell from his voice that he is most weary from his trial. It is no easy thing to kill, and he has no doubt slain more in one day than most men do in a lifetime. He needs time."

Philonoe's heart tightened at the thought of what must have been raging through Bellerophon's mind, but she wondered if Polyidus was right about it. Bellerophon needed time to purify himself, wash, and rest. *Then, I will go to him.*

In his rooms, alone again, Bellerophon breathed deeply and coughed, still feeling the sting of the smoke in his lungs. He removed his helmet and set it upon the floor, along with the greaves and arm guards. He then untied the sash that the princess had given him. It was torn and dirty, but he set it aside to wash. Then, with some difficulty, he undid the buckles of the cuirass and set it down too.

Thank you, Goddess Athena, for protecting me with this armour, and for granting me victory, he thought before going straight to the altar and making offerings to the goddess.

Exhaustion clawed at him, but he sought first to wash, and after removing his soiled tunic, he went to the basin of fresh water, dipped a sponge in, and set to scrubbing himself clean of blood and the numbness that had beset him so.

Bellerophon could have slept for days. The exhaustion was so complete, he thought he might never awaken. However, when he heard the voices in the corridor outside, he rose sleepily from his bed and went to knock upon the doors.

The voices stopped and the bolt outside was slid back.

Philonoe stood there staring at him in the doorway. The guard she had been arguing with stood back. "They were refusing me entry to see you," she said, shocked by his exhausted complexion.

"It was your father's command," Bellerophon said, but then he smiled. "I am glad to see you."

"Have you rested?" she asked, following him into the rooms.

"My lady-" the guard began to protest, but Philonoe turned on him.

"Stay where you are and leave the doors open. I am visiting with our guest, by the laws of Zeus!"

The man backed away.

"Phoebos!" Philonoe called, when she saw the dirty armour and tunic on the floor.

"Yes, mistress?" the slave came running in with the two others.

"I want you to wash Bellerophon's tunic and clean and polish all of his armour for him."

The slave bowed low. "Yes, mistress. Right away!" The three slaves hurried in, gathered the items carefully, and brought them into the hallway, leaving the princess alone with Bellerophon, under the watchful eye of the guards in the corridor.

"Have you eaten?" Philonoe asked, turning to him, her voice tender and concerned.

"A little," he said making his way to the table by the wash basin. He picked up the sash and turned to hand it to her. "I thank you for this. I am sorry it got torn in battle, but I have washed it for you."

She took it and pressed it to her chest. "I hope it helped you."

"You have no idea, Princess." His eyes looked haunted and faraway for a moment. "It gave me hope in that terrible place."

She stepped forward placed her hands upon his crossed arms. "You need not speak of it. Leave it behind now. It is done." She thought he might think her too forward or patronizing, but he sighed and nodded, as if he had needed the permission to stop thinking of the horrors he had seen, and the things he had done. "I actually came to accompany you to the feast if you are willing."

Bellerophon looked outside at the terrace and saw that the sun was setting. "Is it evening already?" he said.

"You have slept for an entire day," she said.

"I must admit, the thought of feasting is not to my liking right now," he muttered, but then he looked at her. "But if you are beside me, I can face it." He managed to smile at her, and she returned it.

"Then we must stay together," she said.

There was no music in the megaron that night, no celebratory atmosphere to welcome Bellerophon, Milyas and his soldiers back from their mission. There was only the sound of muted conversation, the crackle of the fire in the hearth, and the smell of roasted meats and freshly baked breads.

The smell of the fire made Bellerophon cough as he and Philonoe entered the megaron together and all eyes turned to see them.

King Iobates scowled at his daughter when he saw her

accompanying Bellerophon against his wishes. *She grows too fond,* he thought, *and it will only make her pain the greater when Bellerophon dies.*

"Come, Slayer of the Solymi!" King Iobates said aloud when Bellerophon and Philonoe took their seats. "Drink and eat your fill. Regain your strength!"

Bellerophon made no reply, but sat in his usual seat.

To the king's dismay, his daughter whispered to Polyidus, and the seer rose from his own seat beside their guest to yield it to the princess.

Philonoe shot a look as sharp as a barbed arrow at her father, and he decided against chiding her publicly yet again. He had other things on his mind, things which he hoped would bear fruit, one way or another.

"Polyidus," the king said. "You may sit to my left if you wish."

"Thank you, my king," the seer said, moving behind them to the princess' usual seat.

Conversations picked up again around the megaron and Bellerophon settled into his chair. He felt the exhaustion receding little by little, and when a slave filled his wine cup, he tipped some to the Gods without a word from the king, and drank.

"Captain Milyas has told me of your strategy for rooting out the Solymi, Bellerophon," the king said eventually, after they had eaten for a time. "It was most ingenious."

Bellerophon did not answer at first, but then set his cup down and turned to the king. "It was a slaughter."

The king scoffed. "They deserved it for all they have put our people through."

"They are mere shepherds," Bellerophon said, "and though Captain Milyas made me aware of the terrible things they had done to Lykia, I wonder why you have such a personal hatred of them. Solimos, I understand - he was an abomination - but his people? They did not seem so different from others I have seen in my travels."

"You do not understand," the king said curtly. "You are a stranger here, and you have not seen how the Solymi have abused my people over the years. You should be happy with your victory, Bellerophon."

"I might be, if that were an end to it. But, by Zeus Xenios, you have declared that you have another task for me, haven't you?"

King Iobates stared sidelong at Bellerophon. He was starting to hate the Corinthian, and told himself that he probably did do what his eldest daughter had accused him of. He slammed his fist upon the table and stood. "I was going to wait until later to announce it, but since you press me, since you seem so eager to know your next trial, I will tell you now!"

Everyone around the megaron grew absolutely silent and stared at the king who looked down on his guest, ignoring his daughter's pleading face behind Bellerophon.

Bellerophon set down the meat he was eating and leaned back in his chair. There were few men he absolutely disliked, but King Iobates was fast-becoming one of the foremost. He had thought him honourable at first, but now he could see that he was the same as any other king - greedy, cruel and selfish. *He truly is Stheneboea's father,* he thought. "I am listening, King Iobates," he said. "With the Gods as witnesses, tell us what my second task is."

King Iobates cleared his throat and looked around the room. "To the North, on the Phrygian plateau, there is a tribe of Amazons. They constantly harass my men, steal our livestock and burn our crops."

"What?" Philonoe could not help herself. "I have never heard of this happening."

"Silence!" King Iobates said. "You are not a part of the decisions. While you embroider, the world tears itself apart and our enemies eat away at our borders."

Philonoe reached out to touch Bellerophon's arm but the latter kept his eyes on the king.

"The Amazons are daughters of Ares," Bellerophon said.

"Yes, and I want you to kill the entire tribe, especially their queen, Otrera."

"What has this queen done to you, King Iobates, that you would sentence her to death?"

"She has done much. That is all you need to know. Either you do this, or you die on the morrow." The king's gaze was cold and hate-filled.

Bellerophon stood. "I will do this, and likely die, King Iobates. This seems to be what you want, though the Gods themselves know my innocence." He could feel Philonoe pulling at his arm to sit again. He could hear her protestations to her father and the general incredulous murmur of the courtiers, but he was resigned to the hatred of the man before him. It was not new. "I must go and rest now," Bellerophon said, stepping away from his chair. "I will leave the day after next."

"You will leave tomorrow," the king commanded as Bellerophon walked away.

"I never thought you to be such a man, Father," Philonoe said as she left her seat, pulling away from her father's grasp, and marched away after Bellerophon.

"She will be greatly disappointed when he is slain, Polyidus," King Iobates said as he leaned to his other side.

"I do believe a great many people in Xanthos will be, sire," the seer said. "Are you sure you want to set him this task? It may bring greater pain than you know."

"I am certain. If Bellerophon is slain, then I will be free of his poisonous presence. And if he succeeds, I will finally be free of my worst enemies."

"Enemies, sire?" Polyidus said doubtfully. "They have not done the things you have said," he whispered. "Sending Bellerophon will make the Amazons your enemies for certain."

"Make no mistake, Polyidus," Iobates warned. "They *are* my enemies."

"Bellerophon, wait!"

Philonoe's voice echoed in the empty, moonlit court outside of the propylon gate.

Bellerophon stopped to look up at the night sky, his broad shoulders slumped and tired as he breathed.

"You cannot do this thing for my father!" she said.

Bellerophon closed and opened his eyes and looked at her. "I do not do it for him," he said. "I do it to prove my innocence to you. I do not care for any of the others."

"But I do believe you!" Philonoe said, gripping him. "I know what my sister is like. I was not so young as that when she left. I could see how she manipulated people. You have nothing to prove to me, can't you see that?"

Bellerophon looked into her bright eyes and held her hand gently in his, which had been covered in blood just the day before. He looked back up at the sky and sighed. It was a sound of tiredness and exhaustion, and a part of him longed to tap into the anger he had rallied in himself before fighting the Solymi. But he could not. *Death is certain this time.*

"When I was young," he said to her, "I had no ambitions for myself or my life. Why would I have, when no one else did for me? I simply existed. Perhaps I should have dreamed of doing something, for now it seems that the Gods have chosen for me."

"The Gods bless you, Bellerophon," she whispered. "Polyidus has seen it. Even I can see it. Why can you not simply run away and…and never come back? I fear your death more than never seeing you again."

He smiled at her, and he wondered that even in the midst of his dark resignation, she could make him do so. However, he knew what awaited him in the days to come. "Philonoe, I do not know what will await me in Phrygia, but I must go. The Amazons are no tribe of armed shepherds. They are the Daughters of Ares, born and bread for war. And me? I am just a Corinthian refugee whom nobody wants."

"*I* want you!" Philonoe realized immediately what she had said.

Bellerophon's eyes were wide and he was about to speak when Captain Milyas approached.

"There you are!" Milyas said. "Forgive me, Princess, but the king commanded me to seek Bellerophon." He turned to the latter. "I regret that the king has declared that me and my men may not attend you on this task. You must go alone this time."

"I understand," Bellerophon said, not at all surprised by this turn of events.

"He cannot march all the way to Phrygia by himself!" Philonoe said, growing more and more angry with every second.

"I'm sorry, my lady. It is the king's wish," Milyas said, his head bowed to her.

"I will go alone," Bellerophon said. But at least tell me which way to go."

"You must follow the river north for some days until you reach the open plains that are the beginning of the Phrygian lands. From there, you turn northwest keeping the snow-caped mountains to your left. It is dry and rocky terrain, so you will need to bring supplies with you. Ahead, at the end of that long road, you will see a mountain rising up before you in the distance. High on that Phrygian plateau is where you will find the Amazons or, rather, where they will find you."

"Captain, please," Philonoe said. "Can you at least prevail upon my father to allow you and your men to go with Bellerophon?"

"I am sorry, my lady. I did try. It seems… Lately, your father is not himself." He turned back to Bellerophon. "I know you do not like to ride horses, but if you would, the journey would take half as much time."

Bellerophon shook his head.

"On foot it will take you at least seven days," Milyas said.

"Then I have a long walk ahead of me," Bellerophon answered. "I'll take a mule to carry my provisions though. I don't mind mules."

Milyas chuckled. "You are strange, Bellerophon."

Philonoe looked at the two of them, incredulous. "How can you both laugh?"

"What choice do we have, my lady?" Milyas said.

"You can get Bellerophon out of Xanthos this night," she said, her voice low.

Milyas shook his head. "Then it would be my head upon the gates, beside that of Solimos."

"Philonoe," Bellerophon said. "I will not run. All I have is my truth, and I will not throw that away."

Philonoe shook her head and walked away, frustrated, angry, and utterly baffled by everyone's acceptance of her father's will.

"The princess is fond of you," Milyas said.

"She is very kind," Bellerophon answered. "Kinder to me than anyone has ever been."

"More's the reason for the king to wish you dead. And now I think he's picked his method."

"I thought I would die the other day in Pisidia against the Solymi, and yet… I live."

"You will need all your skills against the Amazons if you are to survive," Milyas said darkly. *He will certainly die.*

"It's in the Gods hands now."

When Bellerophon reached his rooms and Milyas set the guard at his door, as commanded, he found his amour and weapons upon a stand in the middle of the main room, before the door onto the terrace. They had been polished to a brilliance he had never seen before, so much so that they cast their own light onto the floor and walls of the room. The horsehair crest fluttered in the evening breeze that came in at the window.

Bellerophon turned and saw that his tunic was also washed and folded upon his bed beside a thick black cloak.

It seemed the slaves had already found out what his next task was, and that they were preparing him for his journey into Phrygia.

Bellerophon walked outside onto the terrace, took the tinder box and a bundle of herbs from the basket and went to the altar where he lit them and raised his hands to the night sky.

"Oh, Goddess Athena… You have brought me through this

first task, and for that I am grateful. Guide me in this second task. Guide my weapons, and my mind that I may have even the slimmest chance of success...of coming back to Philonoe..."

You must remain focussed, Bellerophon, the voice said.

Bellerophon looked up to see the goddess' brilliant and terrifying eyes looking down at him from the other side of the altar.

The princess is not your concern now. The road ahead, and battle are. The Daughters of Ares show no mercy toward their enemies. They are formidable.

"I understand, oh Goddess, and I put myself at the Gods' mercy. I will go, and I will fight."

Athena looked down on Bellerophon's bowed head and, for a moment, she reached out, her luminescent hand hovering above his head. *You are not alone, son of Glaucus. You never were.*

When Bellerophon looked up, she was gone.

Mourning doves cooed on the rooftops of the palace in the early morning haze. The palace corridors were silent, but in the great court Milyas and his men had gathered to see Bellerophon off on his journey.

When the son of Glaucus arrived, fully armed and brilliant in the dim morning light, he found Milyas and the others gathered around a mule.

Milyas smiled at Bellerophon and nodded toward the person loading up the mule.

Philonoe was busy loading provisions of food, pelts, and weapons onto the wooden frame on the mule's back while the beast stood placidly by. When she saw Bellerophon approach, she stopped and looked at him. "Forgive me for my harsh words last night. It is not how I wanted to send you off."

Bellerophon felt his heart lighten at the very sight of her and smiled. "There is nothing to apologize for, Princess." He stepped closer, the mule between them and the soldiers standing by. "Thank you for coming to see me before I go."

She shook her head. "It is nothing. I... I just wanted to make sure you have plenty of provisions. It is a long journey and... And I've also fastened more spears to the mule for you." She placed her hand on the animal's back.

"I thank you," Bellerophon said. He looked into her brilliant green eyes. They were a little red from sleeplessness, but no less beautiful and kind. Her red hair fell about her shoulders, and the freckles about her face danced when she smiled.

"Here," she said, reaching up to unclasp something from about her neck. "Take this." She pulled at a thin rope, and from beneath her peplos rose a golden, double-headed battle-axe. "My father used to tell me this was my mother's favourite charm, and that she wore it always." Her voice was sad and longing then, but he could tell that she was proud of the piece. "I've been told she preferred this to any set of glittering jewels. I want you to wear it."

"I couldn't!" he said. "If I do not return, then it will be lost to you."

"Please!" she said vehemently. "If there is the slightest chance that it will protect you, I want you to have it." Without waiting for him to answer again, she reached up and tied it around his neck so that it hung over the edge of his breastplate, above the gorgon's head. "Come back to Xanthos, Bellerophon. Find a way."

"I will," he said, and he took her hand and kissed it. "Thank you, Princess."

Philonoe looked at him, her eyes glossy in the early morning light, but she did not cry, not yet. "May the Gods protect you on your journey," she said, her voice a little hoarse.

He nodded and placed the helmet upon his head, his long black hair falling over his shoulders from beneath the edges.

As Philonoe backed away, silent prayers upon her lips, Bellerophon took up the mule's lead rope and turned to Milyas and the soldiers who had accompanied him into Pisidia.

"Come back to us, son of Glaucus!" Milyas said as Bellerophon went out of the palace gates to find the road that led to the river and north.

Bellerophon looked back one last time at Philonoe, only to see King Iobates standing behind her, his expression grim and determined.

"His guilt will determine his fate in Phrygia," the king said to his daughter.

She turned quickly, and stepped back from him. Words escaped her, but in her eyes there was no mistaking the utter disappointment she felt in him.

It was in that moment that King Iobates knew that he had lost his daughter's love, as certainly as Death would soon take the son of Glaucus.

The road north into Phrygia was long and lonely, for Bellerophon felt as if he were back at the beginning of his trials once more. The dejected feeling that he had felt before was back in full force, and if it were not for the memory of Philonoe's face, her kindness, he might simply have thrown himself into the rushing river to his left.

As it was, however, the charm about his neck gave him comfort, and reminded him that there was kindness in the world. And so he walked, pulling his pack mule along the way.

The creature that accompanied him was docile and calm, and followed without one iota of the stubbornness for which mules were known. With food and weapons upon its back, the mule clipped along the rocky road, always behind the armoured warrior who led it.

At first, Bellerophon kept looking back at the creature, unsure if he wanted such a companion for so long a journey, but the mule seemed quite disinterested, and certainly not hungry for his flesh.

If my father could see me now... Bellerophon wondered as he walked past the olive and citrus groves surrounding Xanthos, and then along the river.

The air smelled of juniper and fig, the fruit of which was only recently ripe. Pink and white oleander swayed in the hot wind, and along the river, brilliant tufts of tamarisk moved as if nymphs were hiding within them.

Indeed, he felt as though he were being watched the entire time, and yet he saw no one, spoke with no one. In the distance to the northeast, smoke began to rise, and Bellerophon wondered what was causing it, for in merely observing the fires, a deep feeling of dread, which he could not help, came over him.

When the road began to rise to a point where he could see farther, he stopped to look at the pluming smoke and listen to what he thought were very distant screams, though it could have been the hawks diving in among the carob groves to sink their talons into their next meal.

The days were long and quiet upon the northern road, but the nights were anything but restful. Wherever Bellerophon chose to sleep, be it beneath the boughs of oak, plane, or pine trees, or against a rock down by the river, every time he closed his eyes he could hear that same, deep growling that had haunted him for so long, see the rearing form of a wild stallion, and hear its own gut-wrenching squeals. More often than not, Bellerophon would sit and gaze up at the star-riddled sky and watch the shifting forms the Gods had placed there, or stare into the flames of his campfire until his eyes were so heavy that he could not help but fall into a tortured sleep.

After a few days, the terrain became inhospitable to any vegetation but the most hearty of scrub. As the land rose up, it became rockier and more windswept, as if anything that attempted to grow was burned for being so much closer to the sun. But mountains did rise up in the distance all around him, snow-capped and menacing.

The Phrygian sky was wide and endless, a pale blue raked with stretches of cloud. The rocky plain over which Bellerophon now travelled, many days after he had left Xanthos, no longer offered cover of any sort. He knew that if anyone was watching him, they would have seen him by then. He also knew that that wild, inhospitable landscape was not as devoid of life as it appeared, for upon the earth he did mark the tracks of horses in many places.

Cavalry... he thought to himself as he bent to look at yet another set of tracks. His eyes followed the general direction of the tracks whenever he found some, and they always seemed to be going to, or orbiting, a distant, rocky plateau overlooking the valley through which he travelled.

It was then, as he bent to look at the tracks, that he heard a deep growl approaching. His mule began to pull violently at the rope he held in his left hand.

Bellerophon turned to see a lion approaching, crouched as if ready to pounce. He could see his shield and helmet hanging from the mule's pack saddle and knew that he would not reach them in time.

The lion's tawny face contorted in an aggressive growl as it bared its teeth.

Bellerophon slowly drew his sword from its scabbard, but not before the lion lunged for the mule's flailing legs.

The mule heaved a great, painful cry as it kicked and spun, ripping the rope from Bellerophon's hand as he ran directly for the lion.

The mule bolted, but the lion caught up with it and in moments both beasts crashed to the ground in a cloud of dust from which emanated blood-curdling cries.

Bellerophon could hear the mule's flesh tearing as the lion's claws and teeth tore into it.

"Stop it!" he yelled, lunging with his blade out to take the lion in the back thigh.

The lion spun on him, swiping at him with its bloodied claws before turning back to the mule and sinking its teeth into the mule's neck.

Bellerophon kicked out as hard as he could at the lion's ribs, and it was then that the lion turned to face him fully, now that its prey was no longer able to run. Bellerophon crouched ready for the attack, his heart pounding, his eyes searching for a target.

The lion charged and lunged with both of its thick forelegs out as if to take the man in a death embrace.

Bellerophon screamed as he spun, his thigh caught by a single claw, and swept his blade down into the side of the lion's neck.

The beast crashed and began to turn quickly, but not so quickly as Bellerophon whose blade stabbed directly into its open jaws and up into its brain. The lion's eyes shot wide and it fell with a thud in the dust.

"Ahhh!" Bellerophon cried out as he fell to one knee, gripping his torn thigh. Breathing heavily, and blinded by the stinging sun overhead, he turned and crawled over to the mule only to see that its eyes were glazed and lifeless, the flies already massing about them and the blood leaking from its wounds. "I'm sorry," he said, shaking his head as he leaned over the animal's body.

Make camp, Bellerophon. Seal your wound.

Athena's voice was unmistakable, and a part of him felt like weeping for hearing it. But there was no time for softness. The goddess was right. He needed to seal the wound before he fainted.

As quickly as he could, Bellerophon took some of the dried branches he had tied to the mule's back and made a fire in the shelter from the wind provided by the body. Soon, his dagger blade was in the flames, heating until it was red hot.

Bellerophon cut a piece of leather from the ties on the mule's back and bit down on it. Then, he leaned against the body and braced himself as he removed the blade from the fire.

He pulled back the armoured skirt to reveal his wounded thigh and hovered the blade over it for a few second before pressing the burning brand to his flesh as hard as he could manage.

His scream echoed over the valley before his ears began to ring and he passed out.

It was dark when Bellerophon began to rouse, his eyes fluttering open very slowly to see the stars in the night sky and the faint embers of the fire he had lit. He groaned, and then felt the searing, stiff pain in his leg. His shaking hand reached for his thigh and he felt the raw, charred skin, but no fresh blood.

"Ahh!" he sighed. "Athena, help me…" he said as his eyes lolled in his head, trying to wake himself.

"Men!" a voice said mockingly. "Such a little wound!"

"But a big lion," added another voice.

Bellerophon shook his head and opened his eyes to see four shapes standing over him. He grasped wildly for his sword but found only rock.

"Looking for this?" one said, holding up his blade.

Before he could answer, a fist pounded into the side of his head and all went dark once more.

In the darkness, Bellerophon could see Athena walking ahead of him, her helmet tilted back on her head and a long spear in her pale hand. She glanced back at him and smiled occasionally, and he would have spoken but for the loud drumming. He listened more intently and realized it was the blood pounding in his ears, and that he was seeing the goddess from an awkward angle, almost upside down as he bobbed over the rocky earth.

Wind howled, and then the sound of war drums rang out. Dizzy now, Bellerophon vomited and was taken by darkness again.

"We are almost there, lion-slayer," a voice said.

In the darkness in which he found himself, Bellerophon crouched beneath enormous flailing hooves and a writhing mane that moved like pale wheat in the winter wind. A stallion reared, its jaws opening and closing, snapping as its hooves pounded the earth and wind rushed about him.

He wanted to scream, but then he heard an even more terrible sound and turned to see a great set of fiery eyes coming toward him, accompanied by a deadly hissing and a growl that seemed to shake the earth. Claws gripped and broke stone and flames shot up into the air above his head.

Bellerophon reached for his weapons but his hands grasped only air. *No!!!*

The terror before him lunged and his voice rang out its last desperate notes…

"No!" he yelled, but death did not come.

Instead, Bellerophon found himself bound to a pole of some sort, and sweaty, staring at a fire in the darkness before him. As his eyes adjusted, he saw his weapons lying on the other side of the fire, out of reach.

A young girl held the enormous shield on its edge and was polishing it with doeskin, while another held up his sword to the firelight.

"You were dreaming," the one girl said.

Bellerophon looked at them, lost for words as his head spun. They could not have been more than thirteen summers old, and yet they looked like warriors already, the way they handled his weapons comfortably and cared for them. The one had dark hair, and the other blonde, but they looked similar in features, proud, strong and long of limb. Both had their hair tied back tightly with several braids falling down, secured with beads or leather thongs. One had a bruise beneath her eyes, and the other swollen knuckles on one hand.

"Where am I?" Bellerophon asked, his voice hoarse. He

coughed, and the dark-haired one got up to press a cup of water to his lips.

"If you flail, I will beat you," the girl said. "And I will enjoy it."

"I believe you," he answered before drinking. He spluttered and coughed again as the girls giggled. "Thank you for the water," he managed. He then looked down at his thigh and saw the bandage. "Did you bind my wound?"

"Our mother did," said the blonde-haired girl.

"That lion had been skulking around and hunting our herds for a long time," added the other girl. "We have not been able to hunt it down. How did you find it and kill it?"

"It found me," Bellerophon answered.

The girls looked at each other and observed him closely.

"Why am I tied up?" he finally asked.

It was a different voice that answered him.

"Because you are unknown to us, and we do not trust easily."

At the entrance of the large, round house, a tall, beautiful woman stood looking at him. She was not, however, dressed in a peplos or flowing silks. She was armed for battle with a polished, scale armour shirt that reached down to her thighs, over an armoured skirt. Greaves protected her long shins, and matching arm guards covered her forearms. The metal was strange, and glinted in the firelight. A long sword jutted from her back over her right shoulder, and a helmet with double, red horsehair crests was tucked beneath her left arm. She wore no crown, but the way the other warriors stood behind her, protective and proud, and all of them armed, she was certainly their leader.

"Who are you and why are you here?" the mighty woman

asked as she stepped forward, the two young girls going to her side.

"I am Bellerophon, son of Glaucus, of Corinthos."

"You are a long way from home, Bellerophon of Corinthos," she said. She did not smile, but stared steadily at him. "Why are you in Phrygia?"

"I'm looking for someone," he said, finished with pretence.

"Who?"

"The Amazons."

The woman laughed, as did the others behind her, each one of them utterly confident, each carrying weapons that had seen war many times over. The leader looked back at him. "I think rather that the Amazons have found you."

"You are the Daughters of Ares?" Bellerophon asked, sitting up now as best he could.

She nodded, her eyes narrowed.

"Queen Otrera?"

"I am," she said plainly. "And these are my daughters, Hippolyta and Penthesilea. They have been tending you until the poison from the lion's claws was out of your system.

He looked at the young girls. "Thank you," he said, but they made no reply. "How long have I been here?"

"Three days," the queen said, as she came forward and sat upon a fur-covered log across from him, beside his weapons. "Check the food," she told her dark-haired daughter, Penthesilea. "So, Bellerophon of Corinthos, why do you seek me? Men rarely come to our home and if they do, they rarely leave."

"I've been sent to seek you out. All of you."

"For what purpose?" Otrera asked.

Bellerophon looked directly at her, meeting her blue-eyed gaze. "To kill you."

There was a momentary silence. It was uncomfortable, but then the Amazons all burst out laughing, all except the queen who held his gaze and spoke when the laughing had stopped.

"And who asked you to undertake this fool's errand?" she asked.

"King Iobates of Lykia."

They were all silent at that, and Queen Otrera's face hardened. There was no mercy in her eyes then as she stared at Bellerophon. "And why has the king sent a lone assassin?" she asked.

"Because your tribe constantly harasses Lykia, burning crops and taking livestock."

"That's a lie!" one of the warriors behind the queen said.

"Quiet, Cyme!" the queen commanded. "Of course it's a lie." She looked back at Bellerophon. "You do not strike me as stupid, like most men. What is the real reason Iobates has sent you?"

Bellerophon wanted to collapse in on himself, he was so tired of the world, but he found he could not do so before those proud warriors. He looked up at the queen. "Because he wants me dead."

Queen Otrera looked at Bellerophon with curiosity then and turned to Hippolyta. "Untie him and give him a bowl of stew."

"I have just told you I was here to kill you, and you want to untie me?" Bellerophon asked.

"You are my guest," she said plainly. Besides, I am not that easy to kill."

Bellerophon felt the bonds that had fastened him to the post slacken and he rubbed his wrists before accepting a wooden bowl filled with steaming stew.

"Come, sit around the fire with us," the queen said as the

others joined them. "Tell me how you came to be at King Iobates' court."

It was strange to be sitting around the fire with all of them in such a way, the people he had been sent to kill. He felt welcomed, despite his purpose, and felt comfortable telling them his story from his banishment from Corinthos, to the reasons that brought him there. When Bellerophon had finished, the dwelling was filled with warriors who had come in to listen, to see the guest-assassin in their midst.

"You tell an interesting tale, Bellerophon of Corinthos," Queen Otrera said.

"I am not offended if you do not believe me," he said. "I stopped caring long ago."

"I did not say that I don't believe you. It is no secret that I hate King Iobates. Neither is it a secret that his spiteful daughter, Stheneboea, is much like him. In truth, your story is much more believable than hers, from what you have told us. But though I hate Iobates, I have never ordered my warriors to raid his lands or harm his people, least of all..." She stopper herself. "But...I am also impressed by your victory over the Solymi."

"Impressed?" Bellerophon asked, confused. "I slew many men, and some women and children burned in the flames I set alight."

"They are animals, and have no honour," she said coldly.

Bellerophon shook his head. "I am no warrior, and I would not have willingly gone into battle to carry out such an act."

"Though you did for King Iobates!" she said.

"No!" Bellerophon insisted. "Not for him. I did it to prove

my innocence…because that is what the goddess, Athena, told me I should do."

Queen Otrera looked around the faces of her warriors and then back at Bellerophon. "The wise and warlike goddess speaks to you?"

Bellerophon did not answer, but stared into the flames.

Queen Otrera had met a few great men in her lifetime, and many more pitiful ones, but as she looked upon the Corinthian before her, she saw something different. He was a man without greed, though he was strong and capable of leading. He was also, strangely, a man who leaned toward kindness, but whose path led him to violence. He was being used by lesser men, and that upset her greatly.

"You say King Iobates has set you three tasks to prove your innocence?" she asked.

"Yes," Bellerophon answered. "Though slaying you is the second."

"I cannot allow you to harm my people, Bellerophon. You know this."

"Yes, Queen Otrera."

"Do you know what Iobates' third task is?" she asked.

"No. He waits to see if I return to tell me."

"Because he believes you will not return," she added.

"No doubt."

"He is correct," she said. "But, as the Gods demanded that you undertake this quest, you must be given a fair chance. We could kill you right now, if we wanted…drag you outside and cut you into myriad pieces."

"Yes, Queen Otrera. You could do that, I am aware, and I would fight as long as I could." Bellerophon felt saddened at this prospect, but not for the pitiful and painful end, but that he would not see Philonoe again. *I am sorry, Princess*, he thought. *I will not be leaving this place.*

"You will not fight all of us," the queen said. "You will fight one of us, and if you win, which you will not, you will carry back with you an olive bough of peace, in honour of Athena herself."

"I do not ask for fairness, Queen Otrera. That is something I am not accustomed to. I will fight as many as you send against me." He looked around the fire at the faces of the warriors, at those at the back of the room, and saw a strength and vitality in each of their eyes that he had rarely seen in any man's. They were all ready to fight and to die for each other at a moment's notice. *They truly are the Daughters of Warlike Ares,* he thought. *I don't think I could die at the hands of a greater enemy.*

The queen shook her head but stopped short of smiling at his courage, for in the shadows behind Bellerophon, there she spied the glimmer of Athena Parthenos with her spear and aegis. Were it not for all those around her, Otrera would have fallen to her knees and offered winged words to the goddess. As it were, however, there was only one thing she could offer.

"You will not fight all of us, Bellerophon of Corinthos, though you display great courage - or foolhardiness - in offering to do so. No." She stood and looked down at him and the warriors all around her. "Tomorrow, when the sun reaches its zenith, you shall fight me to the death."

"Mother, no!" Penthesilea burst out, but Queen Otrera put her hand up to stop her and the others' protests. "It is my command. Bellerophon has come a long way, and we must honour the Gods' will and our divine father's love of combat."

Bellerophon stood to face Queen Otrera, his leg burning as

he did so. "I thank you," he said, placing his hand on the gorgon upon his chest which resembled Athena's aegis.

"Rest now, for tomorrow, we fight...and you will die."

Bellerophon slept peacefully that night. There was a peace that came with certainty, and he embraced it, even though it pertained to his own death. When he awoke, it was to find both Penthesilea and Hippolyta sitting across the fire again, stirring porridge in a pot above the fire.

"Good morning," Hippolyta said when she saw his eyes open. "Did you sleep well?"

"Yes," Bellerophon answered.

"Why are you speaking to him?" Penthesilea demanded of her sister. "He is going to try and kill our mother and queen!"

Bellerophon found it strange that he was more trusted in the Amazon camp than he had ever been anywhere else. He had fully admitted to coming to kill them all - or rather, being sent to - and yet the queen's very own daughters were alone with him, sent to tend to him. He smiled sadly at them.

"Have no fear. I know that your mother is a great warrior and that I will not last long against her. I am grateful to you all for your kindness. Truly."

"You're a strange man, Corinthian," Penthesilea said, picking up her own dagger and sharpening it.

"Pay her no mind," Hippolyta added, smiling. "Our mother asked us to feed you so that you are strong for the coming fight." She then ladled some of the porridge into a wooden bowl and handed it to him, along with a cup of water. "Eat and drink."

As Bellerophon ate, Penthesilea observed him closely. "Is it true that you defeated all of the Solymi?"

Bellerophon shook his head. "Only some of them. Their warriors, and their chief, Solimos."

"Hmph!" Penthesilea scoffed brushing a dark strand of hair away from her eyes. "They do not have warriors. But I have heard that Solimos was a giant."

Bellerophon smiled at that. "No. Not a giant. But a bear of a man."

"How did you fight him? How did you win?" Penthesilea asked.

"Stop it sister!" Hippolyta said.

"What?"

"You are trying to divine his strategy so that you can tell our mother. It is dishonourable," Hippolyta chided.

"You are too soft," her sister bit back. But she did turn to Bellerophon and smiled. "I should have liked to see that battle."

He did not respond, but finished eating and drinking. When he was done, he stood and stretched.

"Are you ready?" Hippolyta asked.

"Yes, though I do need to relieve myself," he said shyly.

"Over there, behind that curtain," Penthesilea said. "There is a pot. We will wait outside while you do whatever men do." With that, the two girls turned and went out of the roundhouse.

When he was finished, Bellerophon looked around the vast, round structure and wondered that he had been given this all to himself. It was not a prison, but rather a gathering place. The walls were hung with weapons which had been taken in battle, and they glinted dully in the firelight.

He looked for his things and found them piled behind the post to which he had been tied the day before. He was going to pick them up, but he decided against it. *What's the point?* he thought. *I only need my weapons. Philonoe, I would have liked to see you again,* he thought as he pulled the double-headed axe from beneath the rim of his breastplate, kissed it gently, and then tucked it back again.

Bellerophon placed his crested helmet on his head, and then strapped on his sword and dagger. He then bent to pick up his great shield, and slung the quiver of throwing spears over his shoulder.

It had been peaceful in the roundhouse, homely even, but he did not know what to expect when he went outside. He stopped just shy of the threshold and closed his eyes.

"Goddess Athena...I honour you now, as I always have. I do not know what fate awaits me out there, but please, if it is my time to die, stand by me so that I do not do so alone. And protect Philonoe, whatever should happen."

He then opened his eyes and stepped outside, only to be blinded by the brilliant sunlight.

Immediately, a deep, steady drumming began and when Bellerophon was able to open his eyes properly and adjust to the light, he was shocked by the sight before him.

The Amazon settlement was enormous, made up of a great gathering of roundhouses of similar size for every warrior. This was no tribe, but rather a nation. Beneath the enormous blue expanse of the Phrygian sky, the settlement stretched away to white cliffs that fell like a steady waterfall, the waters there glistening in the sunlight where their warriors bathed.

Red banners - the colour of Ares - snapped in the wind from the rooftops of every dwelling, and beneath them, upon poles, were the grisly trophies of defeated enemies slain by the individual warriors.

However, the size of the settlement was not what was most surprising, but rather it was the long avenue down which he was urged to walk, for it was lined with every warrior of the Amazon nation under Queen Otrera.

Each warrior was tall, muscled and proud, and many were more beautiful than any woman Bellerophon had seen in either Corinthos or Tiryns. He did not make the mistake of thinking he was in a paradise, however, for in each of their eyes there was a slight amount of hatred. He had come to kill them, and they all knew it.

Every Amazon was armed and armoured, and they lived that way always. There was not a peplos in sight. Some sat atop champing horses, while others stood variously dressed in leather jerkins, scale armour, or gleaming bronze breastplates. Many had bows, and all had spears, and swords or daggers. Every warrior was individual and terrifying.

Bellerophon, his armour glinting in the bright sun, followed Penthesilea and Hippolyta down the avenue as the drums beat steadily. Eventually, they arrived at a sort of arena which was a large circle of packed earth. They led him onto the arena floor to where Queen Otrera stood, calm as could be. The drumming stopped.

The queen was dressed in her scale armour and armoured skirt, but she wore no sandals or boots. In her left hand she held a long, thick spear with a long leaf-shaped blade, and in her right hand she carried a half-moon shield with a horse upon it. Her long sword jut up from behind her shoulders. Her double-crested helmet rose high above and gave her the look of a goddess of battle which indeed she was, for along her arms were the criss cross patterns of scars from many battles. She was her father's daughter, and to Bellerophon's surprise, the God of War appeared at her shoulder.

Ares stared down at the Corinthian who was Athena's favourite, and smirked, his dark visage a terror to behold.

For a moment, Bellerophon felt that fear might overtake him, but then a cool breeze arrived at his shoulder and he felt Athena's presence rally his courage.

Queen Otrera's eyes widened and she inclined her head.

All around the arena too, the Amazons made signs of obeisance and good omen having glimpsed, ever-so-briefly, the two gods standing beside the champions.

"Die well, Corinthian," Penthesilea said before she and Hippolyta left to join Otrera's wary commanders Mytilene, Cyme, Pitane, and Priene.

A moment later, the Gods disappeared, and Bellerophon faced Queen Otrera alone in the middle of the arena.

"Are you rested and able to fight?" the queen asked. Her voice was harder then, but not devoid of concern for her guest.

Bellerophon bowed his head, his blue crest fluttering in the wind. "I am. Thank you. You have treated me…well… I thank you, Queen Otrera."

She smiled sadly, but her grip on the long spear at her side was easy and strong. "What weapons do you choose?"

"Only what I have." He spread his arms wide to show his sword and dagger, and the throwing spears.

"Those will encumber you," she said, nodding at the quiver hanging from his shoulder.

"It is how I am accustomed to fighting," he said.

"I want you to know that when you die, your remains will be given every honour so that you can make your way through the Underworld without issue."

The words chilled Bellerophon, and he knew then that it was time. He inclined his head.

Then, the commander, Mytilene, stepped to their sides. She carried a long staff, thick enough to crack a man's skull in two, and wore a crimson cloak which covered thick, bull's hide armour. "Are you ready?"

The queen held Bellerophon's eyes and nodded slowly in answer.

"Yes," Bellerophon said.

Commander Mytilene put the staff out between them and held it there for a few heartbeats before shouting, "Begin!"

More quickly than Bellerophon could possibly have imagined, the queen's long, greaved leg struck out and kicked him full force in the chest, sending him several feet backwards where he landed in the dirt.

Suddenly, an explosion of sound reverberated all about the arena as the Amazons roared for their queen and called for her to kill Bellerophon.

Bellerophon heard the rushing footfalls of his opponent and quickly rolled away to gain his feet, just as the queen's spear plunged into the earth where he had fallen. His shield swept to the left and right, up and down to meet the darting spear shaft which the queen so expertly thrust at him without mercy.

"I see the fear in your eyes," she said. "Like all men, you're filled with doubt!"

Then, with a sudden, great cry, Otrera leapt into the air to come down on Bellerophon.

He spun to her shield arm side and hit her in the back as she landed, sending her rolling several feet away, until she landed on her feet.

Bellerophon drew his throwing spears one after another, sending them at the queen as she rushed him for another attack. She darted and dodged with unnatural speed, but a couple of the spears clipped her arm and thigh before she was able to hurl her long spear which ripped through the now-empty quiver and pinned Bellerophon to the ground.

He panicked and flailed where he landed, trying to free himself, but she was on top of him, trying to retrieve her spear which he grabbed and would not let go.

She kicked down in great sweeping arcs, catching him in the shoulder and the side of the head, but he would not relinquish the weapon.

Bellerophon kicked up hard, bracing himself against the planted spear shaft and took the queen on the jaw, sending her helmet into the dirt with a thud as she stumbled. He stood as quickly as he could and ripped through the leather of the quiver to free himself, drawing his sword and taking up his shield again from where it had fallen. He turned back and sliced at the spear shaft, cutting it in half and making the weapon less effective.

The Amazons, including Penthesilea and Hippolyta, cried out for the queen to finish him and as the queen crouched, like a lioness ready to pounce, her long hair fell in dishevelled strands over her shoulders. Her blue eyes sought an opening, and blood dripped from her mouth.

Bellerophon saw the horse upon her shield, the blade weaving as if to strike at any moment, and he crouched too, to meet the attack.

But she was too fast.

Queen Otrera darted left then right and left again before feinting with her long blade and sweeping her half-moon shield across his face to knock the helmet from his head.

Sweat poured down from Bellerophon's brow, and he squinted as he watched her. He breathed heavily, but she seemed only to have gotten started.

It was then that Otrera unleashed a furious attack upon him

with sword and shield, attacking and deflecting his own desperate counter-attacks with her arm guards, greaves and shield. He began to feel desperation then, but not for the fight. Rather he wanted an end to it all. A great weariness came over him, even as he penetrated her defences and cut her again and again.

Then, he felt his legs swept from under him as Otrera dropped beneath her shield, spun her leg, and sent him to the earth. She leapt on top of him, but Bellerophon's legs caught her and sent her over his head. He scrambled, ripping his dagger free and leapt on top of her.

The dagger's tip touched the queen's scale armour but her arms caught his with all of her strength and held them fast as Bellerophon stared down at her wild-eyed.

"Why won't you kill me?" he screamed at her, even as he pressed the blade down. "KILL ME!" he cried.

Then a glint of gold caught the queen's eye where it hung beneath his chin. With renewed strength, she pushed him off.

Bellerophon's body rose up into the air and crashed down again.

Queen Otrera swept the dagger away and straddled him, pounding her fists into this face.

He stopped fighting, and in his eyes, mingled with the sweat and blood upon his face, Queen Otrera saw that there were tears.

But he wept not for fear, but for a weariness greater than anything else. A weariness of life.

"Kill him, my queen!" Commander Pitane yelled, and more of the Amazons took up the cry.

Bellerophon's eyes sought hers and a calm came over him. "Please...kill me," he sputtered from his bleeding mouth.

She hit him again, and again in the side of the head, but he was unresponsive to the pain she inflicted.

Suddenly, Bellerophon's head struck Otrera in the face and she fell sideways. He was on her then, his blade to her throat. "I don't want to kill you!" he cried, his blood, sweat and tears dripping onto her chest.

"You must!" she replied.

He shook his head, and threw his dagger away.

Confused cries went around the arena, and angry shouts of disappointment, but Bellerophon ignored them, even as the Amazons closed in around him.

He spat blood, and bent over to extend his hand to Queen Otrera, pulling her to her feet. He then turned, breathing heavily, to address the crowd. "Your queen has beaten me!" he said. "If she will not kill me, one of you must!" He turned back to Otrera and put his fists up to continue the fight.

The queen squared off, and when he swung, she dodged it and brought her elbow to his face.

Bellerophon fell hard and felt the queen poised above him, her hands on his throat.

But she did not squeeze. Instead, she ripped the golden battle-axe from his neck and held it in his face. "Where did you get this?" she demanded.

"Philonoe…" he said before he fell into darkness.

It was night out, for behind the ringing in Bellerophon's ears, he could hear the faint sound of crickets, the screech of an owl, and the howl of the wind.

Am I upon the plains of the Underworld? he wondered, for he could see the obscure glow of fire around him. "I am in Hades' realm," he said through his swollen mouth.

"No. You are not," said another voice from nearby.

Bellerophon's eyes flickered open and peered beyond the flames in the direction of the voice. "Goddess…Athena?" he asked.

"No," Queen Otrera responded.

Bellerophon opened his eyes wider as they adjusted to the light and saw that he was back in the roundhouse, laying before the fire, bandages upon his arms and legs, and a resin upon his battered face.

The queen lay opposite him, likewise bruised and bandaged. She sat up and moved closer to him, grunting as she did so.

He moved to sit up but she laid her hand upon his shoulder.

"Sit still for now," Otrera said. "I would speak with you, Bellerophon of Corinthos."

He shook his head and sat up anyway. The pain was great as he did so, but like the rest of his life, he bore it. She handed him a cup of water, and he drank slowly, feeling the blood wash around in his mouth.

"Why are you so keen to die?" she asked.

Bellerophon settled and stared into the fire. He shrugged his shoulders. "What is there to live for?" he said. "More betrayal and distrust?" He sighed. "I am so very tired…"

"And you fought like no other man I have ever seen," she answered. "You fought like you wanted to live. Tell me for what? There must be something…"

He shook his head and looked at the dirt floor. A glint of reflected light caught his eye and he looked up to see the queen holding up the golden battle-axe charm that had been around his neck.

"And this?" she asked. "Is this worth living for?"

He put out his hand and Otrera gently placed it in his palm.

He could see the glint of tears in her eyes, though she allowed none to fall.

"Where did you get it?" she asked.

"Philonoe...the daughter of King-"

"Iobates and Queen Pasandra..." Otrera finished. There was tenderness in her voice, regret and resentment.

Bellerophon looked up at her. "Yes. Philonoe is the only person to have ever believed me or been truly kind to me."

"She gets that kindness from her mother," Queen Otrera said, straightening up and staring into the fire as she sipped from her cup.

It was then that Bellerophon noticed the shadowed faces of the silent Amazons sitting around the wall of the roundhouse, including Hippolyta, Penthesilea, and the generals. They listened and watched as their queen turned to face Bellerophon, to reach out and hang the double-headed axe about his neck for him.

"You knew Queen Pasandra?" he asked.

Otera nodded. "I knew her well. We all did, apart from my daughters. She was once one of us."

The sound of the flickering flames was loud then as Bellerophon thought of Philonoe's beautiful, freckled face and fiery hair, similar to so many around him in that moment. Philonoe looked nothing like her father or older sister. In fact, she seemed a world apart from anyone in Lykia. "I don't understand," he said, looking the queen in the eyes.

"Pasandra was once my greatest general. She taught all of them..." Queen Otrera motioned to her generals seated not far off and they all nodded in agreement. "She was also my dearest friend. We grew up together and fought many battles side by side. Then, one day, we fought a new foe - the son of the dying queen of Lykia."

"Iobates," Bellerophon said.

"Yes," Otrera answered, her voice tinged with anger now. "It was a bloody battle. We slaughtered most of their forces, and were about to finish off Iobates. But then, from out of the fire and smoke, the Lykian queen appeared. She was regal and commanded respect. She had never bothered us until then, when she was so old that Death already had his hands about her throat. She asked us for a truce…and an alliance, even as her handsome son stood beside her, bloody from battle."

"Why did you not kill them?" Bellerophon asked.

"I wanted to, but Pasandra urged me to hear them out."

"She did?"

"Yes. But she had already locked eyes with Iobates. Aphrodite and Eros had already begun to toy with them."

"What happened?"

"The Lykian queen said that she wished for one of us to rule in her stead after she died, alongside her son, Iobates. She said that she respected us and our ways, our strength, and knew that Lykia would be safer in the hands of an Amazon queen."

"I don't understand," Bellerophon said. "Why would she offer such a thing when Iobates was set to inherit the throne."

"Because Lykia had always been ruled by a queen. Ascendency had always been matrilineal as far back as anyone can remember."

"And Pasandra stepped forward?" Bellerophon looked at Otrera.

She nodded sadly. "We argued about it. I did not want her to go, and I did not want her to be the queen of Iobates. I could see he was not honest, that he had not fought with honour on the field that day." She shook her head. "But Pasandra was adamant. She insisted that if she became queen of Lykia, it would secure our southern border and allow us to focus on fighting the Hittites to the East, and the Trojans to the North."

"What happened?"

Otrera pursed her lips. "The Lykian queen died six months later, and Pasandra rode to Xanthos to become queen." Otrera pointed at the golden battle-axe around Bellerophon's neck. "I gave her that before she left, to remind her of where she came from."

"And she gave it to Philonoe." Bellerophon began to understand, and his suspicions of Iobates were confirmed.

"Pasandra's daughter is an Amazon. She is one of us, but instead of learning our ways, instead of ruling as queen of Lykia, as is her right, she is locked away in a gilded cage within the palace."

"She is locked away, true," Bellerophon said. "But she is not weak. She is one of the strongest, most honest and true women I have ever met."

"Like her mother used to be..." It was then that Queen Otrera did wipe a single tear from her cheek.

"What happened to Queen Pasandra?"

Her jaw tightened. "Iobates decided that he would use her warlike skills to eliminate his enemies and secure his position. Pasandra did as he asked, I suppose because she loved him, and because she loved to do battle. One by one, she conquered Lykia's enemies, big and small. And then, one day, she moved against the Solymi in Pisidia." Otrera took another drink of water before continuing. "The Solymi had remained quiet until then, sending herds of livestock as tribute to Xanthos. But they had a new leader then - Solimos." She looked at Bellerophon. "The man you slew."

Bellerophon nodded remembering the chieftain draped in bear furs and stinking like an animal.

"The Solymi ambushed Pasandra's small army in their mountains - I suppose Iobates told her that she didn't need a large force for that mission - and they picked off her men, one by one. Pasandra never made it home."

"And Philonoe grew up without her mother," Bellerophon added, "never knowing who she was or where she came from?"

"Philonoe was very young, and she had no idea what the charm she inherited from her mother symbolized," Otrera said. "And Iobates? He never spoke of Pasandra to his daughter. He used Pasandra's death as an opportunity to take the Lykian throne for himself, and the kingdom was no longer ruled by a queen as it always had been."

Everyone in the roundhouse was silent, but for Hippolyta who went to her mother's side.

"Mother... Was it then that the beast arrived?"

"Yes, my heart," Otrera said, kissing her daughter's blonde head.

"What beast?" Bellerophon asked.

"We call it 'Iobates' Bane'," Otrera answered, and it was then, for the first time, that Bellerophon could see fear in all of the Amazon eyes looking at him. "When Iobates broke the sacred laws of Lykia's lands, the Gods grew angry and sent a beast to terrorize him and his people-"

"The Lykians did not stand up for their queen!" the general, Priene, burst out, her voice angry.

"No, they did not," Otrera agreed. "And they have been punished for it."

"Have you seen this beast?" Bellerophon asked.

She shook her head. "No. But I have seen the fires rising into the sky. All who see it do not live to tell of it. It is a beast of the Gods' making…and a fitting punishment for such as Iobates."

"And what of Philonoe?" Bellerophon said. "She too is in danger from this beast!"

"It is no longer our concern," Otrera said. "I would give succour to my friend's daughter, but Philonoe is now a creature of Iobates' making, the same as his bane."

Bellerophon shook his head. "You're wrong!" he yelled, so loudly that the generals drew their blades.

Queen Otrera put up her hand to stay her warriors, and then smiled at Bellerophon. "Something worth living and fighting for then?"

Bellerophon was quiet again, shaking his head. "When I go back to him without having slain you, I will be executed. But I can't leave Philonoe alone in that place."

"Then you must take back something more valuable than our deaths," Otrera said, leaning toward him.

"And what is that?"

"An alliance between the Amazon nation and Lykia,"

There were gasps around the large room, but none spoke against the queen's words.

"An alliance?" Bellerophon thought about it, but he doubted whether Iobates would agree. "I think he would rather see you dead."

"Perhaps," Otrera agreed. "But the Trojans and Hittites are growing in strength again, and Lykia's army is weakened. With the promise of an alliance with us, he has a chance to preserve his kingdom."

"Why would you do that for Iobates? He doesn't deserve it."

"Not for Iobates," Otrera insisted. "But for my friend's daughter… For Philonoe."

. . .

The sun and moon rose and set for another fourteen days before Bellerophon was well enough to travel back to Lykia, and during that time, he had mulled over all that he had learned about the death of Queen Pasandra, and how it seemed that Iobates had used her, perhaps even planned her death.

And it made him angry. He was especially enraged at the betrayal that Iobates perpetrated upon his daughter, Philonoe. She was a descendant of the Daughters of Ares, and yet she was kept in ignorance for the greed and vanity of yet another self-serving king.

As the sun rose on his last morning in the Amazon capital, Queen Otrera, her daughters, and her generals accompanied Bellerophon south to the edge of the border, they on horseback and he on foot, leading a pack mule they had gifted him.

Otrera dismounted and stepped forward to bid farewell to Bellerophon. She took him by the shoulders and kissed him on both cheeks as she might a younger brother.

"It has been an honour to fight you and to get to know you, Bellerophon of Corinthos," she said. "Go with our good will and offer of alliance back to Iobates."

"I will," he said, "and I will make him listen."

A tenderness came into her eyes then. "Be careful of Iobates. He is not an honest man, and he loathes those who are braver than he."

"I will."

"And…" She turned to remove a long bundle of linen that was tucked beside her horse's saddle. "When you see her… when you see Philonoe… Give this to her." She handed the bundle to Bellerophon.

"What is it?" he asked as he accepted the bundle and drew back one end of the linen. There he spied the leather handle and bronze hilt of a sword, decorated with charging horses and Amazon warriors in battle. He looked up at Otrera.

"It was one of Pasandra's favourite weapons. She slew many enemies with it and wielded it with honour. She gave it to me when she left here. Now, I would be grateful if you gave it to her daughter."

Bellerophon covered the hilt again and bowed his head. "I will. And I will tell her the truth when I am able."

"I believe you," Otrera said, placing her palm flat upon the golden battle-axe around his neck. "May Athena guide and protect you in the time to come."

"I thank you," Bellerophon said, looking at the queen, her daughters, and the faces of her generals, "for everything."

With that, Bellerophon tucked the sword into the saddle-bags on the mule, and set off down the dusty road out of Phrygia toward Lykia once more.

"Will we see him again, Mother?" Penthesilea asked, her voice saddened to see such a warrior go.

"I do not think so," Otrera said, smiling sadly. "But I don't think we've heard the last of Bellerophon.

HYMN III

THE JAWS OF FEAR

CHAPTER 9

THE THIRD TASK

The sun was only just beginning to rise when Bellerophon finally caught sight of the river that led away toward Xanthos and the distant sea. Green swathes of olive, orange and fig filled his eyes, but there was something more. There was fire.

Great pillars of smoke rose up from crops that had burned in the night and previous days, as if Lykia had been under attack. Yet there were no armies, no troops. At the farms and hovels Bellerophon passed as he went, he saw terror-stricken eyes peering out at him from the darkness within. When he tried to approach the people to ask them what had happened, they were incapable of speech. Doors and shutters were slammed in his face and he was left to pull his mule down the road toward the capital which rose up from the smoke like an island in a misty sea.

Philonoe.

Bellerophon was suddenly very worried. She had been on his mind constantly since leaving the Amazons, the words of

Queen Otrera foremost, that Philonoe was a descendant of the Daughters of Ares, and she did not even know it.

He also remembered that Otrera had told him not to trust Iobates at all, and so Bellerophon decided to go forward into Xanthos with greater caution than he might have done.

Goddess Athena…guide me…

The city was quiet, and the streets were empty. Even in the agora, the merchants had dispersed and trade had ground to a halt. Broken and charred market stalls lay everywhere, and pieces of amphora once filled with wine and oil lay scattered like leaves on a forest floor in autumn.

Bellerophon paused to look around as he approached the main gate of the palace, and there he saw the helmeted heads of the guards looking down at him.

"Open the gates!" he called up, his voice echoing off of the empty streets and outer walls of the palace.

"Who goes there?" one of the guards yelled back.

"It is Bellerophon, son of Glaucus!" he called up.

"Open the gates!" Captain Milyas' voice ordered from somewhere at the top, and slowly the double doors creaked open.

Bellerophon walked forward with the pack mule and stepped into the courtyard where he saw men of the palace guard being tended to by servants. Many were wounded, and a few others lay still beneath sooty sheets, their chests no longer rising and falling with breath.

"Bellerophon!" Milyas said, coming down from the battlements to see him. "You live?"

Bellerophon turned to the captain and clasped his arm. "Yes. What happened here?"

Milyas removed his helmet and tucked it beneath his arm before leading him a few steps away to talk quietly, away from the wounded. "The beast... It attacked three times while you were gone. The last time was during the night, last night. It's never attacked the capital before..." his voice faded out as if he could not comprehend the terror even he felt. "We could do nothing."

"Philonoe...is she-"

"She's safe. The king ordered her to remain in the palace vaults during the attack. She is now in her rooms." Milyas looked Bellerophon over, as if seeing him for the first time. "You survived, but barely it seems."

"Barely, yes. But I did survive," Bellerophon answered.

"And the Amazons? Are they...are they all dead?" Milyas had a strange look in his eyes, as if he did not really want to know, as if he had not expected Bellerophon to ever be standing there. Truthfully, no one had expected that.

Yet there he was, battered and scarred, but alive.

"Take me to the king," Bellerophon said, taking the olive bough from Queen Otrera from off the mule's back.

Milyas looked strangely at the branch and nodded. "He is in the megaron with his advisors." He turned to one of his men. "Inform King Iobates that Bellerophon of Corinthos has returned!"

"Yes, Captain!" the man said before rushing off.

Milyas led Bellerophon quickly through the palace to the court before the great hall, and just as they were about to enter the propylon before the megaron, rapid foot falls approached from the side, and he turned to see Philonoe, as brilliant as a single light in that dark and oppressive place.

She made to throw her arms about him, but stopped short when she saw Milyas there too. "Thank Athena you're safe!" she said, her eyes glossy as she gripped his arm tightly. "I prayed everyday for your safe return." She reached up to touch the bruising on his face, took in the cuts upon his arms. "What has happened to you?"

"Much," Bellerophon answered. "But it does me good to see you safe, lady."

"What happened?" Philonoe asked.

"Princess," Milyas said, "we are just about to go in to see the king. He is waiting."

"I will go with you," Philonoe said, her voice strong, not to be deterred. She placed her hand upon Bellerophon's armoured chest, and then turned to lead the way into the megaron.

The guards standing there bowed to her and opened the great doors of the propylon, and the three of them passed through.

King Iobates was standing before the hearth fire surrounded by several courtiers and advisors, each of them pleading with him for a decision or some aid for a particularly hard-hit part of the city or kingdom.

Polyidus stood beside the king, silent, listening to all that the men of the court demanded of their king. He felt the king growing angrier and angrier with every demand made of him. Since Bellerophon had been sent on his second task, the seer had felt a lightness in the king's countenance, but then the beast had attacked, and his lord's anger, his desperation, had known no limits.

"Father!" Philonoe said aloud, her voice clear above the buzz of the courtiers. "Father, Bellerophon has returned!" she called out.

"Silence!" King Iobates shouted at those near him, and the

circle around him fell away as they all made room and turned to see the son of Glaucus led before the king by the princess and captain of the palace guard.

Without saying anything, King Iobates mounted his throne and turned to look down at Bellerophon. He glanced at his daughter sternly and looked to the seat on his left.

Philonoe, however, did not move from Bellerophon's side. "He brings news of the Amazons!" she said aloud, and turned to let Bellerophon speak.

Bellerophon looked at the expectant faces about him, and finally rested his gaze on the king.

Iobates' face was dark, a little excited even, for he had been waiting for news either of Bellerophon's death, or of the removal of the Amazon spear between his shoulder blades.

"By the look of you, Bellerophon," the king began, "you have been in a great battle. Tell me, are the Amazons of Phrygia no more? Did you defeat them?"

The megaron was silent as all waited to hear what the returning Corinthian had to say.

Bellerophon searched for the appropriate words, as well as for the ability to keep his anger at bay. Standing before Iobates, he realized how much he disliked the king, how all that Queen Otrera had said made perfect sense.

"King Iobates," he began, "I have travelled far at your bidding in order to prove my innocence and the falsity of the accusations levelled against me. I went into the heart of Phrygia, and I did indeed confront the Amazon queen, Otrera, and her people."

King Iobates leaned forward at this, excited at the prospect of what he might hear, biting his lip in anticipation. "Tell me, son of Glaucus… Are they all dead? Did you slay them?"

Bellerophon held his head up high. *I will not be cowed by*

this man. "I fought Queen Otrera, the daughter of Ares, in single combat-"

"Is she dead, or not?" Iobates yelled.

Philonoe looked at her father, shocked and wary of his reaction, for she had never seen him that way before.

Bellerophon shook his head. "She is a mighty warrior, King Iobates, and an honourable opponent."

"So you bring back nothing but your own cuts and bruises?" Iobates was on his feet then, his finger pointed directly at Bellerophon.

"I bring back something better than death, King Iobates," Bellerophon said calmly, but loudly enough for all to hear. "I bring back the word of the Amazons that they will agree to a truce with Lykia and King Iobates. They have agreed to be Lykia's allies from now on. You need no longer worry about your northern border, King Iobates. It is safe and secure, and guarded by powerful allies." He paused to let the news register with everyone there. "Queen Otrera sends this olive bough as a symbol of her word and the alliance." Bellerophon stepped forward and handed the branch to the king.

Iobates' hands shook, and he seethed where he stood, even though his courtiers began to smile and sigh with relief at the much-needed good news. The king sat down upon his throne again and threw the olive branch into the hearth fire. "I sent you to kill Otrera and her people! You," he pointed, again, "were not to be an ambassador, but an assassin!" he shouted and his voice reverberated about the walls. "You have failed!" he turned to Milyas. "Captain!"

"Yes, my king?" Milyas responded.

"This man is to be kept under guard until his appointed execution day."

There were stunned gasps about the megaron.

"Father, no!" Philonoe said, stepping forward. "For shame! Bellerophon has proved most honourable in this and secured an alliance with a powerful force. Surely, it is better to have obtained new allies rather than eliminate a foe and allow the Hittites to sweep through to replace them?"

"You know nothing, Daughter. You are a child and I command you to refrain from speaking any more, lest you wish to be locked in the dungeons yourself!"

Philonoe stared back at her father with fire in her eyes, and Bellerophon could see the truth of what Otrera had said. She was her mother's daughter. Beneath the peplos and perfume, beneath the beautiful, gilded exterior, Philonoe was indeed a descendant of the Daughters of Ares.

"There is more," Bellerophon suddenly said. "Queen Otrera declares that she will abide by the truce, and be a strong ally of Lykia…in honour of the memory of her dearest friend, Queen Pasandra, and of the late queen's daughter, Philonoe…" He turned to face Philonoe who looked at him, speechless.

The princess then looked to her father, and saw the changed look in his eyes. It was not a look of pain or nostalgia, however, but a look of guilt. She could see her father look with true hate upon Bellerophon, and that scared her.

"King Iobates," Bellerophon said, stepping closer. "By Zeus Xenios, I believe I have better than achieved the task you set me, and brought you a greater outcome. I have kept my end of the bargain."

"You think so, do you?" the king growled. He was about to say more when Polyidus leaned in to whisper to him. It took several moments for the seer to relay all that he wanted to say, to urge his advice upon Iobates, but in the end, the king seemed to grow calm again, despite the dark look in his eyes.

"My seer has given me sage counsel once more."

Those in the megaron looked to the blind man beside the king.

"Bellerophon, son of Glaucus of Corinthos…" the king began. "Though you did not achieve the exact task I set for you, I can see the benefit of what you have done, and though I do not trust the Amazons, I do believe they mean to honour the memory of our late queen. The laws of Xenia will be honoured!" he declared. "Tomorrow night, we will feast in your honour, and at that time, I will declare the nature of the third and final task which will prove or disprove your innocence in the matter of my eldest daughter." The king stood then, and looked down at Bellerophon, being sure to avoid his daughter's shocked gaze. "Go now, and heal yourself of your wounds. Captain?"

"Yes, my lord?" Milyas said, stepping forward.

"Bellerophon is free to roam the palace."

"Yes, my king!" Milyas said.

"My daughter, however, is to be confined to her rooms."

Philonoe looked up at her father but before she could say anything, the king had turned and swept out of the megaron, followed by the majority of the courtiers there.

"How could he?" Philonoe whispered to Bellerophon.

He turned to her quickly before Milyas' reluctant guards arrived to take her away. "Go with them, Philonoe. I will find my way to you, for there is more I need to tell you."

She wanted to ask why, but she felt the guards close in around her.

"I'm sorry, Princess," Milyas said. "Your father's orders…"

She pulled her arm away when one of the guards touched

her arm. "I'm coming!" she said, and looked one last time at Bellerophon before walking out of the megaron with her head high.

When she was gone, Bellerophon turned to the seer, Polyidus, who still stood there beside the empty throne. "What did you tell the king, seer?"

Polyidus smiled. "I told him that you had done him a great service, and that now was not the time to anger the Gods."

"And can you tell me what this third task will be?" Bellerophon asked.

Polyidus shook his head slowly. "No. I cannot. But you should go. Rest and prepare yourself for the trial to come, for the Amazons were nothing compared to what is next." He hung his head. "I'm sorry, Bellerophon, but that is all that I can say, on my life, and the princess'."

"Then you had best say nothing."

Polyidus was about to leave, but he turned once more in the direction of Bellerophon's voice. "What more did Queen Otrera tell you?"

"She told me a story as our wounds were mended."

"And what was this story?" Polyidus asked.

Bellerophon looked at those milky eyes, and there he did not see any hatred or cunning. He knew Polyidus admired the princess. "That is not for me to tell you."

Polyidus nodded. "As it should be," he said. "But I suspect, it is for someone else to hear."

With that, the seer disappeared out the back of the megaron, his staff clicking on the paving stones as he went.

.   .   .

It was strange to be back in the palace again after the long, dusty road, and the warm hospitality of the Amazon camp. The palace was quiet, and somewhat lifeless in comparison.

When Bellerophon returned to his chambers to wash, and gave his armour into the care of the servant, Phoebos, for cleaning, he did not go out into the palace as Iobates had said he could. Once he was clean, he sat upon the terrace to eat heartily of the food that had been brought to him, and to stare at the bundle which Queen Otrera had given him. He needed to get it to Philonoe, for it was hers by right, as was the information he had also brought back.

Such betrayal... he thought, shaking his head and realizing that he and Philonoe had been treated, in some ways, the same by their respective surviving parents. *How will she take this news of her father and mother?* he wondered, but he knew he could not keep it to himself any longer, for he might not live long enough to tell her otherwise.

Once darkness fell over Xanthos, and the night air began to fill with the scent of jasmine, Bellerophon made offerings to Athena upon the altar overlooking the river, and the smoke from those offerings wove about him, thick and fragrant, rising up like a mist to cover the terrace walls.

"Thank you, Goddess," he said softly when he realized that Athena was aiding him. And so, as his offerings burned in the darkness of that star-pocked night, Bellerophon slung the bundle over his shoulders and began to climb.

The stonework was thick, and smooth in places, but not so perfect that he could not find handholds, and not so high that he would fall to his death should he slip. The terraces of the upper palace were close, like the soft levels of a mountainside olive grove. He knew the king's apartments were at the top, and that the princess' were one below that, but there was another between hers and the one Bellerophon inhabited.

He reached the second terrace and stopped when he saw the form of a man standing there in the darkness, waiting.

"Promise me you will be honourable with her," the man said.

Bellerophon stepped closer, his heart beating, but then he saw who was waiting for him. It was Polyidus.

"I do not bring her harm or pain, seer," Bellerophon said. "Only the truth she has a right to know."

Polyidus turned his head to Bellerophon in the darkness and nodded. "Truth often is pain… But this is a truth she must learn. I have kept this secret for far too long."

"Surely others know?"

The seer shook his head. "Have you noticed how young the guards are? Even the courtiers? Few, if any, were old enough to know what had happened to the queen, let alone the Lykian traditions which my king did away with."

"Then how do you know?" Bellerophon asked.

"The king's guilt was overwhelming when his bane arrived and began to ravage the land. He confided in me and asked me to consult the Gods."

"And what did the Gods tell you?"

"They said that after years of suffering, a hero would come from across the sea to help us."

"I am no hero, Polyidus," Bellerophon stated as he went to the wall to continue his climb. "I am an outcast. You should consult the Gods again."

He then disappeared into the rising smoke from below and continued to climb.

"I have," Polyidus whispered as he heard Bellerophon reach the terrace of the princess' apartments.

. . .

When Bellerophon reached the next terrace above, he peered over the short retaining wall to see open doors covered with flowing silk curtains that rustled gently in the nighttime breeze. Beyond them, Philonoe paced back and forth in the lamplight of her rooms.

He swung over the edge and stood to look up at the king's level above. No one was there. He then moved quietly to the curtains. Philonoe was in distress, it seemed, but she appeared strong and determined as she paced, her head held high, her fists opening and closing. Knowing what he knew about her, Bellerophon now saw her in a much different light, an even stronger, more brilliant light than before. He only hoped that she would not hate him for the news he brought to her.

He spotted two female servants waiting upon her and knew he could not risk being seen there. So, when they were turned, their attention taken up with their tasks, he stuck his hand beyond the veil of the curtains and waved to Philonoe.

The princess stopped dead, but did not speak or squeal in surprise. She knew, and turned to her servants. "I will prepare myself and retire now. You may go."

"Are you certain, my lady?" one of them said.

"Quite. I wish to be alone."

The servants bowed, went to the chamber doors to knock so that the guards opened, and then went out, the doors locked again behind them.

"The princess is retiring for the night. She is not to be disturbed," their faint voices said on the other side of the doors.

When Philonoe was certain they were gone, she rushed to the terrace doors and threw the curtains aside.

Bellerophon stood there in his simple, red tunic, the golden battle-axe she had given him hanging about his neck.

Philonoe reached out and placed her hand upon the charm, feeling the rise and fall of his breathing beneath as she looked upon him with her clear, green eyes. "I thought I would never see you again," she said, her voice low.

"I thought the same, Princess. But this charm you gave me saved my life."

"I am so glad." She gripped his hands tightly.

He could feel that she wanted to kiss him, and he wanted the same also. *She is kind and generous and brave, and so very beautiful... But now is not the time. I must tell her!*

Bellerophon raised her hands and kissed them, his eyes closed as he did so. When he opened them, he looked into hers. "There is much I must tell you."

"The guard will hear us if we speak inside, but my father is in his gardens and will not hear us outside." She looked into the darkness of the terrace. "Polyidus may hear us. He is below."

"He knows I am here."

"What?" She looked panicked for a moment, then understood. "He knows what you have come to tell me."

"Yes. But he is determined that you should know the truth."

"He has always been kind to me," Philonoe said, leading Bellerophon to a couch that lay against the outer wall, hidden and lit by a single brazier, surrounded by jasmine and bougainvillea. "Tell me."

Now that it came to it, Bellerophon did not know if he had the words to tell her the truth in the way it should be told. But, he had always spoken plainly and honestly, and that is what he decided to do then.

"The Amazons were never your enemy, Philonoe. They received me well and honoured the laws of Xenia, though I had been sent to kill them. They are the most honourable people I have ever met…apart from you."

"But how did Queen Otrera know of my mother, or of me for that matter?" she asked, no longer able to wait.

"Philonoe," Bellerophon began. "Your mother, Pasandra, *was* an Amazon."

"What?" Philonoe's composure collapsed and shock overtook her.

"This charm you gave me…" he touched the battle-axe about his neck. "It saved me because Queen Otrera recognized it. It broke open the truth which the queen told me, and which she asked me to pass along to you."

"My…my mother was one of them?" Philonoe was incredulous.

"As are you, Philonoe. Your mother, Pasandra, was one of their greatest warriors. She was Queen Otrera's general and closest friend." He could see Philonoe's eyes glossing over as the realization swept her up, but he pressed on for fear he would not be able to tell the rest. "You are a descendant of the Daughters of Ares, Philonoe. And Queen Otrera honours you, as she honoured your mother. She sent this…"

Bellerophon unslung the bundle from his shoulders and laid it in her lap. "The queen said this was one of your mother's favourite blades which she used in battle. She wanted you to have it."

Philonoe looked at the bundle laid across her lap for a few shocked moments before slowly pulling back the folds to reveal the handle and hilt, and the gleaming bronze of the oiled, battle-worn blade. "I can't believe this…" she said, touching her finger to the edge and recoiling quickly when it cut her. "It's so sharp," she said, putting her finger in her mouth to stop the blood.

"It is a warrior's blade," Bellerophon said softly. "And it's yours."

Philonoe looked up at him, her eyes pleading. "How could my father keep this from me?"

Bellerophon looked away from her eyes to the ground, and then back again. "There is more..."

For some time, Bellerophon explained all that Queen Otrera had told him about the battle between Lykia and the Amazons, and of how her father's mother had wanted to pass her throne to Pasandra after she married Iobates. He told Philonoe of her father's betrayal of the traditions of Lykia, and of how he had sent her mother to her death against the Solymi - deliberately or not - and then taken the queen's throne for himself.

Philonoe wept at first to hear all of it, but then anger at the great betrayal filled her heart and without knowing it, she gripped the handle of her mother's sword tightly in her hand, staring at the length of the blade.

"The beast then," Philonoe said. "It is my father's doing. The Gods have punished him for what he has done."

"I cannot claim to know the will of the Gods, Philonoe. That is Polyidus' domain. But I do know that Queen Otrera was not lying. And I know that if you were to take your rightful place upon the throne of Lykia, the Amazon nation would be your staunchest ally."

"It's too much, Bellerophon," she said, looking younger and more afraid than she had, at odds with the anger and strength she also held within herself. "And what of you? If my father finds out what you've told me, he will have you killed."

Bellerophon smiled sadly. "I think he will have me killed anyway. Besides…I have yet to complete a third task."

"Whatever it is," she said, "I know you will succeed." She looked up at the dark night sky then, her eyes tracing the lines of the constellations, and wondered where her mother was and whether she now knew her daughter was aware of the truth. *Oh, Mother…I miss you…* She looked back at Bellerophon. "What would I have done if you had not come into my life?"

He smiled at her. "You would have continued as the strong, honourable woman you already were when I met you. The Gods have a way of helping us along our paths."

"Yes. They do, though I don't think you believe that about yourself, Bellerophon."

"I go where Athena wills me," he conceded. "She has always been there for me."

"And so will I," Philonoe whispered.

Bellerophon felt his heart full then, of what he was not sure, but he knew that he would do anything for the woman before him. He then remembered the charm about his neck and reached up to remove it. "This belongs to you," he said.

But she reached out and stopped him. "Keep it. There is yet another task. If it protected you before, it will protect you again."

"Thank you," he smiled, and kissed her hand. "Whatever happens to me in this third task, Philonoe, I am happier than I have ever been in my life just for having met you."

She moved to kiss him then, unable to control the urge, but he had already stood and was climbing down the wall once more.

When he was gone, she held up her mother's sword to the moonlight to look upon it as a single tear traced a line down her cheek. "Goddess, protect him," she whispered.

. . .

Bellerophon did not sleep that night, not because he worried about the third task to be set for him. He had resigned himself to dying long ago. Sleep escaped him because he thought of Philonoe, and of the effects of the news he had brought her, the painful truth.

When sleep finally took him, he dozed through the sun-drenched morning into the afternoon of the next day. A part of him wanted to climb back up the walls to see Philonoe, but he felt it right that she should be alone to mull over the knowledge she now possessed. A part of him also wanted to burst in on King Iobates and confront him for what he truly was, but that would be a betrayal of the laws of Xenia also. Iobates might have been willing to betray Zeus' laws as a host, but Bellerophon knew that he would not do so as a guest.

And so he waited until evening fell, and the servants came to tell him that the feast was about to begin.

The megaron was brightly lit and filled with the men and some of the women of the court. The young entourage of Lykian nobles, Bellerophon now knew, were ignorant of their old king's past machinations. They laughed and talked and cele-brated, but they were ignorant of all that had gone before.

When the king spied Bellerophon, however, there was something strange in his eyes.

Bellerophon knew then that Iobates suspected that he knew everything, and that was something the king did not want anyone else knowing.

"Will the princess be joining us to celebrate?" Bellerophon asked as he seated himself on the king's right for the feast.

King Iobates shook his head. "The princess has taken ill and will remain in her chambers." Without another word, the king pounded his fist upon the table and raised his golden wine cup to the room. "Tonight, we celebrate the truce with our long-time enemies, the Amazons of Phrygia!"

People around the room cheered, raised their cups, and poured some onto the floor for the Gods.

"And to Bellerophon, son of Glaucus of Corinthos, who made this truce possible."

"Bellerophon!" the other guests cheered and drank.

"Let there be music!" Iobates said, and immediately, the musicians with tambourines, lyres, and auloi began to play from the far corner of the megaron. Platters of steaming meats and breads were placed upon the tables, and more wine was poured. Iobates turned to Bellerophon then. "Are you rested, Bellerophon? You have had a long journey, and such a battle!"

Bellerophon sipped his wine and looked at Iobates. "I am rested, thank you, King Iobates."

"Good." The king set his cup down. "Tell me, what else did Queen Otrera say to you?"

Bellerophon wondered if he should tell Iobates that he knew everything that had happened, but then he glimpsed the shimmering form of Athena in the shadows.

The goddess stood there, bright-eyed and stern, and shook her head slowly before disappearing. *Do not trust him...*

Bellerophon cleared his throat. "Queen Otrera spoke very highly of the late queen, Pasandra. She said that she was a wondrous woman."

For a fleeting moment, a veil of sadness covered Iobates' face as he remembered days long ago, of passion, and of joy when his daughters had been born. But then he remembered his strong belief that Pasandra had intentionally given him daughters and no sons. *The Amazons have their ways of assuring that!* he had thought. He looked at the man beside him, still living, and felt great hatred then, jealously even, for his beloved youngest daughter, he knew, had fallen for Bellerophon, as easily as Pasandra had fallen for him in the beginning. *The Gods toy with me!*

"Do you know, Queen Otrera?" Bellerophon asked when the king did not speak.

Iobates' face darkened and he nodded. "Oh, yes. I know her. She loved my wife, and hated me for also loving her."

A part of Bellerophon felt for the old king, pitied him for his lonely existence. *Perhaps he did not mean for her to die?* he wondered. *But he should have been there to fight alongside her.* He was tempted to ask the king if all of what he heard from Otrera was true, but the goddess and Otrera's warnings echoed in the corners of his mind. "Queen Pasandra must have been a magnificent woman."

"She was," Iobates said flatly, and it was then that Bellerophon knew that the old king had never truly loved the Amazon. He had used her, usurped the Queen's throne of Lykia, and now his people suffered as a result of his iniquity.

Bellerophon looked about the megaron at the faces of the young courtiers, the commanders, and then at the still-silent face of Polyidus who leaned in to hear all that was said. He then turned back to Iobates.

"King Iobates… We have eaten, and drunk, and spoken of many things. I still claim my innocence in the matter of your eldest daughter. And so, I would know what the third and final task is that I must complete to prove what the Gods already know of me. Tell me, what is my final task."

A gleam came into the king's eyes then as he took up his

cup in one hand and pounded the table with his other before standing to address the room.

"My people!" King Iobates said aloud and a hush fell over the room. "Thus far, Bellerophon, son of Glaucus of Corinthos, has proved himself a strong and skilled warrior. He has survived the first two tasks we demanded of him, and though the result of this last brought about a different outcome from what I had commanded, it still benefits our kingdom greatly." He looked about the room at the faces of his sycophants, and his soldiers. He knew they suffered, and in some ways they suffered because of his own actions. *Now is my chance to end their suffering, and the tool to help me achieve that end is sitting beside me!*

"It is time to announce Bellerophon's third and final task! If he should complete this task, it will prove that he is innocent of the accusations levelled against him by King Proetus and my eldest daughter, Queen Stheneboea." The king looked down at Bellerophon then, and waited.

Bellerophon felt Polyidus' hand upon his arm as the seer leaned in to whisper to him. "You must stand before the king now. Trust in the Gods…"

Bellerophon felt a chill then. He felt very alone in that room full of people absent Philonoe. But he stood and walked slowly around the dining tables to stand before the king.

King Iobates looked down on him, his eyes hard and unfeeling. It was a look Bellerophon was much used to.

"The third task you must complete is the most perilous, and yet it will benefit our kingdom the most. If you complete this task, Bellerophon, you will be welcomed into Lykia for all time, and I will grant you the hand of my youngest daughter, Philonoe, who would be yours ever after, as long as you live."

Bellerophon listened to the words the king uttered, understood their meaning, and yet, he did not believe their sincerity. *He is lying,* he thought. "And what is this perilous task, King Iobates?" he asked aloud.

"Bellerophon, son of Glaucus of Corinthos... You are to travel into the mountains, hunt down and kill the beast that has been ravaging my kingdom and terrorizing my people for many years. You are to kill the Chimera!"

There was an immediate and confused uproar around the megaron then, for the people had come to admire Bellerophon for what he had done thus far, despite the accusations against him, but all knew that this final task was impossible.

Amidst the chaos and cacophony of courtiers and guards about them, Bellerophon stood still as he heard the pronouncement of his third task. He stared the king directly in the eyes and saw the absolute hatred which the king had for him. *I know the truth, and he wants me to die.*

"What say you, Bellerophon?" the king asked. "Do you accept this third and final challenge in order to prove your innocence?"

The room grew a little more quiet then as people crowded around the Corinthian to hear his response.

"I accept," Bellerophon said, and the people around him cheered.

The king smiled haughtily, and stepped down from his dais to stand before Bellerophon.

"Do not think that you will live to marry my daughter," Iobates said so only Bellerophon could hear. "You will die, and painfully too, and then the world, and I, shall be rid of you."

With those final words, King Iobates left the megaron as courtiers patted and slapped Bellerophon on the back, barking empty words of encouragement.

Bellerophon stood there amidst the noise, his ears ringing, his death certain, and all he could think of was Philonoe.

"Bellerophon," came the voice of Polyidus who had finally made his way to the Corinthian's side. "The princess is unharmed, but you must focus now. Trust in the Gods, Bellerophon. Trust them."

Bellerophon looked at the seer's blank eyes and, without a word, left the megaron through the propylon.

CHAPTER 10

DIVINE COUNSEL

There was darkness all around, and it was so deep as to make one believe the cosmos had caved in on itself, leaving nothing left to fill the eyes, not a speck of beauty or of light.

And then the ground, the air, the very sinew of Bellerophon's gasping body began to shake in concert with the deep, menacing growl that erupted in that darkness from every direction. This was accompanied by a hideous hissing that preceded violent, stabbing pains before finally, fire exploded from every direction.

It was in those brief bursts of killing light that Bellerophon, grasping and gasping in the dark, felt the rush of wind from every side, and the high-pitched screams of a stallion bent on devouring him the same as his own father had been devoured, torn limb from limb.

In one last burst of firelight, great jaws opened up before him, and behind, the rearing form of a death-bringing stallion rose high above him to crash down…

．　．　．

"NO!"

Bellerophon shot up in his bed, his eyes wild and darting, searching about the room for the beasts who had come to destroy him. But all he saw was the open doorway onto the terrace where curtains blew in a strong breeze, touched by the light of a new day.

Suddenly, he bent over and vomited into the bronze basin that sat upon the floor beside the bed. Sweat poured from his head, neck, and chest, and his heart beat without proper cadence or rhythm.

"Just breathe…" he said to himself, forcing his breath to slow, and his mind to focus. "It was just a dream." For a moment, he wondered if King Iobates had poisoned him, but the ill feeling and pain in his gut soon passed after he washed, ate, and drank cool water from a nearby pitcher. *Fear is poison,* he thought, and all of the previous night returned to his clouded mind, the banquet, Philonoe's absence, and the third task which he had been commanded to perform on pain of death.

Bellerophon looked down at his hands as he moved into the morning light on the terrace, and he saw that they were shaking. He then bent to pick up oil and herbs and set them upon the altar where he lit them. He fell to his knees as the smoke enveloped him.

"Oh, Goddess Athena… Fear has finally taken hold of me. Not of death, but of the unknown monster I must face. I am tired, and do no know if I can perform this task." He felt the desperation in his voice, the exhaustion in his limbs, and he gripped the sides of the altar tightly. "I will willingly go to fight this beast, and am prepared to die doing so, if you will keep Philonoe safe from harm. May she one day replace her father upon the throne that is rightfully hers. Will you do this, oh Goddess, if I fight this beast on my own, alone, as I have lived?"

The air then grew cool and the smoke whiter and thicker, and after a brief ringing in Bellerophon's ears, he opened his eyes to see Athena standing on the other side of the altar towering over it with her spear and aegis, her helmeted head looking down on him with strength and kindness.

You cannot defeat the Chimera alone, Bellerophon, she said, his mind echoing with her winged words.

"Am I then to simply march to my death?" he asked.

The goddess' face was severe and the gorgon head upon her aegis writhed, gaped-mouthed and terrifying. She shook her head slowly.

You forget that I have been with you since you were young...that I have protected you and aided you...

"Forgive me," Bellerophon bowed his head. "I do not forget. If I cannot do this alone, how else am I to defeat the Chimera? Will you fight alongside me, divine Goddess?"

I cannot. It is against the laws of Father Zeus. Even as she spoke the words, there was thunder in the distance, a warning. *There is only one way to defeat Iobates' bane, one ally who can help you in the attack.*

"Who?" Bellerophon asked, looking directly into those shining eyes.

The offspring of Poseidon and Medusa... Pegasus.

Bellerophon did feel fear then, cold and clawing about him. He shook his head. "No. I can't. I won't."

He had heard of the winged stallion but, like all horses, he had never spared a conscious thought for it. *Of course!* he realized as he looked at the goddess. "Please do not insist on this, my goddess. I have seen it in my dreams. Pegasus will kill me as surely as the Chimera. The stallion has been prowling my dreams. He has been hunting me and seeks only my death."

The disappointment upon the goddess' face was as black clouds passing before the sun. *You allow your fears to choke your judgement, Bellerophon,* she chided. *Pegasus will help you, and he is your only way to avoid being torn body and soul by the Chimera. There is no other way.*

"But my father? His death…"

She stepped closer and reached out to raise him to his feet. Her hands were as hot iron upon his skin, her eyes blinding and beautiful. *You are not your father, Bellerophon. This is the task to which your life has led you. You must take up the challenge, or Lykia and Philonoe are lost…*

Philonoe… He thought of the princess, her kindness toward him, her care and honesty…her strength. Then, as if the goddess had blown them away, Bellerophon's deep fear and reticence fell away, even as flashes of his father's fate pulsed in his mind. "Very well, oh Goddess… I will do as you ask. But how am I to ally myself with such an animal as Pegasus?" Even as he said it, he felt fear of the winged beast fill him again.

Athena stepped back from Bellerophon and the altar then. She was unsmiling, stern, and her voice was flat and commanding. *You must conquer your fear and decide for what you will fight. When you have done that, visit the seer, Polyidus, for I have put into his mind the method for you to join forces with mighty Pegasus.*

Light flashed, and a moment later, the goddess was gone, leaving Bellerophon alone upon the terrace. When he opened his eyes, he was lying on his back staring up at the blue sky and morning sun.

On the terrace overlooking him, he saw the dark form of

Polyidus against the sky, looking down at him with wide, blank eyes.

"Walk with me."

That is all Polyidus said when Bellerophon found him in the great court of the palace, near the outer gates of the precinct.

Bellerophon wanted ask many questions, but Polyidus reached out to grip his arm and squeeze. "There is something I must show you."

The guards watched as the seer led Bellerophon toward the gates, but then Captain Milyas approached them.

"Polyidus, where are you taking Bellerophon?" he asked. "The king commanded he be kept under guard." Milyas looked at Bellerophon his lips pursed, his face apologetic.

"Captain," Polyidus said, "I am helping the son of Glaucus to prepare for his trial. It is the Gods' will."

Milyas shifted uneasily, but Polyidus continued.

"He does not plan on fleeing, I assure you," the seer added.

Milyas looked at Bellerophon.

"I have nowhere else to go, Milyas," Bellerophon said. "I'm not going anywhere."

"Very well." Captain Milyas turned to his men. "Open the gates!" he ordered, and the men pulled at the high double doors to reveal the empty agora beyond where Polyidus and Bellerophon ventured.

It was strange to roam the market and streets of Xanthos, so empty and tired, devoid of life. Though Bellerophon could see the people in the windows peering down at him and the seer, he heard not a peep, or whimper. Even the dogs had stopped their barking. It was as if the entire populace held its collective breath.

Fools! Bellerophon thought, shaking his head as he followed Polyidus down the sloping streets to the southern end of the city and out into the olive groves.

"The people pray to the Gods for your success, Bellerophon," Polyidus said. "I can hear their whispered hopes upon their lips."

"I can't hear anything," Bellerophon answered. "What are we doing here anyway? I must prepare."

"You are preparing. And I will aid you in this. Athena commands it."

"The goddess has asked too much of me," Bellerophon answered, immediately regretting the words.

Polyidus sighed and stuck his staff out until he found a large boulder upon which he settled himself. "Sit for a moment."

Bellerophon sat upon another boulder opposite. It was peaceful in the olive grove, the hot wind rustling the silver-green leaves and unripened fruit adorning the branches.

"Do you know how I came to be here, in this place? How I lost my eyesight?" Polyidus' face turned toward Bellerophon, his clouded and scarred eyes seeming to look directly at the Corinthian.

"No. Tell me," Bellerophon said, unable to look directly at the seer's face.

"I had a gift from an early age. That much was evident. For some reason, the Gods had chosen me among my people. I dreamed dreams that could help with crops. I knew when invaders would be coming, and so could give warning. I am from an island, and so there were many invaders. I didn't know exactly what I was doing. I was young, you see. I simply dreamed things, and told my parents."

"Were your parents afraid of you?" Bellerophon asked.

Polyidus shook his head. "No. They loved me very much. They protected me." Polyidus' voice lowered.

"What happened?"

"The Gods continued to speak to me. One day, when I was ten, I dreamed that wolves were coming to destroy the village flocks."

"And did they?" Bellerophon asked.

"Yes. That very morning, the people awoke to find the streets littered with the corpses - ewes, lambs, rams. All gone. The people were angry and needed to direct their anger. They yelled at my parents. Told them that I had not given them enough warning. They believed I had kept the dream to myself for a time, that they would otherwise have been prepared. Of course, my parents defended me. They calmed the villagers down."

"What happened after that? Did your dreams stop?"

"No. I continued to dream, only the visions that the Gods sent me changed. I began to dream of death."

"Death?"

"Yes. Plague came to the village, and I began to dream who would die next. The first victims were my parents."

Polyidus was silent, his face like that of a child's once again, scared and alone.

"I am sorry. That must have been terrible."

"It was. But things got worse. I kept dreaming and tried to warn every family I dreamed of, but I was always too late. People were afraid of me. *I* was afraid! Even as I mourned my parents' passing, the villagers I grew up with turned on me. I was an outcast. But despite that, I persevered and tried to warn them of each vision I had. The Gods began to warn me sooner and I went to people to tell them to leave the village, that they could save themselves. But by that time, people were so afraid of me, they would not listen. People died, though I tried to save them."

"You tried though," Bellerophon said. "What more could you have done?"

"Nothing. I was but a boy, newly-orphaned. As I slept one night, the older boys in the village came and dragged me from my home. They shouted at me, and beat me. They told me that the plague was my fault. They blamed my visions and me for all that had happened. While some of the boys held me down, one of them stuck sharpened sticks in my eyes. He shouted, 'Now you will stop having your visions!' as he blinded me."

Polyidus stopped talking, and Bellerophon could see his hands shaking as he relived that terrible experience in the retelling. He felt a deep anger toward the ignorant villagers. "I'm guessing the Gods punished those ignorant villagers for what they did to you?"

Polyidus shrugged. "I don't know. The Gods did not show me that. The following day, the village elders traded me for a new flock of sheep. The merchant they dealt with was Lykian and had just come to the island to do business. They saw their opportunity to be rid of me. That is how I ended up here. The king heard of my gifts among the outlying settlements and sent for me."

"What did he want?" Bellerophon asked.

"He wanted to use my gifts to help him overcome a new threat to his kingdom. The Chimera had come."

"Did he expect you to fight it?"

"No. Of course not, but he wanted my advice. He wanted to know why it had come. And the Gods showed me this. The

Gods showed me in a dream what King Iobates had done to incur their wrath, what he had done to his queen and kingdom… When I told him what I had seen, he threatened to have me killed, but I explained that I would not speak of it. I told him that my visions were true and that I could help him in the running of his kingdom if he wished."

"And he agreed?"

Polyidus nodded. "Yes. I have advised him in war, and politics, though he has not always taken my counsel. And then I told him that one day, a hero would come to rid him of the Chimera."

"I told you, Polyidus, I am no hero." Bellerophon stood and peered through the olive grove, shimmering in the heat and dust of the plain.

"I speak only what the Gods tell me. You have done the impossible until now, Bellerophon. Why can you not see it?"

"I have been lucky."

"You don't really believe that. I tell you…I saw the things you would do when you arrived here…the subduing of the Solymi…and the alliance with the Amazons."

"Then why didn't you tell the king?" Bellerophon asked.

Polyidus stood slowly and shuffled over to Bellerophon's side. "King Iobates does not have the Gods' favour, and I serve them, not him. But this kingdom needs our help, Bellerophon. We have been brought here, to this place and time, for a reason. It is time now for you to strike a final blow for Lykia. That is why the Gods have sent you here. And now, the goddess has shown me the way. You can defeat the beast, but only with help."

"Why should I do so for Iobates, or for Lykia? They will turn their backs on me anyway, the same as your village turned on you."

"Not for Lykia then, and certainly not for Iobates. You are here to do it for Philonoe, and for your children."

Bellerophon stepped back from the seer. He felt his heart racing, winded as if he had been punched in the gut.

Polyidus stood still before him though, confident in the words he had uttered. "You must do this thing, or die in the attempt. It is the Gods' will."

"So you have seen me die?" Bellerophon thought about leaving then, leaving and never coming back. But then he thought of Philonoe's face where she was locked in her chambers, held prisoner by her own father simply for defending him. *Would I repay her by fleeing?* Bellerophon thought. He shook his head. "It can't be done, Polyidus."

"It can," the seer said with absolute certainty. "But only if you join with a new ally."

"Pegasus."

"Yes," Polyidus confirmed.

"I can't…" Bellerophon could hear the screeching of a stallion in his mind, he could see his father's blood in the dirt as his own horses tore him to pieces. He could feel the emptiness that was left after that terrible end.

"You are not your father, Bellerophon," Polyidus said softly. "And Pegasus is no mere horse. He is a god among horses, the son of Poseidon."

"How will I even ride him?" Bellerophon said. "I haven't ridden a horse since I was a child!"

Polyidus shook his head. "You do not ride Pegasus. He will help you. He will decide whether or not to ally with *you*!"

Bellerophon walked a few paces into the grove and leaned upon the trunk of an ancient, gnarled olive tree. He was sweating, and could feel his heart beating wildly. *Athena…* he prayed. *I ask for your help in this.* Then, he turned to Polyidus. "What must I do?"

"At the end of this grove lies the great altar dedicated to Athena. This evening, just before nightfall, you are to return and make offerings to the goddess there. When you have done that, you must go to sleep at its foot. The goddess will then show you the way."

The fear Bellerophon felt was tangible. It reached out to strangle him as he stood upon a great precipice, frozen and shaking, but then he felt the seer's hand upon his shoulder, one friend to another.

"I do not lie to you, Bellerophon. For if I am wrong, Iobates will kill me also. I was once afraid of my gifts... But peace only came when I finally accepted those gifts, and my purpose. Our destinies are interwoven, Bellerophon of Corinthos. It is the Gods' will."

CHAPTER 11

PEGASUS

Nightfall came more quickly than Bellerophon would have wished. Indeed, he would have delayed further, were it in his power, but it was not. He thought constantly of the immortal stallion, and of the beast he was to hunt. He still did not know much of the Chimera, nor where he could find it, for the people of Lykia did not utter its dreaded name.

As he walked back toward the windswept olive grove, and the altar of Athena located there, Bellerophon focused upon the task at hand. He wore his armour again, and carried his weapons and offerings for the goddess. Soon, gleaming in the moonlight with the shadows of the surrounding olive grove spreading across it, the white marble of the altar came into view. Upon its face was a great gorgon head that seemed to writhe in the darkness, and on the sides were scenes of the great competition between Athena and Earth-Shaking Poseidon for the patronage of the city that now bore the goddess' name.

He arrived at the altar, which was much larger than he had expected, and began to place his offerings upon it - bundles of herbs and flowers, a small amphora of olive oil, and thick chunks of frankincense - items which Polyidus had helped him acquire. He lit the incense, knelt before the altar and raised his hands to the dark sky and stars above, just visible behind the shuddering canopy of branches overhead.

"Oh, Goddess Athena..." he began. "Forgive me for my stubbornness. I know that you have always been there to help me, and to guide me. You are the only one who has ever cared for me. I place all of my trust in you, Bright-Eyed Goddess. Tell me how to defeat the Chimera and ensure Philonoe's safety, and the safety of this land, if it is possible to do so..."

He leaned upon the cold edge of the altar as the smoke swept around it. A great exhaustion came over him as he released the worries that had been haranguing him the entirety of that day, and he lay down at the foot of the altar, his head upon the quiver of spears which he had with him.

Sound and light faded away as Bellerophon's lids grew heavy and sleep finally overtook him...

Some time later - Bellerophon knew not how much had elapsed, nor how long he had slept - the light in the grove changed. It was neither day, nor night, but rather the grove had grown still and existed in some kind of strange, orange twilight, such that one might have thought the world was burning all around him.

But there were no fires on the wind, no tang to sting the nostrils. The air smelled of jasmine and honeysuckle, and the ground was wet with dew.

Bellerophon opened his eyes. He felt calm. His heart was steady within his chest as he sat up, his back against the altar with the gorgon visible just over his left shoulder.

Rise, Bellerophon.

As soon as he heard the voice, he knew the goddess had come. Bellerophon stood quickly and turned to see Athena standing tall and brilliant on the other side of the broad marble surface. He bowed his head immediately.

"Forgive me, oh goddess!" he said. "I was rash, and my fear got the better of me."

Look at me, she commanded.

Slowly, Bellerophon unbowed his head and looked into those timeless eyes.

I have never led you astray, have I? she asked.

"No. You have not," he replied, standing before her.

Then heed what I tell you, for it may save your life. Athena waited a few moments before continuing, ensured that the mortal before her was listening closely. *I accept your offerings, and your apology, and now you must listen, or perish...*

"I understand."

Your entire life has been building to this moment in time, Bellerophon, but you cannot achieve victory alone. If you are to defeat the Chimera, you must join forces with the son of Poseidon.

"Pegasus," he said, forcing his voice to remain steady.

Yes. Only with Pegasus' help can you do this and achieve your destiny.

"But how do I do such a thing?"

As soon as the sun's chariot is high above Xanthos, you must sacrifice a pure white bull - freely-given - to Poseidon, Tamer of Horses, so that he might grant you an audience with his son. When that is finished, you must find the spring sacred to the nymphs which lies across the river, west of the city.

"What do I do there?"

You wait, Athena said firmly. *If the lord Poseidon has*

accepted your offering, Pegasus will appear sometime before Dawn paints the eastern sky. When Pegasus drinks of the sacred spring, you are to harness him.

"If I try to harness the son of Poseidon, he will kill me!"

The dark look Athena cast in Bellerophon's direction chilled him. He had let his fear get the better of him again.

"Forgive me. I will do as you say."

And I will help you to harness him. But you must believe, Bellerophon. Believe in yourself and your abilities. And trust in the Gods...

"I do," he responded. "I will."

The goddess rose up before him, taller and more brilliant than ever, and he had to look away for fear of burning his eyes.

"But tell me of the Chimera, Goddess! What is it and where am I to find it? No one will speak of it in this place!"

Athena's bright eyes narrowed. *The Chimera is an abomination. She is the offspring of Typhon and Echidna, and the sister of Cerberos and the Hydra of Lerna. She is both lion, goat and viper. Pain, and fire, and venom are her allies. She sees all, hears all. She crawls into you and will maul your soul if you let her. The world is aflame when she is near. She is merciless...she is death.*

Bellerophon then realized why no one would speak of the beast, for the thought of it was not only terrifying, but impossible to comprehend. His hands began to shake with the thought as he tried to make sense of the goddess' words, but then he closed his eyes before Athena, breathed, and stilled himself.

"Where will I find this monster, Goddess?"

Athena smiled, even as her form shimmered and faded into the branches of that sacred grove. *Only the bravest person in this land will tell you that... First, harness your greatest ally...*

. . .

When Bellerophon awoke, the sky was awash in pale pink light, and the branches in the trees above him were still and drooping under the weight of their unripened fruit. He rubbed his eyes and shook his head.

It was not long before the goddess' words rushed back to him, and he stood up quickly. To him, it seemed that his eyesight was sharper and more brilliant, that every muscle and sinew in his body felt stronger and quicker when he moved. He stretched and flexed and found that the pain that had wracked his body after his fight with Otrera was completely gone.

He turned to face the altar and gasped when he looked upon the surface.

In place of the offerings he had given, there lay an enormous bridle entirely of gold, the brow band and head piece, the cheek pieces and the bit itself. Long reins flowed around it like shimmering serpents and attached to the bit, golden gorgon heads served as bit ends and a reminder of Athena's gift.

Bellerophon reached out slowly to gather up the goddess' gift before putting it carefully into the satchel in which he had carried the offerings. He looked up at the sky then, and felt the early morning sun alight upon his face.

"Thank you, Goddess… Thank you."

When Bellerophon arrived back at the palace in Xanthos, Polyidus and Captain Milyas were waiting for him in the court with several other soldiers.

"You see, Captain," Polyidus said. "He returns to us."

Milyas looked sheepish.

Polyidus approached Bellerophon. "The captain thought you might have flown in the night."

"I'm sorry, Bellerophon," Milyas said. "Orders." He stepped closer. "No one would blame you for fleeing. The beast is…it's just that-"

Bellerophon held up his hand. "Speak not of it. I am here, Milyas, and I will do what I can."

The captain and the soldiers did not look convinced. They left Bellerophon and Polyidus alone in the court.

"Did the goddess come to you?" Polyidus asked. "Did she accept your offerings?"

"She did," Bellerophon answered, "but there is more to do. I must obtain a white bull and sacrifice it to the Lord Poseidon."

"Then there is no time to waste," Polyidus said. "Come with me."

Sometime later, Bellerophon and Polyidus finally found the farm which the seer had claimed to know of. It lay along the river to the south of the city, outside of the sacred groves, and was made up of a small plot of land with expertly-tended crops, however minute in scale.

There were a few animal pens containing chickens and sheep, but within the enclosure alongside the river, just beyond the humble dwelling, there stood the object of their visit.

"Do you see it?" Polyidus asked, gripping Bellerophon's arm as they walked along the path toward the dwelling. "The bull?"

Bellerophon looked and there, standing in the tall grass along the river, stood a brilliant, white bull. "Yes. I see it." He looked doubtful. "But that is probably the most valuable things these people have. Why would they want to give it up?"

"The Lykians are full of fear, but they are kind-hearted and will do their part if they can. Let me speak with him."

Just then, a young farmer came out of the dwelling, his footfalls crunching on the path as he walked toward them. He wore a simple, homespun tunic and sandals, and carried a thick, oak staff. "Can I help you?" he said. Then, he spotted Polyidus. "Forgive me, sir. I did not see you there. How may I serve the king?"

Polyidus reached out to find the farmer's hands. "I do not come on behalf of the king this day, Apollodoros," Polyidus said. "I come on behalf of the Gods, and the people of Lykia…"

The man froze, but Polyidus carried on.

"When I first came to this land, your father provided me with offerings most pleasing to the Gods. He helped me to fulfill my duties to this land. And now I must ask the same of you."

"You want my bull," the farmer said without hesitation, though his voice told of his reluctance. He leaned heavily upon his staff.

"Yes," Polyidus said. "The Gods demand it."

"There are other bulls, aren't there?" he said, and he glanced at the armed man standing beside the seer. "Why do you require mine? I was going to use him to buy more land for my family."

"We need yours, Apollodoros, and we must not pay for it."

"Pfft!" the farmer said, clearly shocked by the seer's brazenness. "You are the king's man, Seer. Clearly the king can take what he wants, but you will have to kill me for it. That bull is my most valuable possession!"

"We don't want to kill you, lad," Bellerophon said, stepping forward.

The farmer put out his staff to stay him. "Stay back stranger, or I'll crack your skull."

"Apollodoros, listen to me," Polyidus said, stepping between the two men. "I will not take the bull from you, and we will certainly not slay you. Everyone must do their part for Lykia at some point in time. This now falls to you."

"Give me one good reason!" Apollodoros growled, glancing back at the bull which was now leaning against the fence as if to stare at them and listen.

"Because, by sacrificing him, our land will at long last be rid of the beast that has tormented it these many years."

An uncomfortable silence hung between them, but Bellerophon could tell that the mention of the beast had hit home.

Polyidus softened his voice. "I know that your father was killed by the beast while visiting your uncle's farm in the north. How much longer do you think it will be before the creature ravages all of the lands in this part of the kingdom?"

"You cannot kill the beast," the farmer stated, a haunted look upon his face.

"Well," Bellerophon said. "I am going to try."

Apollodoros took in the brilliant armour and the gorgon in the middle of Bellerophon's breastplate. He shook his head slowly. "Why do you want to die, stranger?"

Bellerophon thought about it for a moment. Previously, he *had* wanted to die. He had stopped caring, so exhausted with life had he been. But now, he thought of Philonoe, of repaying her kindness. He felt the golden axe upon his breast and breathed deeply. "It is true, I may die. But, by the Gods, I will take that beast with me if I can." *And I would do so for you, Philonoe...*

Without another word, the farmer turned and walked to the fence where the bull stood still and serene, unlike it had ever done before. "I'm sorry boy," Apollodoros said. "It seems I must give you away." He looked into the large, glossy eyes and saw a serenity there, as if the bull already knew what must be done, and he wondered if the Gods were there, present, whispering into the beast's ear. He nodded, and took a lead rope from around the fence post before going into the enclosure and tying it around the animal's neck.

"He is going to give it to us," Bellerophon whispered to Polyidus, and the seer sighed with relief.

"Here," Apollodoros said, handing the rope to Bellerophon. "Take him, and may the Gods grant you victory so that we may have peace."

"Thank you," Bellerophon said.

The altar of Poseidon lay along the rushing river, near to the southern end of Xanthos, hidden beneath a canopy of broad, black pines and plane trees.

It was a deceptive scene, for the serenity of the flowing river, the deep green and birdsong, were at odds with Bellerophon's dark thoughts. He wondered if it would be the last time he stood before a river, the last time he felt the comfort of shade on a sun-drenched day. He listened to the birds in the trees, and thought that the sound would soon be replaced by the chorus of his nightmares, for even then, the roaring and hissing of his dreams echoed in his waking mind.

The bull tugged at Bellerophon and this brought him to. He led the animal to the altar beside the water. It consisted of a flat marble platform, worn and stained with years of use, and at the end closest to the river, it rose up, the bowl supported by carved tridents and a great conch horn in the middle.

It was as if, standing there, one could hear the sound of crashing waves, though the river revealed no such thing. Bellerophon pulled the bull forward and tied it to a bronze ring set into the base of the altar.

It was strange, how serene the animal was, now peacefully it came to meet its death.

Bellerophon wondered if it knew that its death would benefit the land which had born it. He sighed and shrugged his armoured shoulders. *I suppose I must also accept the possibility of my own death, and hope that some good will come of it.* He stroked the bull's white head and the big eyes closed and opened slowly.

It was then that he felt the presence of others in the wood about him, in the water of the river, and he knew that water nymphs watched and waited as he prepared to sacrifice to their lord.

"It is time," he whispered to the animal, before taking a fistful of grain from his satchel, placing his hand upon the bull's head, and opening it.

The grain fell over the animal's brow and it bent down to eat what fell upon the altar's lower platform.

Bellerophon drew his dagger and raised his hands to the river and sky.

"Horse-Taming Poseidon... I honour you, and I offer you this pure white bull in sacrifice... Help me, Lord, to defeat the Chimera... Send me your son, Pegasus, that we may win this battle together..."

Bellerophon looked down then and, just as the bull was finishing the last of the grains, he reached down, gripped one of the short horns, and slashed quickly and deeply across the animal's neck.

The bull screeched in surprise, flailing with what little strength it had, even as Bellerophon bore down on the horns with both hands. Blood sprayed everywhere at first, and then flowed out slowly and thickly upon the white marble of the altar. It filled the channels about the edges which flowed into the water of the river to be carried away to the sea.

The beast let out a final, deep, shuddering groan, and then was still.

Bellerophon stood slowly, and leaned with his bloody hands upon the altar. "Accept my offering..." He spied the eyes and forms of the nymphs closing in, reaching out to touch the sacrifice, to partake of its purity for their lord, but then they scattered and disappeared back into the river and wood.

Voices approached slowly, and when Bellerophon turned, it was to see three people approaching - Captain Milyas, Polyidus, and in between them, leading them, Philonoe.

Bellerophon stepped down from the altar and she made to rush to him, but Polyidus grasped her arm to stop her.

"You mustn't touch him, Princess. He is in the middle of the sacrifice and must still cross over."

"Are you here to arrest me, Captain?" Bellerophon asked Milyas.

But the captain shook his head. "Are you really going to do this thing? Are you going to slay the beast?"

Bellerophon shrugged. "One of us will die, that is certain," he said, his eyes going straight to Philonoe.

She looked beautiful to him, strong. She did not weep or wail, but stood tall before him. "I would go with you on this task," she said, firmly. "I would fight at your side."

"I know, Princess," Bellerophon answered. "And I thank

the Gods for it…for knowing you. But there is only one being who can help me in this battle, and I must go now to meet him."

"Do you remember where to go?" Polyidus asked, his eyes straying across the river.

"Yes," Bellerophon answered. "The spring lies in the wood upon the mountain slopes, on the other side of the river."

"Straight ahead from here," Polyidus confirmed.

Bellerophon dared to step a little closer to Philonoe, and she moved toward him. "I am grateful to have come into your life, lady."

"As am I for your arrival," she said, shaking her head. "There is so much I would say to you…so much I have to thank you for."

"Then pray that the Gods give us that chance, lady."

"I will."

Bellerophon glanced over her shoulder at Captain Milyas. "And you, Captain? How do you come to be here in disobedience to your king?"

Milyas sighed. "My princess has told me the truth of what happened, of the lost secrets of this land. And Polyidus has confirmed it. I thought it right that she should be here to see you. I serve her now."

"Good." He stared at the captain for a moment. "If I do not return in three days, you will know that I have failed, and that you must prepare to defend the city."

"Bellerophon," Philonoe said, straining not to reach out and hold him. "You will succeed!"

He reached beneath his breastplate and pulled out the golden battle-axe to kiss it. "You are with me, lady."

"I am."

"One last thing," he said. "Tell me where I can find the

beast."

Philonoe turned to look at Polyidus and Milyas then back to Bellerophon. "They say that its lair lies in the mountains to the northeast. They say that there are no trees upon the rocky slopes, and that the Chimera's fires burn incessantly."

"My lady!" Milyas gasped when she said the beast's name.

But she turned on him. "I am no longer afraid to say it!" she said. "The Chimera has terrorized my land long enough!"

It was then that Polyidus felt a chill, the moment that the princess, in her own mind, reclaimed that land for herself.

Philonoe turned back to Bellerophon. "My heart and strength go with you, Bellerophon. Come back to me."

The Corinthian stood tall and proud, and in that moment, he felt his fears dry up. "By the Gods' grace, Princess, I will."

With that, Bellerophon tore himself away from her, took up his weapons, set his helmet upon his head, and turned toward the rushing river.

He stepped down the embankment and waded into the shallows, moving across slowly.

The water rushed more violently the farther out he went, and the riverbed deepened so that it was up to his chest, pulling at him and his quiver of spears.

"Careful!" Milyas shouted.

But the current was too strong and Bellerophon was swept under.

"NO!" Philonoe yelled, rushing forward to the shoreline. "Bellerophon!"

For a few, dreadful heartbeats, there was nothing, but then a hand grasped one of the boulders on the far side and Bellerophon's blue crest emerged from the dark water. He pulled himself and his weapons out, slowly grunting with the effort and stood to face them.

"He has been cleansed," Polyidus said, breathing a sigh of relief.

On the other side, Bellerophon looked down to check that the had not lost any of his weapons, his shield, or the satchel containing the bridle, and saw that he had not. The blood of his offering had also been completely washed away from his face, hands and armour, and when he turned to wave one last time at the others, they saw a gleaming warrior before them.

"Farewell," Philonoe whispered as she watched him disappear into the wood beyond.

"May the Gods guide him," Polyidus said as he felt Philonoe take his arm. "Yes, my lady?"

"I would speak with my father now," she said. Her voice was determined and angry, for she had thought long and hard about all that she had learned, and what she would say. "I must tell him that I know the truth."

"I beg you to wait, Princess," Polyidus said. "Let Bellerophon set off. There will be a time for reckoning, but it is not now. If Bellerophon succeeds, then the king will have to honour his victory."

"He is right, my lady," Milyas added. "The king is not in his right mind. Let this trial pass."

Frustrated, Philonoe looked back across the river and saw that Bellerophon was gone. She turned to Milyas and Polyidus. "Very well. But one day, and soon, I will confront my father for what has done."

"And we will stand by you, my lady," Milyas said.

The forest on the western side of the river was thick and uninhabited, but for the spirits of wood and stream who dwelt there in that place protected by the Gods' grace. Sound travelled strangely on the slopes of that mountain, and the angled sunlight looked different as it filtered through the pine, gnarled oak, and towering juniper.

After he had crossed the river, and climbed a short distance up the slopes, Bellerophon had turned to catch a last look of Philonoe as she had stood there with Milyas and Polyidus. He was relieved that she had allies in the palace, and that freed his mind to focus on the task before him.

Such a task! He had accepted that the beast he was to slay would probably be the death of him. He had seen the fear in people's eyes when there was any sort of inference regarding it and the fires that took farms and families' lives. But now, he had to face another beast. *A god among horses!* And he had to ally himself to it.

As Bellerophon picked his way up the mountainside and through the forest, he prayed to Athena for the strength to do what needed doing, the strength to face a fear that had long robbed him of courage and reason.

He did not see the dark faces of the wood nymphs and satyrs watching him, the curious looks in their wild eyes as he passed, as they ensured that he found the spring as ordered by the goddess Athena herself. They looked on with wonder and fear at the armoured man in their midst, observed the weapons that he carried, and the glow emanating from the satchel slung over his shoulder.

After what seemed like an entire day of climbing, Bellerophon reached a plateau upon the mountainside. The trickle of water tickled his senses as he reached the edge of the forest, and when he stepped out onto the flatter ground, it was night.

The plateau was lit by Selene's silver light, and the stars whirled overhead in a way that was completely foreign to

Bellerophon. He knew that he was in a supremely liminal space, a place between worlds.

"The spring must be here," he said to himself as he turned around, trying to locate the source of the trickling. He stopped walking, and took a deep breath, for his heart had begun to beat wildly. *Goddess, guide me,* he thought. When he opened his eyes, they were drawn to a rough circle of rocks, ahead and to his left.

Bellerophon approached the rocks, stopping when a great serpent slithered away into the forest at the sound of his footsteps. When it was gone, he continued.

"The spring!" he said, his voice swallowed by the surrounding wood. He looked into the broad pool and for a moment he thought that he had fallen, for in it the Gods' firmament was perfectly reflected, alive, and writhing with every expression of the cosmos.

Though he was thirsty, he dared not drink. He stepped back and looked for a place to sit and wait. On the other side of the clearing, he spotted a broad oak surrounded by moss-covered rocks. He walked over to it and, after searching the surrounding shadows for any threats, he laid down his helmet, spears, and the satchel containing the bridle which he held in his lap.

Weariness began to overtake him, but Bellerophon strained against it, his eyes searching night's canopy for the writhing forms that had been set there by the Gods so very long ago. It was, however, no use to fight his exhaustion. The wind picked up and rustled the trees as if Hypnos whispered all about him, and so Bellerophon's lids grew heavier and heavier until with a last glance at the far spring, he fell into a deep slumber.

. . .

Night had never been Bellerophon's friend, for ever since his father's hideous death, it had brought only remorseless anguish. As the mortal man slept in the embrace of that hidden place, his fears crept in upon him from the shadows of the mountain, their claws extended, tearing at him as he slept.

In the darkness, Bellerophon cried out, surrounded by the stomping hooves and gnashing jaws of his father's horses as they tore him to pieces. Glaucus' eyes were wide with shock and fright, their whites pooling with blood as he met his end, as he heard his own flesh being torn from his body.

Bellerophon wept, unable to help, unable to stop his father's suffering. The feeling of utter uselessness that had dogged him the whole of his life swept in to strangle him. Faces of the past stood by, watching and laughing at him beyond the pounding hooves and bloody teeth - his mother, his brother and sisters, his cousin, Belleros, and others.

My son! Glaucus cried out, his bloody arm reaching toward Bellerophon. *Help me!*

But Bellerophon was frozen, unable to approach. However, a thought occurred to him as he stared at the massacre, and the words of Athena echoed in his mind.

You are not your father!

"Forgive me, Father, but you did this to yourself! You left me to the wolves! I cannot help you."

NO! Glaucus screamed as his chest was torn out, his voice drowned in his own blood.

Bellerophon then turned from the scene of terror and fear that had long haunted his life, and as he did so, he found Bright-Eyed Athena standing before him.

Well done, the goddess said before a great wind rushed around him, sweeping her and the grisly scene at his back away.

. . .

Bellerophon opened his eyes and saw the forest limbs all around him swaying, as if a great storm were announcing itself. He stood up, grasping his sword, leaving the satchel upon the ground. As he moved into the clearing to stare up at the pale sky, he saw a brilliant apparition in white circling in a great arc overhead.

It was blinding against the rosy, dawn sky, but as Bellerophon strained to look up, he heard a loud neighing that shivered the trees about him as the wind got stronger, and a great flapping sound battered him down to the ground.

Bellerophon retreated to the tree where he had slept and crouched down to watch as the son of Poseidon alighted upon the ground to shake the earth.

Pegasus, he thought as he observed the stallion, knowing that he had never seen anything so powerful, and terrifyingly beautiful in all his life. This was no mere horse. It was a god standing before him.

Pegasus trotted around for a few heartbeats, flapping his enormous, white wings as if to stretch, the action causing a windstorm in the clearing that made Bellerophon cover his eyes.

The stallion reared thrice, and then went to the spring where he bowed his thick neck to drink from the cosmos' mirror.

Bellerophon watched and knew that he must approach Pegasus, that he would only know if Poseidon had accepted his offering if he proved to be successful. He stood, unaware that he still held the sword, and walked into the clearing.

He walked slowly toward the drinking stallion, and the

closer he got to him, the more immense Pegasus seemed. Bellerophon had never seen such a large animal.

Pegasus' coat was of purest white, such that it illuminated the surrounding dark of the forest, and its surface was crisscrossed with thick, fast-flowing veins that pulsed with life and vitality. His mane and tail were long, the colour of pearl, and his legs were thick, sleek and powerful, ending in hooves that could crack open the earth. His wings, by far more broad and powerful than even those of Zeus' eagle, stretched and flexed as he drank deeply of the spring.

Bellerophon knew that it was madness to approach Pegasus, but he also knew that it was the only way he might have a chance of achieving victory. He began to walk, his feet crunching on the rocky ground.

Pegasus continued to drink, but as Bellerophon got closer, the stallion's ears perked up, and he turned his mighty neck slightly, just enough to see the glint of a blade in the man's hand.

Make the mortal work for your friendship, Poseidon had commanded his son before sending him to Lykia.

"Pegasus?" Bellerophon asked, his voice uncertain and tinted with fear.

As quickly as a bolt of lightning from the hand of Zeus, Pegasus' hind legs struck out, one kicking the blade from his grasp, and the other hitting him upon his armoured chest.

The blow sent Bellerophon flying backward through the air to land on his back on the other side of the clearing.

Bellerophon groaned where he landed, and would have lain there, but for the sound of galloping rushing toward him. He rolled to the side quickly as a hoof stomped onto the spot where he had landed, found his feet, and stood only to be kicked in the chest once more.

This last sent him flying back into a pine sapling which cracked upon impact as Bellerophon was flung into the wood beyond.

Pegasus' large, glossy eyes watched for movement for a moment, and then he turned and went back to the spring.

"Ahh!" Bellerophon pulled himself up from the ground and stood again to climb over the broken tree and rocks to reach the clearing once more. "Pegasus!" he said aloud, but the stallion simply glanced at the mortal over his muscular shoulder and continued to drink.

Bellerophon made to pick up his sword again from where it had fallen, but then he remembered the harness given to him by Athena. He picked up the satchel and approached Pegasus once more.

It was then that a strange feeling came over him, strange and critical thoughts. It was as if he were calling himself a coward, full of fear, but he was not conscious of the thought.

That's when he realized that they were not his own thoughts, but those of Pegasus.

Bellerophon stopped his approach, and breathed deeply, struggling to still his racing heart. When he was calm, he carried on, only to have Pegasus whirl on the spot, his wings outstretched.

The stallion reared higher above Bellerophon than the mortal man could have imagined possible.

But Bellerophon stood his ground. "I am not here to harm you. I honour you, Pegasus."

The stallion's front hooves crashed to the ground, sending dirt and rock flying in every direction.

Then, Bellerophon reached inside the satchel and pulled out the brilliant, golden bridle. "I need your help, Pegasus," he said, holding out the bridle given him by Athena.

Pegasus' enormous eyes gazed upon the shining bridle as he leaned his neck forward to sniff at it, his warm breath tickling Bellerophon's hand. He did not recoil anymore, but allowed the mortal to approach closer.

"Thank you," Bellerophon said as he raised the bit and bridle to the stallion's mouth.

Pegasus pulled his head up swiftly, lifting Bellerophon off of his feet into the air.

Bellerophon struggled to reach Pegasus' head, and quickly slung the reins over the stallion's head and neck before turning and holding out the golden bridle. He did not force it, but spread the bridle straps wide to expose the bit.

Pegasus paused and stared down at it, at the writhing gorgon heads upon it.

"Athena has told me that I need your help, Pegasus," Bellerophon said softly, his voice soothing now. "Whoa... Easy... Has your father accepted my offering? If not, I will leave you alone. But I need your help."

It was then that Bellerophon relaxed and leaned against Pegasus' neck, felt the stallion's warmth, and heard the strong breathing deep within, a rhythm which he too fell into.

"Will you help me defeat this beast? Will you help me defeat the Chimera?"

To Bellerophon's great astonishment, Pegasus then bent his head down, took the bit in his mouth, and allowed the mortal man to turn and fasten the straps.

Bellerophon stood back and faced Pegasus directly then, their eyes meeting, and he reached up to place his hands on either side of his head, placing his own forehead to the great soft muzzle. "Thank you," Bellerophon said.

Together they walked across the clearing so that Bellerophon could gather his weapons, shield, and cloak. With everything secure upon his shoulders and back, Bellerophon turned to Pegasus.

"The Chimera's lair lies to the northeast in the treeless mountains, where the fires burn."

Pegasus bobbed his head up and down, turned sideways, and knelt so that Bellerophon could get onto his broad back.

"I've not ridden in many years," Bellerophon said as he settled.

Pegasus rose up to his full height then, the reins held firmly in his rider's grasp. He turned to face the open clearing, now filled with morning sunlight, and charged.

Pegasus' great wings flapped faster and more powerful than ever as he charged, and just before they reached the trees on the far side, he took flight.

Bellerophon felt his stomach tighten as they rose up, as the mountains and the trees fell away. For a moment, he felt as if he would fall to his death, but then he heard Athena's voice reach out to him.

You must trust in Pegasus as you must trust in yourself!

Bellerophon smiled then as he looked along Pegasus' neck from the eye-slits of his crested helmet, and he relaxed and focussed on the trial ahead.

Pegasus and the Gods are on my side in this. Now, I too must be! he thought to himself as they soared over the city of Xanthos where the people rushed out of doors to watch their champions fly overhead.

From the terrace of her apartments, Philonoe watched them, and she felt a great lightening of her heart at the sight.

"May the Gods protect you, Bellerophon," she said as she held her mother's sword.

CHAPTER 12

THE CHIMERA

The wind rushed all around Bellerophon as he and Pegasus soared over the rivers and mountains of Lykia. It was as if he were caught in some unbelievable dream, but not one of the nightmares that had so frequently haunted the lonely nights the whole of his life. He was flying unlike any mortal man before him, seeing the world from such a perspective as to change him for all time.

As he and his new-found ally left Xanthos behind, he finally felt, without any doubt, that the Gods were truly with him. He shared the Gods' view of the world below then, and he knew that it was something he would never be able to forget.

Riding Pegasus, however, required more attention that he was giving it, and he nearly plummeted to his death several times but for the stallion's skill in managing his rider.

Pegasus' wings were strong and broad, the wondrous feather-like span filled with air as they soared and circled in the blue skies.

"The princess said that it was to the northeast, high in the treeless mountains where there are fires constantly burning."

Bellerophon was not sure if Pegasus understood him, but when the stallion adjusted his course, he felt certain he did. He smiled. "By the Gods!" he said as they flew higher and higher, his stomach tightening as he held on tightly with his legs, his fists white about the golden reins. "Look!"

Bellerophon peered along Pegasus' strong neck and mane to see pillars of smoke rising up from the valley below, one after another, more fires than he had seen on his previous journeys through that land. "The beast must be down there somewhere!" Bellerophon said over the sound of the wind, but as they circled lower and lower to get a better view, they found the creature gone, the only sign that it had been there the destruction it had wrought, and the cries of the people far below.

Bellerophon spotted children wailing over the bodies of their slain parents, and the sight fired his determination to slay the creature. It was no longer about proving himself or his innocence. He knew he was innocent. It was about stopping the suffering of Lykia's people, and helping Philonoe. "Keep going, Pegasus!" he said, squeezing with his legs and turning the stallion's head to the northeast and the distant mountains.

As they flew farther, the land grew bleaker, the air more choked with fume and smoke. There were no more crops to speak of, for they had long ago been turned to cinder. Only the hardiest of scrub grew, but after a while, even that disappeared.

Bellerophon felt fear creeping in upon him, subtle and menacing, for he remembered Athena's words, her warning…

Pain, and fire, and venom are her allies. She sees all, hears all. She crawls into you and will maul your soul if you let her. The world is aflame when she is near. She is merciless…she is death.

"How can such a creature exist?" Bellerophon wondered

aloud, unable to comprehend what it might look like. Of course, he knew of the dreaded Hydra at Lerna, but had never ventured there. And Cerberos…well…if things went badly, he would meet Hades' hound soon enough. But a sibling of both? "I've hunted lions before," he said to himself.

The sun's chariot was moving quickly overhead and as Bellerophon looked up at it, he spied Helios himself leaning over in the cab to look at him and Pegasus just before they sped away into the grey and choking clouds of the Chimera's domain.

Suddenly, Pegasus swerved and neighed loudly as rocky peeks swept dangerously close to his underbelly.

Bellerophon fell forward, his arms around the stallion's neck, his shield and quiver of spears falling forward.

Pegasus began to shake his head wildly, trying to regain his equilibrium.

"Are you trying to kill me?" Bellerophon yelled at the stallion when they regained control.

Pegasus glanced back and bucked at that.

"Whoa! Easy!" Bellerophon yelled, unable to see anything but Pegasus' swirling white mane and violently flapping wings. "I'm sorry!" he shouted, clinging to Pegasus with all of his might.

Pegasus softened his airborne stride, and in that moment, the mountain over which they had passed fell away to reveal a long desolate valley of jagged rock.

Bellerophon began to think of how he would be able to fight the beast, for he had never done battle from horseback, let alone from atop a horse whose wings he could injure by swinging a sword or casting a spear. Panic began to take hold of him, and in his mind he could hear the roar and hiss that had taken root in his dreams of late.

Then, Pegasus stumbled slightly, regaining his flight.

Bellerophon looked up to see the stallion's ears pitched forward, listening to something. The roar and hiss came again, and Bellerophon knew then that it was no dream.

Far below, as they dropped from the ceiling of grey cloud and smoke, the rocky ground was lit up by scattered fires that spewed and flickered out of the earth.

"What is all that?" Bellerophon wondered aloud. "How-"

The words stopped in his throat, for as his eyes followed the fires - spread out like rocks thrown from a Titan's fist upon the lifeless valley floor - he spotted the enormous, gaping maw of a cave directly ahead.

Bellerophon felt his heart pound, and doubt arise full force in his mind to prod his deepest fears.

There were fires everywhere, and the rock faces about the cave, radiating from it, appeared to be scratched and scorched in places.

This is my end, Bellerophon could not help but thinking as they flew lower. He could even feel Pegasus skittish beneath him. *I can't fight like this,* he suddenly realized, and when they were low enough, Bellerophon set down the reins and leapt off of Pegasus' back.

He fell hard upon the ground but rolled awkwardly to his feet, crouching as he observed the distant cave rising so high above him that he had to squint to peer through the surrounding flames into the darkness within.

Pegasus pulled up suddenly when his rider jumped and circled back to land beside Bellerophon. He stomped his mighty hooves, his head bobbing up and down, wild and panicked as he urged the mortal to get back on.

"I can't fight from your back, Pegasus!" Bellerophon said, trying not to yell. Nevertheless, his voice echoed off of the surrounding rock. "Take to the air! You'll be safer!" he said, waving the stallion away. "Go, you stubborn beast!" Bellerophon said.

Pegasus continued in his attempts to urge Bellerophon onto his back again, but the mortal refused.

"Go! You've brought me here. You've done your part. Now, it's for me to finish."

You will die!

Pegasus' thoughts suddenly burst in upon Bellerophon's own, but it made no difference.

Bellerophon stepped closer and placed his hand upon the stallion's forehead. "Go, my friend. If I am to die, I will die."

Pegasus reared angrily, his forelegs kicking out in frustration, and then he took to the air, the wind flattening the fires all about Bellerophon for a few seconds.

Bellerophon watched the stallion take flight, and soar higher and higher into the sky before he disappeared into the grey, overcast that bore down on that desolate place.

Suddenly, it was quiet and very lonely as Bellerophon looked about him. The fires spewing out of the ground all around him seemed silent and menacing, like fiery pillars in an unseen hall of Hades' making. Except, this was not the Underworld. It was the lair of a beast born of hatred and greed, a devourer of men, women, and children, the tormentor of Lykia.

"Athena…I am here… Guide my sword and spears in this fight that I may take this beast as it takes me." Bellerophon crouched then to look around at the terrain, the places where there was no fire, the spots of higher ground from which he might be able to attack and defend. In his mind he traced a path around the mouth of the cave. When he had surveyed the battlefield, he reached beneath the collar of his breastplate and pulled out the golden battle-axe to kiss it before tucking it back. "Be safe, Philonoe... Thank you..."

He stood then, and looked up to see no sign of Pegasus. Then, he drew his sword and raised his shield before him as he walked slowly forward toward the cave. His heavily-filled quiver of throwing spears pulled at his shoulder and neck, and his cloak billowed in the suddenly growing wind that swept about him and jostled the surrounding fires.

"Where are you?" he said to himself, as he approached the cave, closer and closer, step by hesitant step.

The gorgon head upon his shield and armour peered directly ahead too, urging the foe to emerge, challenging it.

But there was only the whistling of the wind upon the surrounding rocks, and the flickering of the fires out of the ground.

Bellerophon now stood before the cave entrance, dwarfed by its magnitude. He looked around the entrance to see the titanic claw marks in the rockface, and the places where fire had melted that rock.

"Gods...let us finish this," he said, bending over to pick up a rock. He pulled it back and heaved it into the cave as far as he could throw it into the darkness.

Nothing happened.

Perhaps the beast is still ravaging the countryside? Bellerophon thought. *I will stay here, and wait for it.*

Only, in that moment, as Bellerophon turned and stared down the long, fiery path along which he had come, the ground began to shake, and a deep growl seemed to rise up out of the shuddering earth at his feet. A great hissing joined with the growl, and the sound of it chilled Bellerophon's blood, made his limbs shake. He breathed slowly, and turned back toward the cave then.

"Gods," he whispered, his eyes wide beneath his crested helmet as he backed away, staring up as if to the sky.

It was the Chimera.

In all of the darkest, most terror-stricken thoughts he had ever had, Bellerophon could never have imagined such a creature as the one that now rose up before him, approaching slowly, hungrily.

The monster's head and powerful legs were those of a tawny lion, only larger than any beast that roamed the plains of the earth. Its mane was bristling and angry, shifting about the massive jaws and brow like a wreath of bronze rather than of hair. But it was those frowning eyes of fiery amber that struck deep, as if it knew it looked upon easy prey.

As it stepped forward, after the slowly retreating Bellerophon, there appeared more, for out of the Chimera's back bent the grey and black head of a horned goat with dead-looking eyes larger than a man's fist. It weaved and bobbed unnaturally upon the lion's back, shifting to get a glimpse of the man before it.

Bellerophon noticed something strange within the goat's head. Its throat glowed, as if it were on fire, and as a result, the goat constantly worked its crooked jaws, yawning and snorting through its nostrils.

They continued to size each other up, the lion walking slowly, crouching, its deep growl utterly disconcerting.

Another sound joined, and as Bellerophon shifted to try and move around the back of the beast, his shield before him, the hissing started.

The beast's tail rose up from the back, swaying and darting, and Bellerophon noticed that it was a fanged serpent, black as adamant with eyes like emeralds at the bottom of a bog.

Bellerophon felt his heart racing faster and faster, for the sounds of his nightmares, the doom of the world, had been made flesh. And with his fear, the Chimera paused to sniff at the air, as if to savour the moment to come. It was a beast of pure violence, and more terrifying than any Titan or giant.

We shall bite you, and burn you, and feast upon your flesh... The time of your death has come...

How the voice reached into Bellerophon's mind, he did not know, but somehow the beast spoke to him, taunted his soul as if to petrify his body with the deep fear that attacked all of its victims.

Bellerophon crouched, his shield up, his sword out, his eyes searching desperately for a weakness.

Suddenly, a ball of flame shot from the goat's head, to engulf him, and the lion's jaws closed in amid Bellerophon's screams.

The sky was blue, beautiful, and vast as the laneways to Olympus stretched out before Pegasus. The stallion's wings swept the air and shuddered the trees over which he soared.

But he was skittish, and uncertain, his flight interrupted as the sound of screaming rent the air. Pegasus' ears bent back and he thought of the mortal who had befriended him, despite his deep fear. He circled in the sky, his large eyes searching the eastern peaks from which he had just come. His muzzle sniffed at the air and snorted.

Pegasus smelled the impending death upon the wind and it saddened his mighty heart no end to think of what would happen. Though he too feared death, he found that he feared the suffering of the mortal even more. He remembered the man's soft but wary voice, the hesitant but gentle touch of

Bellerophon's hands upon his neck, and the beating of his strong heart.

Return to him! The voice of Horse-Taming Poseidon commanded. *Fight!*

But Pegasus was already flying as quickly as he could in the direction of the sounds of terrible battle and the Chimera's fires.

Bellerophon found himself, flying, tumbling through the air, his body still aching from the strike upon his shield and the fireball that followed his arcing flesh.

"Ahh!" he cried as he slammed into the rock wall of the valley and fell in a heap of jagged slate. He rolled immediately, slashing his sword out blindly, even as he untangled himself from his quiver of spears.

He tried to reach for a spear but the Chimera rushed at him before he had the chance, and he was running again, circling the monster, trying desperately to penetrate its defences. But he could not from any side, for everywhere he sought to attack, he was met by sweeping claws, fire and, perhaps most terrifyingly, the dripping fangs of the long, darting serpent.

My time has come, Bellerophon thought, his breathing ragged as he crouched behind his shield to meet another fireball. *I'm sorry, Philonoe... I tried.*

When the fire around Bellerophon petered out, his cloak and helmet's crest singed and smoking, he straightened and pointed his sword at the Chimera's black heart. He began to run, lunging over the serpent's head as it struck at his feet, and readied to plunge his sword into the lion's chest.

The great claws raked out again and sent him flying to land with a crack upon the rocky, flame-drenched ground.

Bellerophon groaned as he lay there, his sword knocked from his grasp, the earth shaking as the Chimera ran at him, and his thoughts were not of the painful death that lay moments away, but of blue seas and mountains, of soaring through the skies...of the only joy and kindness which Philonoe had given him. *Athena, make it quick!* He prayed as the Chimera's roaring jaws opened above him like a chasm.

Then, there was a loud, booming neigh from out of the heavens, a battle cry, and the Chimera's head shot sideways from a great impact.

Wind was everywhere, rushing, cooling, driving the shooting flames in the other direction.

Pegasus! Bellerophon's heart cried out, renewed and emboldened.

The stallion reared bravely before the Chimera, is hooves striking out at the jaws as if the Gods' own spears were levelled at the monster.

The Chimera retreated a few steps to prepare for a brutal attack, and it was then that Bellerophon rushed and leapt upon Pegasus' back! They set off at a gallop and took flight, just as the lion's jaws slammed into the rocky ground where they had been.

Fire followed them, but they flew high, out of reach and circled the valley as if watching a deadly insect in the bottom of a bowl.

The Chimera roared and shook the mountains, charging this way and that as all of its eyes sought out the soaring pair.

Bellerophon gripped the golden reins tightly, trying to control Pegasus, but the equine god pulled at the reins and shook his great mane.

He is your ally! Athena's voice sped toward him. *Fight together!*

It was then that Bellerophon released the reins and gave Pegasus his head.

"Fly close to it for me, Pegasus! And beware of fire and fangs!"

Pegasus circled in the air, his head and neck strong, proud, and a moment later, they were flying at the Chimera from above.

Bellerophon felt the wind in his face as he pulled one of his spears from his quiver and poised himself to launch.

The fire rushed at them, but Pegasus swerved and dodged, and as he began to pull up from the fast-approaching earth, Bellerophon released a spear!

The leaf-shaped blade cut through the air to graze the serpent's neck as it struck out, and the lion roared in dismay as the goat breathed fire in the wake of the flying man and horse who took to the sky once more.

"Again!" Bellerophon yelled as Pegasus peaked, and turned back to earth for another attack. He could see the serpent's head bobbing strangely, wounded as it was, and took aim.

Pegasus fell at an unnatural angle, but Bellerophon gripped tightly with his legs, holding on with force and faith in his mount, another spear poised, and when he threw, it struck home, pinning the serpent's head to the rocky earth where the flames spewed out.

The Chimera roared, and when the goat head bobbed to shoot its deadly flames at them, it was taken in one eye by another of Bellerophon's spears. The Chimera launched itself skyward after the pair, but was pulled back down as its hideous serpent-headed tail was severed clean by the mortal's spear.

Blood seeped over the rocks, cooking in the Chimera's surrounding fires, and somewhere in the depths of the Underworld, and the swamps of Lerna, the monster's siblings cried out in anger.

The goat head flailed wildly from the Chimera's back, fire shooting everywhere, fanning out into the sky as it sought to engulf the horse and rider.

Pegasus was faster than flame however, and dodged and weaved in and out of the fiery tunnels in the sky, as if all of the winds conspired to help him and Bellerophon move where they would.

Bellerophon looked down as Pegasus circled, preparing for another attack. He grasped two spears now, his shield slung over his back once more.

They attacked again.

The Chimera circled wildly, its two remaining heads turned up, the one full of rage, the other pained and bloody and seeking vengeance.

The fire rushed toward Pegasus and Bellerophon, and the beast and the earth disappeared from view for a moment. When their sight was renewed, the Chimera's jaws were open to snatch them, but Pegasus swerved quickly and Bellerophon's spears planted themselves in the goat's throat so that they punctured its fiery innards, causing it to implode.

Pegasus crashed onto the ground at a run, and they continued up into the sky, just as one of the Chimera's claws raked his hind quarter. The stallion screamed in pain as it tried to climb higher, this time with unimaginable effort as blood streamed behind him, staining his brilliant white coat.

Bellerophon leaned forward to pat the stallion's neck. "We've almost got him, Pegasus! One more attack! This time, head-on!"

Pegasus circled, his great neck straining toward the

Chimera, and then he shot down toward the valley floor, swerving in among the fires reaching for them out of the earth.

The Chimera charged, its great claws tearing the rock beneath its feet, its roar echoing off of the surrounding mountains, such that Bellerophon thought that his ears would burst.

With his spears poised, Bellerophon launched the first only to have it bounce off of the beast's bristling mane. But his second plunged deep into one of those death-seeking eyes.

There was a moment's rush of excitement, but then everything was a blur as the Chimera's claw struck Pegasus' chest.

Poseidon's son screamed and the air was filled with pain and blood, and Bellerophon tumbled over the Chimera's back, slamming into the lifeless goat head and down the bloody, split length of the serpent.

"AHHH!" he screamed as fire shot out of the rocky ground, singeing his skin before he could roll away, dizzy from his fall. "Pegasus!" he yelled, but he could not even hear himself above the stallion's pained cries and the earth-shaking roars of the Chimera as it crept toward Pegasus, jaws open, claws extended to tear him to pieces.

"NO!" Bellerophon yelled as he rushed forward.

Pegasus backed against the rocky wall of the valley, his wings flapping wildly, sprayed with his own blood, his hooves slipping on the ground of crushed shale.

The Chimera's claws struck out, but Pegasus darted and struck back, only to stumble again, as if he were a mouse being taunted and played with by a stable cat.

It was then that the son of Poseidon sent up a prayer to the Gods that they remember his deeds, and thanked them for the life they had given him. His great eyes closed, exhausted and resigned to the death that lunged toward him without mercy.

"NO!" Bellerophon suddenly cried.

When Pegasus looked, it was to see three spears planted in the side of the Chimera's lion head, and Bellerophon holding his last one poised as the Chimera turned toward him.

"Fight me!" Bellerophon roared back at the monster. "FIGHT ME!"

The Chimera's jaws gaped open to take the mortal man in one violent, crushing bite, but Bellerophon moved to one side with the speed of a god.

Pegasus then rushed and kicked at the Chimera's ribs with all of his remaining might.

The beast reared upon its hind legs and it was then that Bellerophon's spear cut through the air, planted in the flesh, and punctured its wicked heart.

The Chimera crashed to the earth and before it could breathe its last, Bellerophon leaped upon its back, grasping the sword he had picked up again, and planted it into the monster's skull with a sickening crack.

The air was silent then, as if a great storm had just ended.

The world spun as Bellerophon stood upon his fallen foe and looked to where Pegasus limped, bloody and exhausted toward him.

Philonoe, he thought, *we did it...* even as he fell to the hard ground and into darkness.

The night was strange and silent, and the stars overhead spun and sparkled in the blackness of the heavens.

The Gods had seen the battle, admired the courage of both man and beast who lay prostrate upon the ground beside their defeated foe.

They must be healed, for it is not over, Athena said to Poseidon as she passed her glowing hands over Bellerophon.

No, it is not, Horse-Taming Poseidon said as he poured life-giving water over his beloved son to wash and seal his grievous wounds. *I shall have him set among the stars for his courage,* Poseidon said as he stroked Pegasus' soft jaw and looked into the stallion's dazed and exhausted, glossy eyes.

Such courage... Athena said, stroking Bellerophon's hair. *Your trials are nearly at an end, Bellerophon, but not yet... not yet...*

When morning came, it was with a new hope and brilliant light.

Bellerophon's mind and body were silent and still, but his breath was strong and the rise and fall of his chest beneath his armour was a relief to the godlike stallion that stood over him.

Pegasus bent down to him, his hot breath upon his cheek to rouse the mortal man, his friend, his ally.

Bellerophon's breathing became more rapid and regular and when he opened his eyes, it was to see the winged stallion standing over him. "I dreamed that the Gods were here with us."

Pegasus' great head bobbed up and down and he stomped the rocky ground. *Victory, friend... Victory!*

"Yes," Bellerophon groaned and stood to look at the monstrous body of the Chimera beside them. "Victory." He walked to Pegasus and wrapped his arms about the stallion's neck. "Thank you for coming back."

In that moment, the two of them felt great appreciation and gratitude for each other, and the world about them was a different one than what had gone before.

Bellerophon remembered the goddess' words from the night before however, and knew that he was not quite finished.

He remembered the Amazon queen's warning of King Iobates too, and knew that his own return to Xanthos would be most unwelcome.

"Can you fly?" Bellerophon asked Pegasus.

The stallion reared and flapped his wings.

Bellerophon smiled. "Good." He then pulled his sword from the Chimera's lifeless head and gazed upon the entirety of that fallen beast. In that moment, he felt the last vestiges of fear, of resentment, and of anger fade to nothing, and he let out a great cry that echoed over the mountains of Lykia to the sky above.

CHAPTER 13
A HERO'S TRIUMPH

The sun shone differently over the kingdom of Lykia that day, for the fires that had darkened the skies for so many years no longer burned. Distant farmers spoke of the sounds of hideous battle, of a rumbling in the mountains which, at first, they took to be the Gods' final punishment of them all. But as the people had cowered in their hovels, praying for the Gods' mercy while the sounds of battle had raged on, it so happened that their world did not end.

Dawn arrived bright and glorious, painted across a sky as beautiful as any in recent memory.

The true relief came when, coming out of their homes to breathe the fresh air and thank the Gods for the continuance of their lives, they looked up to see Pegasus and his rider, the Corinthian, Bellerophon, of whom they had heard so much, flying toward Xanthos.

"Could it be true?" people asked. "Have Bellerophon and Pegasus slain the Chimera? Are we free at last?"

The Gods' altars burned brightly that day, and every day afterward, with the people's offerings of gratitude and relief.

. . .

King Iobates had heard the rumours which had spread like summer fire.

Bellerophon had succeeded. The Chimera had been slain.

The king knew that he should be overjoyed that his kingdom's long-time tormentor was no more, but he was not. The victory was bitter and tainted, for he knew that he must still, somehow, dispose of the son of Glaucus for what he had done to his eldest daughter. As he paced in the megaron of the palace, he tried not to think of his youngest child, however, for she believed in Bellerophon's innocence. That is why he had refused to see her for so many days since the announcement of the third and final task.

"She has fallen prey to Bellerophon's lies," the king said to himself as he mulled over what to do. "I have given shelter to this fugitive, this wandering liar... I have fulfilled the requirements of Xenia."

Even as he said the words, doubt wormed its way into his mind.

"It's impossible. No mortal man could have slain the monster. It must be lies. Another trick!" The king nodded to himself. "That's it. The people have been fooled!" Iobates then turned to one of the guards near the propylon. "Call for Captain Milyas!"

"Yes, my king!" the man replied, and then ran off to fetch the captain of the guard.

Philonoe had been in her chambers for days, locked away like a prisoner in her own home. But that did not mean she was not aware of the stories raging through the city streets, of a great victory in the northeast. Night and day she had prayed for it, and at last the confirmation of her hopes had arrived.

So, when she heard Polyidus' voice from the other side of her door, she rushed to meet him.

The guards let him through and the moment she saw his face, she knew something was not right.

"How are you, my lady?" he asked, his hand squeezing hers tightly.

"How should I be? I have been kept prisoner for many days," she responded, leading him to the terrace on the other side of her rooms. "What news? My servants told me that Bellerophon has been victorious, that the people are singing and dancing in the streets!" She could barely contain her relief.

Polyidus cocked his head to listen for the guards' footsteps nearby and knew that they had remained in the corridor. "Listen, Princess!" he said, his voice low but urgent. "The king plans to betray Bellerophon. He has sent Milyas and two battalions to intercept him at the altar of Athena in the olive grove. He was just seen flying in that direction upon Pegasus."

"He *was* victorious, then? The Chimera is dead?"

"Yes, but so too will Bellerophon be if he is not warned!"

She had never seen Polyidus so anxious, so upset. "But the laws of Xenia?"

"My princess, your father no longer cares for the laws of Zeus. He has abandoned reason and is about to commit a terrible crime. He is going to have Bellerophon slain."

"We have to help him!" Philonoe said. "But how? How can we help him?"

"*We* can't, my lady. But you can. You must go and warn him. Show yourself to the troops. Convince them. The time has come for you to take your mother's place."

Athena help me, Philonoe thought as she stood upon that

cliff of decision. She breathed deeply and thought of all the risks Bellerophon had taken. It was time for her to risk all now. Philonoe nodded and went to her bed where she took up her mother's sword, her talisman during her imprisonment. "We need to take care of the guards," she whispered.

"Leave that to me," Polyidus said as he walked with his staff toward the doors and knocked.

When the two guards opened the doors, he emerged and leaned in close to the one to speak to him. "The princess is in need of fresh air. She must be allowed out of her rooms."

"No," the one guard said. "King's orders are that she does not come out and-"

Before the man could finish, Polyidus' staff struck the side of his head so hard that he crumpled to the ground.

Immediately, the other guard grabbed the seer from behind, and just as he drew his dagger high above his head, he felt the full force of the pommel of Philonoe's sword on the side of his head. He fell like a stone upon the paving slabs of the corridor and both Philonoe and Polyidus stepped over the guards to rush away.

"You must take your horse from the stables, my lady. I have asked the stable boy to have it ready. Ride as quickly as you can. Most of the palace guards have gone to intercept Bellerophon."

"But what can I do, Polyidus?" There was fear in her voice, for she was suddenly swept up in her father's betrayal, the only person who could help Bellerophon.

"You are your mother's daughter, Princess. You are the rightful ruler of Lykia. The Gods will guide you!"

She nodded, her heart beating wildly within her chest. "Thank you, Polyidus!" she said, and then rushed down the corridor as quickly as she could before anyone else spotted her.

"Now…" Polyidus said to himself. "To the king."

Bellerophon had never felt so strong as he did that morning, soaring through the skies upon Pegasus' back as the sun shone brightly over the mountains, rivers, forests and fields of Lykia. He knew that the Gods were indeed on his side. He also knew at last that he was not alone in the world, that there were those who had believed him, Polyidus, Milyas, and most of all, Philonoe.

The princess had been unwavering in her belief in him, and had shown him every kindness, and as he looked down to see the battle-axe charm hanging from his neck, he knew that he would do anything for her. He wanted to spend the entirety of his life with her, he knew that now, and he wished with all of his heart that she wanted the same. The king had promised the hand of his daughter to Bellerophon, should he succeed in slaying the Chimera, but Bellerophon would not accept it unless it was her will.

Pegasus and Bellerophon followed the line of the river south, soaring high over the city of Xanthos where the sounds of laughter and song rose up to greet them.

Bellerophon strained to see if the princess stood upon her terrace of the palace, and could not see her, hoped that she was safe.

Once again, the warnings of Athena and the Amazon queen came to mind. *King Iobates is not to be trusted!* This thought tempered his feelings of triumph, for he knew that somehow, the battle was not yet over. "There is the olive grove, Pegasus," Bellerophon said, as the stallion circled lower and lower to land among the silver-green hectares of trees.

When they landed, Bellerophon slid off of Pegasus' back,

the satchel over his shoulder, he stopped to listen to the whirr of cicadas in the trees but nothing else.

Pegasus stomped the dusty ground and cocked his ears.

"Something's not right," Bellerophon said as he walked forward in the direction of the altar of Athena.

When they reached the altar, Bellerophon set the satchel upon the ground and removed his helmet which he placed upon the altar.

"Oh Bright-Eyed, Goddess… Thank you for guarding me in my trials, for guiding me through this life, to this point in time. I know now that it was always you who helped me." He then pulled the sword from its sheath and laid it upon the altar with the helmet. "Please accept my offerings in gratitude for my victory. I will accept whatever comes next, for I have lived longer than I ever expected to."

Pegasus suddenly reared and flapped his great wings, shuddering the branches of the nearby trees and causing their green fruit to fall to the ground all about them.

Bellerophon, his head still bent as he leaned upon the altar, heard the tramp of hobnailed sandals and knew that the king had no intention of keeping his word. He turned to Pegasus. "It is time for you to go, Pegasus. Fly and live." He waved his hands, but the stallion refused to move and, instead, stepped in front of Bellerophon as King Iobates' soldiers arrayed themselves before him, their shields up, their spears levelled.

Bellerophon stepped forward, no weapon in hand, only his heavy satchel slung over his shoulder.

The troops looked in awe upon the winged stallion. He towered over the Corinthian whose gorgon-headed breastplate seemed to glow and move in the daylight.

From out of the group, Captain Milyas stepped to face Bellerophon. "Welcome back!" the captain said, his eyes looking to either side at his men. "Were you victorious? Did you slay the beast?"

Bellerophon walked toward the captain, Pegasus right at his shoulder. "The Chimera will no longer torment this kingdom."

Milyas sighed and looked relieved, nodding slowly. "Then you have done what no one thought possible."

"He's lying!" one of the troops yelled behind Milyas.

"Kill him!" cried another. "It's the king's command!"

"He dies, or we all die!" said a third, Milyas' second-in-command.

Milyas quickly drew his sword and turned on his men. "The king lies!" he shouted at them, but instead of backing down, they growled, and grew angry, thinking the captain to have been corrupted by the foreigner.

"I'm with you, Bellerophon," Milyas said. "To the end!"

"Bellerophon turned and was about to take his sword off of the altar when the sound of galloping approached and a voice rang out in the olive grove.

"STOP!!!"

A brown stallion with a deep black mane pounded into their midst, between the battle lines, and when the dust cleared, Princess Philonoe came into view, her long red hair like fire in the sunlight and a gleaming sword in her hand.

"I command you to put down your arms!" she cried.

"Princess, get out of the way!" yelled the second-in-command, pointing his spear at Bellerophon. "The king has commanded he be slain at once, or that we all should be executed."

Philonoe looked at Bellerophon and felt her heart filled with love for him, the man who had helped to open her eyes, and who had risked everything for their kingdom. She then turned in her saddle and stared down at the battalion of troops.

"Would you slay the man who saved our kingdom? Would you rather risk the Gods' wrath, over that of my father's?"

"He is our king, lady!" one soldier said.

"My father…has lied to all of us!" she said. "The Chimera was the Gods' punishment for his lies and treachery!"

There were murmurs among the men.

"Would you further anger the Gods by slaying a guest in our kingdom?" She could see the men looking doubtful now. "You have been lied to, all of you! Until my father, Lykia was always ruled by a queen. My mother was the last queen, and she was betrayed by my father." She could feel the tears beginning to sting her eyes as she said the words aloud to the men, but she forced herself not to let them fall. "I will set things right, and make our kingdom great again! Will you join me, your rightful queen? Will you help me?"

The men looked at each other, then up at the princess they had always seen wandering the corridors of the palace, quiet, protected, for she now looked like a warrior herself, sat atop a stomping horse, sword in hand.

Bellerophon smiled, awe-struck by her courage. *She is her mother's daughter,* he thought.

One by one, Philonoe watched as the men lowered their spears and knelt before her.

For you, Mother, she thought. *I will make things right again.*

Captain Milyas stepped forward to look up at Philonoe. "Well done, my lady," he said, his face beaming with pride.

"Thank you for your loyalty, Captain," she said.

"What about the king?" he asked.

"Take the men to the road and wait for me. You will all

enter the city with me and Bellerophon. Then…then we will go to my father."

"Yes…my queen…" he said, bowing low.

When the men had marched off to wait for them, Philonoe dismounted and rushed into Bellerophon's arms, her lips pressed to his, her hands holding his face so that she could look upon him and burn his image into her mind.

"I thought I would never see you again!" she said as they held each other.

"I thought so too," he replied. "I almost did die," he added as he removed the charm from about his neck. "This belongs to you."

But she held his hand and pressed the charm to his chest. "It is yours…as I am yours…and you are mine, if that is your wish."

"So long as you want me, Philonoe, my heart is yours."

They kissed again, softly, happily, but after a moment, Bellerophon felt a nudge at his shoulder and turned to see Pegasus.

Philonoe looked in awe upon the son of Poseidon and reached up to stroke his forehead and jaw. "Pegasus…" she said. "Thank you." She smiled, but then that smile faded, for she knew that the battle was not yet over. "It is time to go," she said. "Will you both come with me?"

"We won't leave your side," Bellerophon answered.

They mounted up, and rode through the sun-drenched olive grove to where the troops were waiting for their queen.

It was something out of a dream for the people of Xanthos. The Lykians had lived in fear for so very long, that it felt strange to celebrate, to sing, and to dance. Many wondered if it was a trick of the Gods' making, something to lure them into a false sense of peace and of hope.

However, when their princess entered the gates of the city at the head of a small army with the Corinthian and Pegasus himself at her side, they knew a new day was dawning for Lykia, and as she passed, they felt the sun full upon their faces at last.

Philonoe rode upon her stallion at the head, a sword in her hand, her sandalled feet coaxing the animal forward as she looked upon the faces of her long-suffering people. She was, however, not smiling, for the closer they got to the palace - no matter how many flower petals fell upon her hair and the ground below - the more she wondered what she would say to her father.

He has lied to all of us, she thought. *But I do not wish his death.*

"Are you all right, Princess?" Bellerophon asked as he and Pegasus drew even with her.

"My father will not easily step aside."

"Then you will convince him," Bellerophon smiled.

The tramp of the troops' feet behind them grew louder as the street narrowed and they passed into the markets and turned toward the great, double-gates of the palace complex.

The guards at the gates stared with wide eyes at the approaching princess and her force, their spears up.

"Open the gates!" Captain Milyas stepped forward. "Princess Philonoe returns!"

Without question, their eyes upon the Corinthian, the winged horse, and their sword-wielding princess, the men quickly turned, pounded on the gate and yelled to the men on the other side to open up.

The great doors creaked open and they all marched into the court.

Philonoe dismounted, as did Bellerophon and together they turned to face Captain Milyas and the men.

"We go now to the megaron where my father, no doubt, has already had word of our arrival. If he orders your comrades to fight you, I want no killing if it can be avoided. And I want my father unharmed!"

"Yes, my queen!" Milyas shouted, and the men echoed his words, for he had told them the truth of what had happened to their kingdom, and it had spread quickly among their ranks.

"Follow me!" she said, and together with Bellerophon and Pegasus, they made their way to the megaron.

King Iobates sat upon his throne, his fists working its arms as his courtiers and advisors stood about him, murmuring, wondering what they would do. They had heard of the princess' approach, of the Corinthian's victory, and of the turning of the troops.

"They will slaughter us all!" one courtier with a long, oiled black beard said, the golden beads set in it jingling as he shook his head back and forth.

"We must leave at once!" said another. "Take ship for Phoenicia!"

"SILENCE!" the king shouted, and as the voices died down, the sound of marching could be heard, nearer and nearer, until finally the propylon doors swung open and Philonoe entered with Bellerophon and the others at her side. *By the Gods!* The king thought when he saw Pegasus at Bellerophon's shoulder, like a loyal hound at his master's heal. *Olympus has turned against me.*

"Daughter!" the king said suddenly, unable to help the anger in his voice, especially when he saw the sword in her hand, the sword with which Pasandra had first fought his mother's armies. "What is the meaning of this?"

A hush fell over the crowd as the troops settled around the fringes of the megaron, behind the trembling courtiers.

"You've taken over my men? My army?" Iobates said accusingly.

"They are Lykia's army, Father," Philonoe said, stepping from between Pegasus and Bellerophon. She could feel her heart beating wildly in her chest, so much that it made her dizzy, but she held fast to her courage and the memory of her mother. Others had risked much to get her to this point in time, and now it was her turn. "I know the truth, Father. I know everything about my mother, about why the Chimera came to torment Lykia, and about your role in all of it." Philonoe tore her eyes from her father's form atop the throne, and looked at the people about her. "My mother was an Amazon, one of their greatest warriors, and he sent her to her death against the Solymi! She was your rightful queen, destined by the laws of this ancient land, *and* the Gods, to rule and bring peace to Lykia. Instead," she turned back to her father, "the king took the throne for himself, despite the sacred law. That is why the beast came to Lykia! That is why the Gods have punished us all for so long!"

Philonoe could feel her anger rising, blinding her to the man before her, a man she felt certain still had some reason within for all that he had done.

"Do you actually believe the lies that this Corinthian has told you, Daughter? He has been shunned all of his life by all who have met him, even by his own family! He is a liar, an abuser of women, and a murderer! Would you take his word over mine? I am your father!"

The sword in Philonoe's hand rose up to point at the king. "Stop!" she yelled. "No more lies, Father! The Gods brought Bellerophon to us to help us. Olympus knows his worth, his honesty, and so do I!" She looked at Bellerophon. "He has proven himself innocent by completing all of the tasks you set him, with the Gods as your witness."

"How do we know he actually slew the Chimera?" Iobates demanded.

With a look at Philonoe, Bellerophon stepped forward for all to see, the heavy satchel hanging from his shoulder.

Pegasus stepped forward too, unafraid among so many men, determined not to leave Bellerophon's side.

The courtiers backed away, afraid and curious all at once as Bellerophon held up the satchel and turned it over.

"The Chimera is slain!" Bellerophon yelled as a set of claws, two curved horns and a set of bloody fangs fell onto the ornate floor of the megaron. "We fought in the mountains, among the spewing fires before its lair. Before the Gods, the beast is slain… And I am innocent of the crimes I have been accused of!"

Many of the courtiers began to weep, for they now knew that the beast was no more, that they need no longer live in terror of fire and death.

King Iobates looked at the grisly remnants of the beast, at Bellerophon, Pegasus, and at his daughter. *I am defeated,* he told himself, resignedly.

Philonoe stepped forward to face her father, her mother's sword hanging by her side. "Father, you have defied the Gods' laws, and flouted those of Xenia. You cannot be king any longer."

"Will you kill me then? Your own father?"

Philonoe looked hurt that he could think such a thing, but then, she realized he had not really made any attempt to know her in that life. He had been too overcome with guilt and lying to be concerned about anyone but himself. *He is still my father...once loved by my mother...* "No, I will not have you killed. I will not lose another parent. But you must step down. Ask the Gods for forgiveness..." She turned to Bellerophon. "And honour the promises you made to Bellerophon of Corinthos for all that he has done for our kingdom."

The king was silent as he looked upon his daughter, and as he stared into the flames of the hearth between them. The shame that seeped through his veins then was intense, and he could feel the anger of Zeus all around him. *Gods, forgive me,* Iobates pleaded in his heart. He turned to Polyidus beside him, for the seer had been silent the entire time. "Polyidus... You have been loyal these many years. What do the Gods advise?"

Polyidus turned his head toward the king. "My lord... I told you that Bellerophon was the one destined to help us, and he has. Olympus demands that you step down, or else face the wrath of Zeus."

Iobates nodded, and it was then that he removed the golden circlet from around his head, turned, and placed it upon the throne. He then descended the steps and went to Philonoe and Bellerophon.

"I did love Pasandra..." he said, "but I could never live up to her. I regret my actions every day of this life." He looked into his daughter's eyes, so like her mother's, and a tear fell down his cheek. "I am sorry," he said, and Philonoe knew that he meant it.

Iobates then turned to Bellerophon. "Bellerophon of

Corinthos…" he said aloud for all to hear. "You have proved your innocence!"

There were cheers from Milyas and the troops around the room. "You have honoured your word, and now, I shall honour mine. My last act as king is to welcome you as a Lykian and to give you the hand of my daughter if she desires it. May you be a more worthy husband than ever I was." He turned to Philonoe then, his eyes glossy as he looked upon her. "Is this what you desire, Daughter?"

Philonoe looked upon Bellerophon and a smile spanned her face. "Yes, it is."

Iobates then reached out to take each of their hands and clasped them together. "May the Gods bless your union, and bless this kingdom from now on."

There was great applause around the megaron then as Philonoe and Bellerophon embraced before all the court and the troops.

In the midst of all that was happening, Iobates slipped out the back entrance of the megaron, leaning over to speak with Polyidus before making his exit.

"Farewell, Polyidus," Iobates whispered before disappearing.

The seer felt a chill running up his body, but so great were the events unfolding before him, that he did not pursue the former king. Instead he turned in his seat to fumble for the crown. "Princess Philonoe!" Polyidus cried aloud.

All eyes turned toward him and the vacant throne.

"Go, Philonoe," Bellerophon said, squeezing her hand. "Take your rightful place."

Philonoe laid her hand upon his armoured chest and turned, her mother's sword still in her hand. She mounted the steps of the dais and turned to face the court and her loyal troops.

Polyidus shuffled behind her with the glinting crown held aloft, and then slowly lowered it upon her fiery brow. "I give you Queen Philonoe!"

"QUEEN PHILONOE!" the crowd roared, and every man and woman, soldier, noble, and slave, bowed.

Bellerophon too bowed, and he was proud to do it. They had both fought long and hard in their own ways, to emerge from the shadows where others had placed them. Now, as their eyes locked and love filled their hearts, they knew that the sun shone fully upon them at last.

CHAPTER 14

A TALE OF GLORIES PAST

The group of boys around the old man was silent as the words flowing from his lips stopped, his tale abruptly ended. The sun was only just beginning to rise, for they had listened intently all through the night.

"What happened next, Daskale?" the eldest boy asked from where he sat at the bottom of the spear on which he had impaled the head of the serpent they had slain the day before.

"You cannot end the story just like that!" protested another.

The old man listened to their entreaties, and tried to rally himself to tell the rest. It had been emotional, revisiting those memories, remembering that time when the sun shone brightest.

"Please, Daskale," the youngest, Daxeos, said at his side. He had been awake all of the night, most interested in the tale. "Tell us what happened to Bellerophon and Philonoe."

"Did the king take revenge on Bellerophon?" another of the boys asked.

"Tell us!" the rest whined in concert.

The old man put up his gnarled hands for peace and when they fell silent again, he cleared his throat.

"Very well. I shall tell you," he said. "After Iobates left the megaron of the palace, with the court and soldiers cheering their rightful queen, he went back to his chambers. He did not seek vengeance, or attempt to kill Bellerophon. He did not want to harm his daughter any more than he already had done."

"Then what did he do?" ask the eldest.

"Iobates prayed to the Gods and the shade of his wife for forgiveness. He got into a hot bath, and he cut his wrists before going to eternal sleep."

The boys all gasped.

"But why?" the eldest asked, disappointed.

"Because he could not live with the guilt of his actions. The Gods accepted his sacrifice in recompense for all that he had done." The old man hung his head at that, leaning low upon his staff.

"What about Queen Philonoe?" asked another of the boys. "What happened to her?"

The old man raised his head and smiled. "The land of Lykia thrived under her rule. There was peace and good harvest. She reestablished the connection with her mother's people, and they became her staunchest allies. The people all across the land loved her and would have died for her, as she would have for them."

"And Bellerophon?" Daxeos asked again, patiently waiting to hear what had happened to the Corinthian who had been shunned by all others until he met Philonoe.

"Bellerophon supported Queen Philonoe in all things. He was her most loyal subject and, for a long time, he never left her side. They loved each other, and they had three beautiful children - two sons named Hippolochus and Isander, and a daughter which they named Laodameia, who was sent to learn the ways of the Daughters of Ares."

"Were they a happy family?" Daxeos asked, saddened when he saw the downcast look upon the old man's face.

"For a long time, they were happy. Yes. But a hero, after his trials, is ever restless, and even for the best among them, hubris is a dangerous companion."

"Was Bellerophon guilty of this?" the eldest boy asked.

"One has to remember, that Bellerophon was just a man. But he was a mortal who had achieved the impossible. He was, and remained, friends with Pegasus, a winged god. Ask yourselves this… How does a man, after such feats, come back into the world? What is considered normal for him? You have all slain a great beast in your minds. Will you see the world, or yourselves for that matter, the same as you did before your deed? Or has your perspective been changed by your experience?"

"Everything is different!" the eldest boy said, and the others nodded.

"And so it was for Bellerophon. He had achieved great deeds, though they were forced upon him. He had flown through the skies! Can you imagine such a thing? It is no wonder Bellerophon yearned for more, not out of arrogance or boredom, but rather out of wonder and an urgent, never-ending need to push the limits of his existence."

"He left the queen and their children?" Daxeos asked.

"He never truly left them, Daxeos, for they were ever in his heart. But he did leave often with Pegasus to explore the world. Some say he took vengeance upon the queen of Tiryns for the lies she had told about him, but I do not believe that. Others say that, having been so near the Gods, he decided he would try to fly up to Mount Olympus itself with Pegasus."

"And did he, Daskale?" another boy asked.

The old man shook his head. "He tried, but the Gods would not allow it. Zeus sent a gadfly to sting Pegasus as they climbed the long pathways of the sky to Olympus, and Bellerophon fell back to the earth."

They all gasped.

"No!" Daxeos cried. "But why? After all that he did! After his loyalty to the Gods and the queen?"

"One should not try to explain the ways of the Gods, Daxeos. Some things are better left a mystery, and Bellerophon discovered that. We all have our place in the world, our role to play, be we noble or servant, coward or hero."

"Did Queen Philonoe and their children mourn his death?" the eldest boy asked, moved at last by the tale.

"Oh, he is not dead…not yet anyway. But he did mourn the passing of his wife, for she died in battle, fighting the Hittites alongside the Daughters of Ares." The old man wiped a tear away at the thought. "They say she died most bravely in battle, and that the people of Lykia mourned her for many moons. Her children rule the kingdom now, and Bellerophon…"

The words died in his throat, but young Daxeos reached out to give him courage, squeezing his hand firmly. The old man smiled down at the young boy, though he could not see him. "Bellerophon still wanders the world, mourning his beloved queen, searching for a trial that will end his life once and for all so that he might join her."

"And has he found it yet? His trial?" Daxeos asked, his voice hoarse.

"I do not know," the old man said, sad at the silence he had blanketed over the young boys. He could feel their hopes for themselves teetering on the edge of doubt and despair, and knew that he needed to make things right once more. "But there is hope, boys. There is always hope, and you must find it within yourselves." He stood slowly and stiffly and turned on the spot so that they could all hear him. "Your destiny is yours, for the Gods will lay many choices before you. Remember... There is a hero in everyone of you. The question you have to ask yourself is this: what kind of hero will you be, and what kind of world will you leave behind when you are gone from it?"

The boy, Daxeos stood and held fast to the old man's hand. "Thank you for the story, Daskale," he said.

"You're very welcome, my boy," the old man said.

"Thank you, Daskale!" the others muttered as they began to leave separately, back to their homes.

"Daskale," said the oldest among them. "We will come back later and bury the serpent. We will make offerings to the Gods for it."

"I'm glad to hear it, lad," the old man said.

When they had all gone, the old man picked up his staff and shuffled his way onto the beach to go to the silent seashore where he felt the water upon his aged feet. He bent over to splash his face and felt the rising sun upon it.

"Still telling tall tales, Polyidus?" a voice said from down the beach.

The old man turned in the direction of the voice, and recognized the limp, always accompanied by the easy trot and cool breeze of the winged stallion at the man's side. "My friend," he said, reaching out to grasp his hands in greeting. "Where have you been?"

"Wandering... Mourning..."

"She died bravely, I hear," the old man said, his voice breaking.

Bellerophon looked upon Polyidus then, how old he looked, how old they had both become. He looked at the rising sun over the sea and sighed. "She did…and I was not with her."

Polyidus grabbed him and pulled hard. "You were always with her, and she knew it. You each had your battles which you fought alone, but you were both with each other… In here!" he said, poking his heart.

Bellerophon nodded, and the tears fell from his cheeks into the surf at their feet.

They stood silent for a time before Polyidus spoke.

"I have food at my home. It isn't much, but I would like for you to join me." He placed his hand gently upon Bellerophon's shoulder. "Please come."

Bellerophon nodded, his long grey hair falling about his shoulders and face. "I'll be along shortly," he answered.

"Good. I'll see you soon," Polyidus said, and he set off slowly along the path up from the beach, his staff clicking on the rocks as he climbed slowly over them.

Bellerophon then turned to face the sea and lean against his long-time friend's thick neck.

"I miss her, Pegasus," he said as he gazed upon the brilliance of that enormous sun, his eyes alight with memory. "She was the only one who was every truly kind to me and believed in me," he said.

The stallion neighed and nudged Bellerophon.

"And you, my friend," he said, smiling, even as his tears fell. "And you." Bellerophon then stood back. "Go now…fly. I will see you later. I mustn't let Polyidus down. He needs me, it seems."

With a great flap of his wondrous wings, Pegasus reared and charged down the beach to take flight in the wake of the sun's chariot.

Bellerophon watched him soar across the blue canvas of the heavens. "Farewell, my friend." He then closed his eyes as the heat of that sun fell upon him, and remembered the face of his beloved queen as she was when he first met her.

I love you, Philonoe... he said to the sky and air that his thoughts might reach her in the Underworld. *I will see you soon, my love...*

THE END

Thank you for reading!

Did you enjoy this book? Here is what you can do next.

If you enjoyed *The Reluctant Hero*, and if you have a minute to spare, please post a short review on the web page where you purchased the book.

Reviews are a wonderful way for new readers to find this series of books and your help in spreading the word is greatly appreciated.

More books in the *Mythologia* series, as well as exciting historical fantasy set in the ancient world, will be coming soon, so be sure to sign-up for e-mail updates at:

https://eaglesanddragonspublishing.com/newsletter-join-the-legions/

Newsletter subscribers get a FREE BOOK, and first access to new releases, special offers, and much more!

AUTHOR'S NOTE

The myth of Bellerophon and the Chimera is one that I have been wanting to explore for some time, not only because it provided an opportunity to tell the story of a good old 'monster battle', but also because it involved the winged horse, Pegasus.

When I was a child of about six, my first taste of Greek Mythology was seeing the original *Clash of the Titans* film, and every time I watched it Pegasus, was always the focus of my attention. I loved seeing Pegasus, and wished for such an ally and friend. It was Pegasus who brought me to Bellerophon, though at first I had only associated him with the hero Perseus.

It is strange that most people will know the myth of Perseus, but have only a passing knowledge of Bellerophon, mainly as it relates to the Chimera, and not the man himself. In truth, Bellerophon is one of the central heroes of Greek Mythology, but we seem to have forgotten about him some-what in the modern age. Perhaps this is due to the film that I, like so many, enjoyed as a child? Popular culture is a powerful thing in the modern age.

I thought it was time to give Bellerophon his due, and the *Mythologia* series was the perfect place to do it.

When it comes to the Greek myths, the primary sources are often sparse and scattered, our knowledge of them pieced together through fragments of text, artwork, and retellings by Roman writers in later centuries.

Many ancient writers mention Bellerophon and the Chimera, such as Hesiod (*Theogony*), Pindar (*Olympian* 13; *Isthmian* 7), Euripides, and Apollodorus. However, the earliest mention of Bellerophon comes from Homer in the sixth book of the *Iliad* in which, Glaucus, the grandson of Bellerophon, tells others of his lineage and the story of his grandfather and the Chimera. It is actually quite a long description of the tale, which is a blessing for later writers and ourselves. Interestingly, the description of Bellerophon's tale by Homer is the first and only mention of actual writing in the *Iliad*. In reference to the letter that King Proetus has Bellerophon carry to King Iobates of Lykia, Homer writes:

To slay him he [King Proetus] *forbare, for his soul had awe of that; but he sent him to Lycia, and gave him baneful tokens, graving in a folded tablet many signs and deadly, and bade him show these to his own wife's father, that he* [Bellerophon] *might be slain.*

(Homer, *Iliad*, Book 6, 170)

The sources are varied to be sure. Homer speaks of Bellerophon fighting and defeating the Solymi, the Amazons, and the Chimera, but makes no mention of Pegasus. However, Hesiod does mention that Pegasus and Bellerophon both defeated the Chimera who was the offspring of Typhon and

Echidna, and the sibling of Cerberos (the three-headed hound of Hades), and the Lernaean Hydra which Herakles later defeated. It is a fascinating, and sometimes difficult, process to link together the various traditions of a particular myth to create a coherent story, but I believe it has worked in the case of Bellerophon and the Chimera.

Some readers may notice that, for the purposes of the story I wanted to tell, I have changed the order of Bellerophon's tasks. In Homer, for instance, Bellerophon first slays the Chimera, then fights the Solymi, and finally, defeats the Amazons. Because I wanted the Chimera to be the climactic battle, I thought that it was acceptable to change this order. However, the battle with the Chimera did not end up being the primary focus of this book. Originally, as mentioned above, I had the idea of writing a 'monster-battle' novel, but as often happens, things changed as the story developed. At its heart, Greek Mythology is often about very human trials and emotions. To me, though the battle with the Chimera is the climax of the book, the main focus is Bellerophon's journey from a shadowy no-one to a true hero as he overcomes his own demons and finally discovers himself.

As usual, I have also tried to set the story in the real-world locations in which it was said to have taken place. I have opted to use the name of Bellerophon's home of Corinthos (modern Corinth) because it is familiar to us today, but in the ancient texts, and at that time, it was known as Ephyra. I visited ancient Corinth on my first trip to Greece many years ago and remembered being overwhelmed by it, but also saddened at the destruction wrought by Rome on that great and ancient city. It was then that I visited the Acrocorinthos, the enormous mountain that overlooks the city. Today, all one sees up there are the remnants of the vast medieval castle, but it was not difficult to imagine the place during the Greek Heroic Age. To stand up there and look down on Corinth and the sweeping beauty of the lands south toward Mycenae and Argos over the mountains is, simply-put, breathtaking. I decided to make that the place where Bellerophon's story begins, where he trains and commits the act that gets him banished from his home, specifically the killing of Belleros which gives Bellerophon his name, 'Belleros Killer'.

There are other sites in the first part of the tale that you might be familiar with, such as Argos, and the great fortress of Tiryns where Bellerophon stays with King Proetus and Queen Stheneboea (also known as Anteia). Having visited those sites, it was a joy to go back to them and write about the landscape and palace of Tiryns especially. To read more about Tiryns, that ancient fortress of myth and legend, you can read a blog post about my visit HERE. Another ancient site that is truly fascinating is the guardhouse where Bellerophon first meets King Proetus' men. I located this guardhouse at the mysterious Pyramid of Hellinikon, just outside of Argos. This site was either believed to be a tomb, or a guardhouse built during the wars between Proetus and his brother, Acrisios. You can read about the pyramid and watch a short video tour of the site HERE.

Once Bellerophon journeyed across the sea, I was in uncharted territory for myself, never having travelled to modern-day Turkey where the ancient Kingdom of Lykia is located. The research for this was fascinating.

Not far from the Greek islands of Rhodes and Kastellorizo is the mouth of the river Xanthos which leads north a short distance to the ancient city of Xanthos (outside modern Kinik). This ancient Greek and Roman city had many structures such as a theatre, agora, monuments and shrines, as well as unique 'pedestal tombs', but there is very little in the way of remains for the period in which this story takes place. There was an acropolis overlooking the river below, and that is where I chose to set King Iobates' palace in the story.

Likewise, I elaborated on the fictional village of the Solymi where Bellerophon fights the leader of their tribe, though their lands were located in the ancient region known as Pisidia.

When it comes to the Amazons, I chose to set their capital in Phrygia since it was said that there were Amazon tribes in that remote region north of Lykia. In searching for a geographic setting, I chose the ancient city of Hierapolis which is located at modern Pamukkale, which is known for the mineral-rich thermal waters flowing down white travertine terraces on a nearby hillside. This was a sort of ancient spa town, but for the purposes of this story, I decided to make it the Amazon base.

In Turkey today, there is a place known as Mount Chimera, and this is located near the sea to the southwest of Xanthos. Though I chose to make this a remote mountain region to the northeast in the story, I did try to remain true to the setting, mainly the Chimera's cave and the strange fires that are constantly burning from out of the rocky earth in that place. These are in fact methane gas emissions that are on fire, and have been for centuries, but for as long as people can remember, they have been called fires of the Chimera. It is here that the climactic battle in the story takes place.

Lastly, there is a bit of a nod to my own heritage at the end of the book when Bellerophon and Polyidus meet on the island of Chios, where the paternal side of my family comes from. The reason I chose to do this is because on the island, just north of Chios town, near the sea, is a site known as 'Homer's

Rock' or 'Daskalopetra'. In Greek, *daskalos*, means teacher, and in the story, the narrator or 'teacher', is the aged Polyidus. It was said that Homer himself used to sit upon this rock and tell his tales of the Trojan War and of Odysseus' travels. This was my acknowledgment of that tradition.

One of the most difficult tasks of writing this story was figuring out the family tree and timelines for the characters inhabiting the story. I soon realized that with so many references over time to various characters, it is not as clean-cut as one might think. One question I wrestled with was whether Perseus lived before or after Bellerophon, for the latter dealt with King Proetus whose brother was King Acrisios, the father of Danae, Perseus' mother. Another question was, which Amazon queen was alive when Bellerophon faced the Amazons. At first I thought it would be Myrina, who was supposedly a friend of Horus (yes, the Egyptian Horus), but then I read that Queen Otrera was the mother of both Hippolyta and Penthesilea. However, Otrera is also said to be the very first Amazon queen. It is all a bit confusing for the modern reader and researcher, but when I decided not to cling to an absolute timeline, the story began to take shape beautifully.

In mythology, Bellerophon's parents are Eurymede (sometimes known as Eurynome) of Megara and Glaucus, the son of Sisyphus who founded Corinth and who was one of the great sinners the Gods imprisoned in Tartarus for all time. Mythology does indeed tell us that Glaucus was eaten by his own horses after losing the chariot race at the funeral games of Pelias, and this trauma haunts Bellerophon in this version of the story.

As I have mentioned, King Proetus of Tiryns was the brother of King Acrisios of Argos, and he was married to

Stheneboea of Lykia, the eldest daughter of King Iobates, who did send troops to help Proetus in the war against his brother.

King Iobates is one of the main characters in the myth, and in this story, but as is often the case in ancient texts, the women who were a part of the tale get little mention. I wanted to change that with *The Reluctant Hero*.

The character of Pasandra, Philonoe's mother, is pure fiction on my part. When I began to read about the Amazons and found out that Lykia was indeed originally a matrilineal society, the idea came to me to make the late queen, Pasandra, an Amazon. This gave the tale an added depth and made it much more interesting to tell that side of the story.

It also allowed me to delve further into Philonoe's character as I wanted to bring her to the fore. To me, she languished in the background in the primary sources. The story is, I feel, much more interesting for it, and for the fact that she is not a damsel in distress, 'saved' by the hero who shows up. In this story, Philonoe is a hero in her own right.

In myth, Bellerophon and Philonoe had three children: Hippolochos, Isander, and Laodameia.

As mentioned above, in Homer, it is the son of Hippolochos, Glaucus, who tells the tale of Bellerophon in the *Iliad*. He led the Lykian army during the Trojan War. As for Isander and Laodameia, they were less fortunate in their lives, for Isander was supposedly killed while fighting the Solymi, slain by Ares, and Laodameia was the mother of Sarpedon by Zeus, later to be killed by Artemis for angering that goddess.

One thing is certain, the mythological family trees are never boring!

But what of Philonoe and Bellerophon?

The ancient texts make no mention of Philonoe's end that I have seen, so I decided that she should meet an end worthy of her Amazon lineage, giving her children the chance to take over the kingdom.

As for Bellerophon, the ancient texts make no mention of his death either, but Homer does say the following:

But when even Bellerophon came to be hated of all the gods, then verily he wandered alone over the Aleian plain, devouring his own soul, and shunning the paths of men...

(Homer, *Iliad*, Book 6, 200)

It is true that most Greek myths, especially those of the heroes, often end in tragedy, but why was Bellerophon shunned by the Gods? In his lost tragic play, *Bellerophon*, Euripides spoke of Bellerophon's attempt to fly up to Mount Olympus upon Pegasus, and Zeus' subsequent anger at this. The king of the gods sent a fly to sting Pegasus, and Bellerophon, the slayer of the Chimera, tumbled back to earth. He survived the fall, but was crippled by it and wandered alone until the end of his days.

It was a sad end for a great and misunderstood hero, and I hope that I have done his story justice.

Thank you for reading.

Adam Alexander Haviaras
Stratford, Ontario
October, 2021

Become a Patron of Eagles and Dragons Publishing!

If you enjoy the books that Eagles and Dragons Publishing puts out, our blogs about history, mythology, and archaeology, our video tours of historic sites and more, then you should consider becoming an official patron.

We love our regular visitors to the website, and of course our wonderful newsletter subscribers, but we want to offer more to our 'super fans', those readers and history-lovers who enjoy everything we do and create.

You can become a patron for as little as $1 per month. For your support, you can also get fantastic rewards as tokens of our appreciation.

If you are interested, just CLICK HERE or visit the website below to go to the Eagles and Dragons Publishing Patreon page to watch the introductory video and check out the patronage levels and exciting rewards.

https://www.patreon.com/EaglesandDragonsPublishing

Join us for an exciting future as we bring the past to life!

ABOUT THE AUTHOR

Adam Alexander Haviaras is a best-selling and award-winning author and historian who has studied ancient and medieval history and archaeology in Canada and the United Kingdom. He currently resides in Stratford, Ontario with his wife and children where he is continuing his research and writing other works of historical fantasy.

Historical Fiction/Fantasy Titles

The Eagles and Dragons Series

The Dragon: Genesis (Prequel)

A Dragon among the Eagles (Prequel)

Children of Apollo (Book I)

Killing the Hydra (Book II)

Warriors of Epona (Book III)

Isle of the Blessed (Book IV)

The Stolen Throne (Book V)

The Blood Road (Book VI)

The Eagles and Dragons Legionary Box Set (Books 0-I-II)

The Eagles and Dragons Tribune Box Set (Books III-IV-V)

The Carpathian Interlude Series

The Carpathian Interlude - Complete Trilogy Box Set

Immortui (Part I)

Lykoi (Part II)

Thanatos (Part III)

The Mythologia Series
Chariot of the Son: The Story of Phaethon
Wheels of Fate: The Story of Pelops and Hippodameia
A Song for the Underworld: The Story of Orpheus and
Eurydice
The Reluctant Hero: The Story of Bellerophon and the
Chimera
Mythologia: First Omnibus Edition

Heart of Fire: A Novel of the Ancient Olympics

**Saturnalia: A Tale of Wickedness and Redemption in
Ancient Rome**

The Etrurian Players
Sincerity is a Goddess (Book I)
An Altar of Indignities (Book II)

Titles in the Historia Non-fiction Series
Historia I: Celtic Literary Archetypes in *The Mabinogion*: A
Study of the Ancient Tale of *Pwyll, Lord of Dyved*
Historia II: Arthurian Romance and the Knightly Ideal: A
study of Medieval Romantic Literature and its Effect upon
Warrior Culture in Europe
Historia III: *Y Gododdin*: The Last Stand of Three Hundred
Britons - Understanding People and Events during Britain's
Heroic Age
Historia IV: Camelot: The Historical, Archaeological and
Toponymic Considerations for South Cadbury Castle as King
Arthur's Capital

Eagles and Dragons Publishing Guides

Writing the Past: The Eagles and Dragons Publishing Guide to Researching, Writing, Publishing and Marketing Historical Fiction and Historical Fantasy

STAY CONNECTED

To connect with Adam and learn more about the ancient world visit www.eaglesanddragonspublishing.com

Sign up for the Eagles and Dragons Publishing Newsletter at www.eaglesanddragonspublishing.com/newsletter-join-the-legions/ to receive a FREE BOOK, first access to new releases and posts on ancient history, special offers, and much more!

Readers can also connect with Adam on Twitter @Adam-Haviaras and Instagram @ adam_haviaras

On Facebook you can 'Like' the Eagles and Dragons page to get regular updates on new historical fiction and non-fiction from Eagles and Dragons Publishing.

To watch Eagles and Dragons Publishing's mini documentaries and other fun videos, be sure to follow us on TikTok and subscribe to our YouTube channel.